ROBERT B. PARKER'S

BAD INFLUENCE

The Sunny Randall Novels

Robert B. Parker's Bad Influence
(BY ALISON GAYLIN)

Robert B. Parker's Revenge Tour
(BY MIKE LUPICA)

Robert B. Parker's Payback
(BY MIKE LUPICA)

Robert B. Parker's Grudge Match
(BY MIKE LUPICA)

Robert B. Parker's Blood Feud
(BY MIKE LUPICA)

Spare Change

Blue Screen

Melancholy Baby

Shrink Rap

Perish Twice

Family Honor

For a comprehensive title list and a preview of upcoming books, visit PRH.com/RobertBParker or Facebook.com/RobertBParkerAuthor.

ROBERT B. PARKER'S

BAD INFLUENCE

A SUNNY RANDALL NOVEL

ALISON GAYLIN

G. P. PUTNAM'S SONS
New York

PUTNAM
— EST. 1838 —

G. P. PUTNAM'S SONS
Publishers Since 1838
An imprint of Penguin Random House LLC
penguinrandomhouse.com

Library of Congress Cataloging-in-Publication Data

Names: Gaylin, Alison, author.
Title: Robert B. Parker's Bad influence / Alison Gaylin.
Other titles: Bad influence
Description: New York: G. P. Putnam's Sons, 2023. |
Series: A Sunny Randall novel; 11
Identifiers: LCCN 2023013015 (print) | LCCN 2023013016 (ebook) |
ISBN 9780593540527 (hardcover) | ISBN 9780593540534 (ebook)
Subjects: LCSH: Randall, Sunny (Fictitious character)—Fiction. |
Women private investigators—Fiction. |
LCGFT: Detective and mystery fiction. | Novels.
Classification: LCC PS3607.A9858 R63 2023 (print) |
LCC PS3607.A9858 (ebook) | DDC 813/.6—dc23/eng/20230324
LC record available at https://lccn.loc.gov/2023013015
LC ebook record available at https://lccn.loc.gov/2023013016
p.   cm.

Printed in the United States of America
1st Printing

Book design by Elke Sigal

ROBERT B. PARKER'S

BAD
INFLUENCE

ONE

"W ere we ever like that?" I said. "Please tell me we weren't."

"We weren't," Spike said. "Believe me."

I was with my best friend in the bar of the restaurant he owns, both of us transfixed by a couple twentysomething influencers sitting at a dimly lit table and taking selfie after selfie, a bottle of pricey cognac looming behind them like a chaperone. I'd been told their names were Blake James and Alena Jade—apparently, last names had gone the way of MySpace. I'd also been told that they were Instagram's "it" couple, and having them here, in Spike's, would be sure to transform it from "just some place" into a "destination."

It made sense. Between them, Blake James and Alena Jade had close to a million followers, and getting them both here in Spike's, together, could ensure a house full of big-spending fans, each one of them desperate to stand in the spot where their inked-up, Fashion Nova–wearing, iron-pumping, duck-face-making idols had stood.

Blake James in particular. In addition to his wildly popular Instagram account, Blake was a YouTube sensation, with legions of viewers tuning in to his workout video channel, The Shred Shed.

As irritating as it may have been to Spike and me, I hoped the presence of these two sentient mannequins would give Spike's a much-needed prestige infusion. Despite a post-pandemic uptick in business, inflation and supply-chain issues had taken their toll on the place—just as they had on most restaurants. And my friend, for all his hard work, was back in the red.

I was worried Spike might do something stupid to keep his tavern afloat. Again. Which is why I listened to a woman named Bethany Rose who called herself a "media concierge" and assured me she could "marshal the power of the Gram" to ensure that Spike would never feel the need to swim with another loan shark. But more on that later.

All you need to know at this point is that Bethany Rose brought us Blake and Alena.

Blake rested his chiseled chin on Alena's bare shoulder, a selfie stick holding the phone high over their heads, the two of them pouting up at it contentedly.

Spike stared at them. "How can anybody spend that much time looking at themselves?"

"Maybe they're looking at each other." I took a swallow of

my pinot noir—a nice year, recommended by Spike, and probably one-twentieth the price of the influencers' cognac. I did have to admire Alena. Looking the way she did took more effort than I could ever imagine mustering—and I'm not exactly low-maintenance.

I once had a drag queen client and I doubted he spent as much time with the contouring brush as Alena did. Her face was so sculpted she seemed almost unreal, and her shimmering hair was perfectly behaved, like a swath of black silk. She had to have spent tens of thousands on plastic surgery to get that body—which was really something you'd see only in comic books or the Kardashian family.

Blake, meanwhile . . . Okay. If I was going to be honest, I didn't mind looking at him. "I'd love to paint that man," I said. I hadn't intended to say it out loud, but sue me. He had the most symmetrical face I'd ever seen.

"Meh," Spike said.

I stared at him. "Are you serious?"

He shrugged. "He's not my type. I've punched too many guys who look like him."

Blake raised his glass for another selfie and smiled, his Caribbean-blue eyes an exact match with the sleeveless jacket he was wearing, his teeth gleaming nearly as much as his exposed, tatted biceps. And then Blake shouted, "Let's do a cheers!" like a five-year-old.

A couple of Spike's regular patrons shot him death glares. The bartender visibly cringed. Even Alena looked embarrassed.

I turned back to Spike. "I get what you're saying."

He sighed. "Is this really necessary?" he said. "I mean . . . the last time this place was in trouble, I handled it."

I raised an eyebrow at him.

"Okay, I guess I shouldn't have—"

"Taken out a loan without reading the fine print?"

"Uh-huh."

"Gotten involved with the Russian Mob?"

"Yep."

"All of the above, plus breaking a loan shark's nose and nearly getting both of us killed?"

"Yeah. Except for the nose-breaking part. I stand by that decision."

I grinned, clinked my glass with his. "Let's do a cheers to that," I said.

"To Spike's," he said.

"To Spike's."

He swallowed his wine, then glanced at his watch. "So . . . the customers should be rushing in any minute now, huh?"

Spike was watching the door. I was, too, but not for the same reasons. Unlike my best friend, there was only one customer I needed to see walk into this place tonight. And that was media concierge Bethany Rose. She was late.

TWO

It wasn't long before new customers began streaming into Spike's—dozens of them, all under thirty, the girls in rompers and sky-high heels, the boys in skintight T-shirts and stinking of Axe spray, all of them spray-tanned within an inch of their lives. It wasn't the typical crowd you'd see in Spike's—or in Boston, for that matter. It was more like Hollywood meets *Jersey Shore*. But Spike didn't seem to mind. When the fourth or fifth group started a tab, I saw him smile for the first time in I couldn't remember how long.

"This media maven—what's her name?" Spike said.

"Bethany Rose. And it's media *concierge*."

"Whatever," he said. "Color me pleasantly surprised."

I had to agree. Even if this wasn't my ideal bar clientele,

money was money. I glanced at the door again. "She should be here."

"Who?"

"Bethany."

"Why?"

I sighed heavily. "We're supposed to talk terms."

I'd spoken to Bethany Rose the previous day at the suggestion of Lee Farrell. It felt weird to hear a no-nonsense cop like Lee use a term like *media concierge*, but as he said himself when I told him Spike might lose his bar again, "Bullshit times call for bullshit measures."

Lee had known about Bethany from his niece Emily Barnes, a pretty college student with a habit of getting herself into un-pretty situations. These days, Emily was earning extra cash and free swag as an influencer—a noble pursuit, comparatively speaking. With Bethany's help, she'd become what they call a micro-influencer, with close to fifty thousand followers. Lee had no idea what that meant, but he was still proud. And who could blame him? It was legal.

Anyway, Emily had done one of those email intros between Bethany Rose and me, and yesterday, Bethany had given me a free consultation via Zoom. She basically looked the way I'd expected her to. Kris Jenner haircut, a rope of expensive-looking pearls, cheekbones that angled out from her face dramatically, and plumped-up lips that were no stranger to the needle. Looking at her, Bethany Rose could have been anywhere from thirty-five to sixty-five. It was impossible to tell—especially since she went so heavy on Zoom's "touch up your appearance" feature. She wore a tailored black jacket that probably cost more than my kitchen renovation, which made me wonder if I was wasting my time. The economy was tough for PIs, too, monthly expenses for my home and office had skyrocketed and, solvent as I may have been, it was hard to justify dropping a small fortune on something as ephemeral as potential word of mouth. I'd decided to keep the consultation short and sweet.

My first question for Bethany: "What the hell is a media concierge?"

"If you have to ask, Sunny, you can't afford me."

I hadn't even cracked a smile.

"I can put your friend's business on the map," she had said.

"How?"

"I have a five-point plan."

"What are the points?"

She'd gone on about reach, demographics, and algorithms for at least six solid minutes, sprinkling her pitch with info about her "stable of influencers" and a lot of social media lingo. "The Gram," she'd said repeatedly, her blue eyes lighting up each time she said it, as though it were some kind of wonder drug.

"Look, Bethany," I'd said, once I could get a word in. "You seem great. And your pitch is . . ." I struggled for the right descriptor. "Well, it's the bomb."

"Thanks."

"But Spike and I don't have much in the way of extra cash these days. I'm thinking you're probably out of our league."

"Don't be so sure," she had said. "Emily told me about your private investigating business."

"Meaning . . ."

"Meaning I have a problem that requires your services."

"You want to barter?"

"Yes."

I'd blinked at the screen, at her flawless image. "Details, please?"

Bethany told me she'd send her two most popular influencers to Spike's the following night pro bono. (I didn't bother to tell her she wasn't using the term properly.) "A few minutes of these two, the business they bring in . . . You'll see what I'm capable of doing for your friend."

"I'm listening."

"I'll come by the place myself at ten p.m. That'll give Blake and Alena enough time to get the word out. You like what you see, I'll give you all the details you need."

I looked around now at the hectic bar. A group of bearded wannabe hipsters was taking selfies with Alena, while Blake and two barely-of-age girls were doing another cheers. The bartender was taking orders faster than he could fill them, and Spike was across the bar talking to his manager, a huge grin on his face. Everyone was drinking and spending as though the world wasn't about to end. There was no denying it. I was liking what I was seeing.

I felt a light tap on my shoulder. "Sunny Randall?"

I spun around on my corner barstool, and there she was. Bethany Rose. In the flesh.

"Sorry I'm a little late. I had a hotel opening on Newbury and traffic was a nightmare." Strangely enough, I still had no idea how old she was. She looked very much the same as she did on Zoom, though she was smaller than I expected. Doll-size. Standing next to my barstool, she was able to look straight into my eyes, and when I stood up to shake her manicured hand, I could fully see the top of her sleek black pixie cut.

She asked if we could talk somewhere quiet, and we found a table near the window. Spike spotted us and came over to introduce himself. Before I could explain who he was, Bethany told him she'd like to place her order and asked for a glass of Blake and Alena's fancy cognac.

"This is the owner," I said. "Bethany, Spike."

"Oh, I'm sorry," Bethany said. "You look so young, I thought you were a hot waiter."

Spike grinned. "She can stay." He pulled up a chair and joined us.

Bethany trained her eyes on Spike. They were hard to look away from—the same color as the sky in Van Gogh's *Starry Night*. They had to be colored contacts. "Your girlfriend's lucky," she said. "Big, strong drink of water like you . . ."

I could have sworn he blushed. "Boyfriend," he said.

She turned to me. "Always the best ones."

Spike blushed even more. No doubt about it. This woman knew how to make friends.

Spike called a waiter over and we all ordered. Pricey cognac for Bethany, more of that good pinot for Spike and me.

After he left, Bethany smiled brightly at both of us, then

gestured around the room like a boat-show model. "You guys like what you see?" she said.

"Absolutely," said Spike. Not even attempting to give her the hard sell.

"How do we know this isn't just a coincidence?" I said. "I think the night game just let out at Fenway."

A reach. And Bethany knew it. "You let me work my magic," she said, "and in a few weeks, you'll consider something like this a slow night."

"Wow," Spike said.

I sighed. "Tell me about your problem."

Bethany removed a file folder from her Birkin bag. "You and I are women, Sunny. We have to work that much harder to prove ourselves every single day, and I think it helps us develop thicker skin than the guys." She glanced at Spike. "Present company excluded, of course."

"Understood."

"I have a lot of young, gorgeous women who are clients. A lot of them have gotten . . . unwanted attention from followers. Alena included."

"I'd imagine," I said.

"Anyway, these girls, like I said, are tough. Assholes slide into their DMs, they do like I would do. Tell 'em to fuck off. Nine times out of ten, it works. That's the end of it." She pushed the folder across the table and gave me a long, meaningful look.

I opened the folder. Inside was a series of printouts—isolated screenshots of direct messages and comments on

Instagram posts, nearly a dozen from different accounts, all saying the same thing.

YOU REAP WHAT YOU SOW.

"Creepy," Spike said.

"I assume you checked out the accounts that posted these comments," I said.

Bethany nodded. "Fakes," she said. "You click on them, they no longer exist." She thumbed through the stack, selected one of the printouts, and tapped on the profile picture. "Recognize this girl?"

I did. Most everybody in Boston did. The profile pic was of Carlotta Espinoza. Influencer. Problematic side piece of a powerful political consultant. Missing person and, ultimately, murder victim. "Nice reference," I said. "Clever."

"I thought so."

The other profile pic choices on the fake profiles weren't as inspired: cats, plant life, household-name celebs like George Clooney and Oprah. It was understandable. Besides Espinoza, I was unaware of any other dead Boston influencers the stalker could have sourced.

"So, you have no idea who might have created these profiles?"

"Nope."

"And your client doesn't, either?" I said. "No enemies? No angry exes?"

"Hell hath no fury like an angry ex," Spike said.

"Don't I know it," Bethany said.

Spike fist-bumped her.

She looked at me. "No troublemakers that I know of."

"Is it possible," I said, "that your client could be keeping something from you?"

She shrugged. "Possible, yes. But highly improbable."

The waiter came by with our drinks and I closed the folder. I'd gotten anonymous threats before. More than once. In my line of work, it was a given.

Not too long ago, I came home to find a picture of my dad, the red light of a rifle scope superimposed onto his face. I knew what that was about: some lowlife, trying to scare me off an investigation. But that didn't make the feeling any easier to handle—all that hate coming at you from an unknown source. It's like being the target of that rifle scope. Someone else has all the power.

Bethany thanked the waiter and drank her cognac, swishing it around in her mouth for a while before swallowing it. I sipped my wine.

"Have you tried going to the police?" I said to her.

"They don't care. They're overworked. They think it's nothing. You know this, Sunny. Kids get bullied online into killing themselves and the cops don't get involved until it's too late. They're not going to waste time looking into some influencer's hate mail."

"Good point," I said.

"Look, this client of mine is sensitive," she said. "And scared."

"So, in exchange for marshaling the Gram or whatever it is you said you can do to put Spike's back on the map," I said, "you'd like me to track down the stalker."

"Well, yes. But also—"

"Also?"

"You can shoot a gun, right? Emily told me—"

"I'm not going to kill for you, Bethany."

"I will," Spike said.

"He's kidding."

"Don't be so sure."

"I don't want you to execute this person," Bethany said. "But I'd like you to spend some time with my client."

I blinked at her. "Like a bodyguard?"

She let out a heavy sigh. "In his case, it would be more like a babysitter."

"*His* case?" Spike and I said it at the same time.

Bethany nodded slowly, and I followed her gaze to Blake, who was standing up on his tiptoes, raising his glass and yelling, *"I'm the king of the world!"* so loudly, the girls next to him were plugging their ears.

"*His* case," she said.

THREE

I may not look it, but I'm a very good bodyguard. Thanks to my experience on the BPD and whatever genes I inherited from my police captain dad, I'm cautious, observant, reasonably calm under pressure, and a pretty good shot—qualities that, believe it or not, tend to trump bulk and muscles when it comes to keeping people safe. And when it doesn't, I've never been shy about calling for backup.

As a result, I've taken on several extremely challenging jobs that could be classified as protection-for-hire, most recently Melanie Joan Hall—yes, *that* Melanie Joan Hall, bestselling novelist/cottage industry/serious handful.

I imagined guarding Blake James would be a piece of cake compared to guarding Melanie Joan—mainly because guarding a rabid honey badger would be a piece of cake compared to guarding Melanie Joan.

But tracking down his stalker was a different matter. Unlike Melanie Joan, whom I'd known for years and who even owned the house I used to rent, Blake James was a complete stranger. If I was going to find out who hated him enough to leave those comments and send him those texts, I needed to learn more about Blake—or at least the world he lived in.

So, once I got home to my loft and gave Rosie her nightly soup bone and belly rub, I poured myself a glass of Malbec, stretched out on my couch, and logged in to Instagram.

It would've probably surprised my closest friends that I did, in fact, have an Instagram profile. It had been created by my older sister, Elizabeth, who, during a rare tender moment following my breakup with Jesse Stone, decided to enroll me on one of the dating apps—one that connected directly to the Gram.

In typical Elizabeth fashion, she'd created it under my given name, Sonya, which she knows I hate. But to her credit she did post some nice photos of me—some with our mom and dad, some with Rosie, some with her (in which she predictably outshone me, but whatever). She even posted a few shots of my paintings—a gesture that I must say I was moved by.

Not enough to use the dating app, though. Despite the fact that it had been around for most of my adult life, I harbored a deep distrust for social media of any kind. The idea of voluntarily revealing all that personal info to strangers had always struck me as dumber than dumb—and I'd seen far too many cases of Internet stalking, fraud, catfishing, and worse to change my mind about it. Ever since my early twenties, when I'd shut down my meager Facebook account after some jerk tried to blackmail me for nudes via private message, I've used the Internet only for work and for the purchasing of shoes—an approach I believed could lead to world peace if more people shared it.

Anyway, a few days after Elizabeth created my Instagram profile, I'd changed the handle to @RosieRandall, switched out my sister's carefully curated snaps for a few glamour shots of my dog, and exited the site forever—well, until now.

The first thing I did was to send a direct message to Blake James. (Glad to be working with you! Best, Sunny -- and Rosie!) Next, I did the same thing his 529,000 followers did: I checked out his pics.

Besides the shots of Blake posing next to Alena at Spike's (which he'd hashtagged #DateNight, #Spikes, and #CognacBuzz), I didn't see anything special at first—a whole lot of selfies, most of them shirtless, in gyms or parks or beaches, doing chin-ups or looking adoringly at bottles of vitamins or protein powder, the comments so full of heart-eye and fire emojis you'd have thought nobody knew how to type actual words anymore.

As I continued to scroll, I couldn't help thinking how shocking it must have been for Blake to spot a threat among these declarations of love. How scary—like finding a bloody knife in a bouquet of flowers. The comments had of course been deleted, nothing remaining but the printed-out screen-shots Bethany had given me. But it made me feel sorry for him—this poor, silly guy who became visibly hurt when people didn't "cheers" with him at Spike's. He must've been terrified.

Alena was different. Whereas Blake was twenty-one with the personality of an eleven-year-old, this Gen Z beauty had a soul as old as the dawn of time. A Bosnian immigrant with a thick accent, a deep, sultry voice, and a thousand-yard stare, she'd stood with her arm around Blake's waist in a way that felt more protective than romantic, and didn't even crack a smile until Bethany told her I was there to help Blake with his "little problem."

"You find the person who posts this evil saying," Alena had said. "I will rip them limb from limb."

"That's probably not necessary, sweetie," Bethany had said.

"Probably not," I had said. "But thanks for the offer."

According to Bethany, Blake and Alena had been "official" for nearly two years. But there wasn't much to show of that relationship on Blake's Instagram—or of any relationship, for that matter. Besides tonight's shots, the most recent picture I could find that wasn't a selfie was one from two months ago—Alena in a dimly lit restaurant, blowing out the candle on a pink-frosted cupcake. The caption: Happy birthday, Babe! #LoewsHotel #NARS #Feelin24 #Blessed. No one else was in the picture. And the first two hashtags were paid promotions.

Strange. But what did I know? In the world of influencers, this post was probably as heartfelt as it got.

I switched over to Alena's Instagram and scrolled through a sea of arched backs, skimpy outfits, pouty faces, and product placement. Alena was the only person in almost all of the snaps, except for the ones taken in Spike's and one from a few weeks ago, in which she posed with a couple other girls in bikinis aboard a yacht in the harbor—all of them as tanned and toned and surgically enhanced as she was. They toasted the camera with cans of some energy drink called Gonzo. (#Gonzo #Boats #BFFs #HotGirlSummer.) I wondered if these girls were really Alena's BFFs, or simply coworkers, arranged on the deck of this fancy boat like Barbie dolls. Looked more like the latter to me.

It was interesting to me that there was no record of Alena's birthday dinner on her Instagram. No solo pictures of Blake, either. If it weren't for those perfectly posed shots with the cognac at Spike's, you'd never know the two of them were a couple.

Rosie whimpered a little, so I scooped her up onto the couch and let her curl in my lap. "You ready for hot girl summer?" I said to Rosie.

She glanced up at me and promptly fell asleep.

"Yeah," I said. "Me neither." I raised the glass of Malbec to my lips and drank, returning to those shots from Spike's—Blake and Alena, still in the blush of their early twenties and "attached at both hips," according to Bethany. #DateNight. Like a long-married couple. Maybe lasting love worked only for the very young. Or maybe I was just in a cynical frame of mind.

I hadn't been on a date in months—not since my fling with Tom Gorman, a sweet newspaper columnist whom I'd promptly dumped as soon as he uttered the word *exclusive*. I knew I was being harsh, but I couldn't help it. I really, really liked him. I could see a future with him. And that was a big fat red flag if there ever was one.

As I'd grown to learn, sexual relationships could come and go for me, but romantic ones were chronic, roiling beneath the surface long after a split and flaring up regularly, no matter how cured I believed myself to be. I started dating Jesse Stone because he reminded me of my ex-husband, Richie Burke. Big mistake. A year after our breakup, I thought of Jesse far too often for my own good, and had more than once succumbed to those thoughts.

And though Richie had remarried, fathered a son, and divorced since we'd parted ways, he still, in all honesty, remained the love of my life. (Yes, I've discussed this in therapy. Repeatedly. As they say on social media, don't @ me.)

I sipped some more Malbec, listening to Rosie's soft snoring, and told myself to snap out of it. I had work to do that included subjecting myself to several episodes of The Shred Shed. I needed to focus.

Before leaving Alena's page, I took another look at the yacht picture. The girl to Alena's left caught my eye, and when I enlarged the image with my fingers, I saw that I was right: I knew her. She'd changed since I saw her last—lip fillers, a new makeup palette, her hair bleached platinum. But she was still Lee Farrell's niece, Emily Barnes.

It wasn't Emily I was most interested in, though. It was the woman captured in the frame behind her—*captured* being the operative word. I enlarged the picture more in order to see her better, caught mid-turn in a chic black shift, both hands fanned in front of her face so that all you could see of her was red nail polish and a shiny black pixie cut.

Rosie shifted in my lap. I patted her head. "Looks like Bethany doesn't like having her picture taken," I said.

FOUR

My breakfast meeting with Bethany and Blake was at The Blue Hut in Southie. The Blue Hut was a classic greasy spoon, open all night. It had stood in the same spot, serving poor-to-middling food, for more than half a century. It was a favorite for area cops because of its location and hours. And as a kid, I'd enjoyed many a breakfast there with my dad, pushing my food around on my plate but reveling in his company.

Mom and Elizabeth wouldn't have been caught dead eating at The Blue Hut. And neither, I imagined, would Blake and Bethany, but they'd asked to meet somewhere "safe," and thanks to its clientele (if not its grade from the health department), this place filled the bill.

I showed up ten minutes early and scored us a booth. Bethany and Blake arrived on time, at eleven. They turned heads—Bethany polished to a high gloss in a sleeveless black dress with the Prada logo on the front, Blake in a tight black T-shirt, tattooed guns out and fully loaded. They both looked like they'd stepped out of one of those bingeable streaming series, where everybody is gorgeous and lives like royalty and yet despite all that privilege, someone winds up getting murdered.

I was hyperaware of all the dropped jaws in the room, all the blue uniforms.

I stood up to greet the two of them. I noticed a tattoo on Bethany's shoulder—a delicate red rose that was as tasteful as the rest of her ensemble. She air-kissed me on both cheeks. I wondered if anybody in here had ever seen a live-and-in-person air-kiss before.

Bethany in particular seemed out of her element. "This place is interesting," she said, before diving into the booth. I half expected her to throw a hand over her face, the way she'd done in Alena's yacht picture.

Blake said hello and shook my hand. His grip was weak for someone with such enormous biceps.

After we were all seated, I looked at Blake. "How are you feeling this morning?" I was referring to what I figured must have been a walloping hangover, considering all the cognac I'd seen him consume the previous night. But he didn't take it that way.

"I was feeling pretty happy," he said, "until about an hour ago."

A waiter approached our table and asked what we'd be

having. I ordered a banana nut muffin and coffee. Blake ordered a burger without the bun, a hard-boiled egg, and a side of bacon. Bethany ordered hot water with lemon and a bowl of berries.

After he left, I asked Blake what happened an hour ago.

He handed me his phone. I looked at the screen and saw a direct message from someone who called themselves AvengingAngel and used a black rose as a profile pic. You reap what you sow, it read.

I tried giving him a smile. "That line's getting kinda old," I said.

"It's from the Bible."

"They're just trying to scare you, sweetie," Bethany said. "And Sunny will find them. Won't you, Sunny?"

"I'm going to try."

"The thing is," Blake said, "I always get these comments and DMs when I'm alone. And I'm not alone that often. It's like . . . like they're watching me."

Bethany patted Blake's hand, then squeezed it—an oddly intimate gesture, I thought, for a manager (concierge, whatever she called herself) and client. Blake turned to Bethany, his gaze soft on her face. "It's gonna be okay," he said. "Right?"

She kept holding his hand. I got a weird feeling—like I should give them their privacy. Then the waiter returned to our table, breaking the spell. He set down my coffee and muffin and Bethany's hot water and berries. "Your keto platter will be up in a second," he said to Blake, smirking.

I looked at Blake. As expected, he was oblivious.

I drank my coffee. Bethany sipped her hot water. Her bowl was full of grayish strawberries, a few shriveled blueberries thrown in for variety. She gave it a disdainful glance and pushed it away. "So," she said. "Did you figure out who the stalker is yet?" She smiled to let me know she was just kidding.

I smiled back. "You guys aren't making it easy."

"What do you mean?"

"I was online for probably two hours last night, researching Blake. Alena. You." I broke off a piece of my muffin and tried to eat it. To call it stale would have been a compliment. "Outside of the products Blake and Alena endorse, I came up with nothing. No hometowns. No family. Not even last names."

"That's intentional," Bethany said.

"I figured. But why?"

"The less complicated your online presence is, the more aspirational you are."

"'Aspirational'?"

"When you're influencing, you're projecting perfection," she said. "It's like your friend's restaurant. When we do his social media, we're obviously not going to show pictures of empty tables and dirty dishes, even though everyone knows those things exist. You use filters, Photoshop. People, places. You want them idealized. Not realized. That's the whole point of creating an image. And the cleaner and simpler that image, the better."

"What about you, Bethany?" I said. "I looked you up. No

Instagram. No Twitter. No TikTok. You have less of a social media presence than my dog."

"Your dog is cute," Blake said. "Nice profile pic."

"Thanks. I think so."

"Will I get to meet her when you're my bodyguard?"

"She usually comes everywhere with me," I said. "Only reason why I didn't take her here is she's picky about her scraps."

Bethany didn't glance away. She sipped her water, her bright gaze locking with mine. "I'm not a star, Sunny, and I have no desire to be. What I am," she said, "is a star-maker."

"Fair enough," I said. "Who's your biggest star?"

"Excuse me?"

"Which of your clients has the most followers? Who rakes in the most money?"

"You're sitting next to him," she said.

"I figured."

Blake grinned.

"We're in talks to make The Shred Shed into a regular TV series, so he stands to be next-level soon."

"What are the odds someone might be trying to get at you," I said, "by scaring your biggest-earning client into hiding?"

She put her cup down. "It's . . . It's possible."

"But it's also possible Blake could have an enemy he doesn't know about."

"I suppose."

"Last night," Blake said, "coming home from Spike's, a car followed my Uber right up until it dropped me off."

Bethany looked at him. "You didn't tell me that."

"I didn't want to scare you."

The waiter came back with Blake's burger, egg, and side of bacon. "Anything else?"

"You have Sriracha?"

The waiter scowled at him.

"We're good," Bethany said.

I took another sip of my coffee and waited for him to leave. "My point is that this stalker could be anybody, because you've given me nothing to help narrow it down," I said. "If I am going to protect Blake—and you—I need more than online personas. I have to know exactly who it is I'm protecting."

Bethany was quiet for several seconds.

Blake sliced up his boiled egg, carefully laying the slices on top of his burger. Then he followed it with all of the bacon. At the next table, a uniformed cop complained to his partner about his Yankees fan brother-in-law. I drank more coffee. Blake cut into his burger. Bethany continued to watch me. Seconds ticked by.

Finally, Bethany spoke. "What do you need to know?"

"Well, for starters," I said. "What are your last names?"

FIVE

Y ou took those people to The Blue Hut?" my dad said.

"Yep," I said.

"What did they think of it?"

"Not a lot."

He nodded. Sipped his scotch. We were sitting in The Street Bar at the Newbury hotel—our standing weekly get-together for drinks and catching up. As usual, I was bending his ear about my latest clients, gleaning whatever info and advice I could from Captain Phil Randall, who, though many years into his retirement and enjoying the fruits of it in elegant surroundings such as these, remained the savviest investigator I knew. "You can't really appreciate The Blue Hut," he said, "unless you're coming off a nine-hour stakeout."

"Or if you're seven years old and willing to risk ptomaine for a little quality time with your father."

"I thought you said you liked the pancakes."

"They were okay," I said. "But TBH, I prefer this place."

"TBH?"

"To be honest."

"Ah."

"Text speak." I took a large swallow of my cosmo. "Less than twenty-four hours with these people and I'm already talking like them. Shoot me now."

My father sighed heavily. "I'm old enough to remember when *influencer* wasn't a real word."

"Same," I said. "It feels like a million years ago."

"So," my dad said. "Any thoughts as to who might want to threaten . . . What's the kid's name?"

"Blake James."

"Sounds like a movie cowboy."

"His full name is Blake Jameson Marshall. Which . . . well, that kinda sounds like a movie cowboy, too."

"It does."

"But he doesn't look like one. Unless you've seen a movie cowboy with a SpongeBob tattoo on the back of his neck."

My dad drank more scotch. "Can't say that I have."

"To answer your question," I said, "it's tricky. Blake says he has no enemies. He loves everybody and everybody loves him. But I don't think he has a realistic view of his surroundings."

"How so?"

"Okay, for example, at The Blue Hut, he asked for Sriracha

to go with his weird keto meal. The waiter looked at him like he wanted to punch him in the face, but Blake was completely oblivious," I said. "Last night at Spike's, he had too much to drink and got very loud. Some of the regulars were clearly pissed off, and Spike himself would have tossed him out of there if he hadn't brought in so many new customers. But Blake . . ."

"Can't read a room."

"That's right."

"Probably has enemies he doesn't even know about."

"Right again."

"Makes him difficult to protect," he said. "Fortunately, I know my little girl is up to the job."

"Thanks, Dad." I raised my glass. "Want to do a cheers?"

"Do a what now?"

I winced. "By the time I finish with these people, I'll have no language skills left."

Dad clinked his glass with mine, and we both drank. "At least I knew what you meant that time," he said.

He asked me if he could help at all, and I told him I hoped so. I let him in on everything I now knew about Blake Jameson Marshall—which, truth be told, wasn't a lot. He was twenty-one. He hailed from a little town in Indiana called Greendale. He'd grown up on a farm. His father had died in a tractor accident about fifteen years ago. Blake's mom, Lisa, ran the place now. His older sister, Rain, was a third-grade teacher, but Blake didn't have much contact with either one of them. Not with anybody from Greendale, he claimed. Not since he decided to leave the farm at eighteen to pursue a modeling career in New York. Lisa and Rain weren't on social media, so they probably didn't even know that Blake got only as far as Boston, where he met Alena during leg day at Equinox and fell in love. ("My very first girlfriend," he said.) Alena introduced him to her manager, Bethany Rose (her real and full name, she insisted; she even showed me her driver's license), and before long, Blake was making more money on the Gram than he'd ever hoped to earn on NYC runways.

"So he doesn't owe anybody," Dad said. "No outstanding debts?"

"According to him? No," I said. "But who knows? Somebody back in Greendale might feel differently."

"A friend of mine from back in the day moved to his old hometown—one of the suburbs of Indianapolis—and became police chief," Dad said. "He's still there, far as I know. Maybe he's got some Greendale connections."

"Can you give me his info?"

"I can when I get home."

I shook my head. "You still haven't learned how to put contacts into your phone."

"Who says I want to learn?" he said. "My paper address book hasn't failed me yet. And it doesn't cost me any data."

Dad. Still on a limited-data plan. Hell, it was less than two years ago that he'd finally given up his flip phone. But he probably had the right idea. There was a lot to be said for relying on one's memory, even for something as simple as phone numbers. My dad was aging. We all were, but he seemed to be doing it more rapidly as of late. He had been using a cane since his gunshot wound last year, and I worried that his reliance on it might be a permanent thing. I also knew from Mom that he was on stronger blood pressure meds, and that he'd recently been diagnosed with what she said was "very mild diabetes." But though he may have been physically frailer, Phil Randall's mind was as sharp as ever. "All the important numbers—like yours—I got right here." He tapped his head and gave me a sly smile, as though he'd been reading my thoughts. Maybe he had been. I wouldn't have put it past the guy.

I smiled back.

"So on a different note," he said, "have you talked to Richie lately?"

I sipped my cosmo, the name a slight stab to my heart. "Not for a while," I said. Such a strange story, Richie and me. When we fell in love, my dad and Richie's father, Desmond Burke, were archenemies. And while they may have tolerated our marriage and subsequent post-divorce friendship, their animosity for each other continued unabated—no surprise, considering the fact that Desmond remained one of Boston's most powerful crime bosses, and Phil had spent much of his career trying to put him behind bars.

But things began to thaw between them around the time of Phil's shooting. They spoke occasionally. They asked each other about "the kids." It may have been a "life's too short" kind of thing, but these two men—who still despised each other above all else—seemed to have found some type of common ground in the idea that they both were still alive, that they both had children who loved them and who, at one time at least, had loved each other.

Yet the closer Desmond and Phil got, the bigger the rift grew between Richie and me. At first I thought it was because I'd rejected his idea of getting back together. But when I texted him one night after too many glasses of wine and told him I was willing to reconsider, he texted back No. You were right. I'd spoken about this to my shrink, Susan Silverman, who suggested that a clean break might be the healthiest thing for both of us. But while that may have indeed been true, it's also a known fact that in life, the healthiest things are often the least pleasurable.

Dad drank his scotch. I finished my cosmo.

"So you probably haven't heard," Dad said, "that Richie is moving away."

I stared at him. *"What?"*

And then, wouldn't you know it, my phone started ringing. "Dad, you can't just say that. I need details."

"I don't have details," he said. "Desmond mentioned it."

"When?"

"A little while ago."

My phone was still ringing. I picked it up, looked at the screen, saw Blake's name. "Shit," I said. "It's the movie cowboy."

"You should answer."

"I know. I know." I tapped the green dot and put the phone to my ear, still thinking of Richie, leaving town without even telling me. "Sunny Randall," I said.

"Is this Sunny Randall?" Blake said. As though I hadn't just answered the phone by saying my own name. I would have told him to call back during work hours or asked if this could wait until tomorrow morning, when I was supposed to accompany him to a meeting with the producers of the upcoming *Shred Shed* TV show. But something in the tone of his voice stopped me—a quavering, as though someone were holding a knife to his throat.

"Blake?" I said. "Are you okay?"

My dad raised his eyebrows.

On the other end of the line, Blake took a shaky breath and made a sound—half sob, half whimper.

"Blake?"

"Can you come over now, please?"

"Sure. But why?"

For a few seconds I thought he'd hung up. But then he spoke, his voice as frightened and pained as a lost little boy's. "The stalker left something in my apartment."

SIX

I asked Blake if I could go home and pick up a few things before heading over to his place, and he said sure. By "a few things," I really just meant my gun and Rosie, so I knew it wouldn't take long. It didn't. Less than thirty minutes elapsed between my phone call with Blake and the moment I arrived at his apartment building. And in that brief window of time, I'd managed to argue with my dad over who would pay the bar tab (he won . . . sigh), put both of us into Ubers, grab my gun and my dog, change out of my vintage Bruno Magli pumps and into my most broken-in pair of Chucks, and take another Uber to Blake's, which was located in a sparkling-new Back Bay high-rise.

I was better than Domino's.

The fact that I'd spent at least twenty-nine of those thirty minutes thinking about Richie leaving Boston—and, by extension, me—was not something I cared to address. I needed to focus on my job right now. It helped that I was dressed for the occasion, in my most no-nonsense black St. John pantsuit, topped off by the black Chucks and of course the .38 Special in my speed holster. Very Secret Service chic.

Blake had said he'd call down to the security guard and put me on a list. So I expected my exchange with him would last five seconds—maybe ten, if he wanted to pet Rosie. It didn't go that way, though. The guard—a towering wall of flesh with tiny, dead eyes—paid no attention to Rosie. (I don't trust people who don't pay attention to Rosie.) But he did take the time to ask questions like "What kind of a name is Sunny supposed to be?," demand two separate forms of ID, and use his height advantage to blatantly look down my blouse.

Riding the elevator up to Blake's twenty-fifth-floor apartment after suffering through that exchange, I found comfort in the pressure of the gun in its holster at the small of my back. It was almost like the embrace of an old friend—which that little snub-nose was, when I thought about it. It had been with me ever since I left the force and struck out on my own. Unlike certain other old friends, the .38 Special hadn't failed me once. And it had no plans to leave town without telling me.

I found the right door and knocked on it.

I heard Blake's voice. "Is that you, Sunny Randall?"

"It is, Blake," I said. "And you can just call me Sun—"

The door opened. Bethany stood there, looking up at me

with her electric-blue eyes and wearing a silk shirtdress that matched them perfectly. "Thank you for coming on such short notice," she said. As though she lived here, which . . . come to think of it, maybe she did?

"Is Blake okay?"

"He's fine," she said. "Just a little shaken up."

Rosie yelped. I undid her leash and scooped her into my arms as Bethany ushered me in.

"You brought your dog," she said.

"I didn't know how long I'd be here," I said. "And she doesn't like to be alone."

"Who does?" Bethany said.

It made me think of Richie again. "I do. Sometimes."

Rosie and I followed Bethany into the apartment. Aesthetically, I wasn't a fan of massive, ultramodern buildings like these, which felt like they'd sprung up overnight, taking over my beautiful city like steel Godzillas. But I could never resist a nice view, and Blake James's pad was a true guilty pleasure. A corner apartment facing the Charles, it boasted two enormous floor-to-ceiling windows—the river straight ahead, the Common to the right, Boston spread out below in all its twinkling, elegant glory. I recognized the view from Blake's Instagram—it appeared as a background in numerous pics, which no doubt paid a good share of his rent. But in person it was breathtaking—literally. I gasped.

"Gorgeous, isn't it?" Bethany said. "Imagine living like this at twenty-one."

"It definitely beats my BU dorm."

"Can I pet your dog?" Blake said. He was sitting on the white leather couch, with Alena beside him, the two of them sipping from large white mugs. They were both all in white, Blake in jeans and a tank top, Alena in a sheer sundress. Two perfect, sad angels, perched on a cloud. I wondered if there was ever a time when the two of them didn't look as though they were in the midst of a photo shoot.

"Of course," I said.

I walked up to them, set Rosie down on the floor, so she could sniff Blake's shoes. She rolled over onto her back and let him scoop her into his arms, his expression softening as she put her paws up on his chest and licked his face. Spike was always telling me I should get Rosie certified as an emotional support dog, and watching her with Blake, I saw he had a point. Even stoic Alena cracked a smile.

After a few minutes, I pulled a dog biscuit out of my purse. Rosie jumped onto the floor, took the biscuit from my hand, and settled down with it beneath the glass-topped coffee table.

"Have a seat," said Bethany, who had made herself comfortable on the other side of Blake.

That was easier said than done. The room felt as though it was designed more for entertaining than for relaxation—big on sculptures and fixtures and screens, but very light on furniture you could sit on. And it felt strange to squeeze in next to Blake, Bethany, and Alena.

I saw a few tall chrome-and-white leather stools lined up in front of a fully stocked wet bar, a flimsy-looking director's chair positioned near a tripod with a ring light on top, and a white beanbag chair about six feet away from the couch, next to a black marble fire feature. I settled on the last choice. Bethany must have read my mind because she got up and slid the beanbag chair closer to the couch and said, "How about a scotch, as long as I'm standing?"

I said sure, then sat down on the beanbag chair as gracefully as I could with the gun digging into my back. My eyes found a manila envelope on the glass coffee table—practically the only object in the room that wasn't white, black, or metallic.

Bethany returned with scotches for herself and me. I took a sip. It was smooth—blended, I thought. But an expensive one. Alena sipped from her mug. Blake lifted his mug from the coffee table and took a big swallow. Rosie crunched on her biscuit.

"So who wants to tell me what happened?" I said.

Bethany was the one to reply. "Blake and Alena went to a party for a new energy drink," she said. "I gave them a ride home."

"You live here, too, Alena?"

"*Ne ne zham.*"

I blinked at her.

"In English, dear," Bethany said.

"No, I do not. I live in the building, though. Twenty-eighth floor."

I nodded.

"Alena and I were kinda wound up from the event," Blake said. "Too much Gonzo."

"Gonzo?"

"The energy drink."

Alena wrinkled her nose. "I hate Gonzo." I remembered the Instagram pic of her and her #BFFs aboard the yacht, those smiles of sheer enjoyment as they toasted the camera with cans of the stuff. So much for truth in advertising.

"After Bethany left, I went to make us some chamomile tea," Blake said. "Chamomile tea always helps break a bad buzz. No carbs, too. I love it. So does Alena."

"I do. Soothing." She took another sip.

"Anyway . . ." Bethany said.

"Anyway. Yeah. Sorry. So I was so busy making the tea, I didn't even notice it," Blake said. "I don't know if I would have seen it at all if Alena hadn't picked it up . . ."

He was looking at the manila envelope on the coffee table. Bethany pushed it toward me, and I opened it. Inside the envelope was a blown-up color photo of Blake, sound asleep on the same white couch that he was sitting on now. He was fully dressed. And I recognized the Caribbean-blue sleeveless jacket.

"You wore that last night," I said.

He nodded slowly, the mug clutched in his hands like a security blanket. "The picture was taken last night," he said.

"You're sure?"

"I got so drunk at your friend's restaurant I couldn't make

it into the bedroom," Blake said, his voice cracking. "That never happens. I hardly ever drink. Because of the carbs."

"Was . . . anybody with you?"

He shook his head vigorously. "Alena took the elevator up to her place. I came in here alone. Passed out on the couch alone," he said. "Someone got into my apartment. Someone came into this building and broke into my apartment and took that picture."

"And then they came back," Alena said. "They came back in here and put the picture under the door. I find the envelope on the floor."

Blake gulped his tea, then set the mug back on the table. "It's just so . . . so fucked up."

Bethany and Alena put their arms around him. "It's okay," Bethany said. "Sunny will fix things. Won't you, Sunny?"

I thought about the building's lobby. The security cameras. That huge, intrusive guard, right next to the elevators. Yet somebody had made it up to Blake's apartment, not once but twice. I looked at Blake. "Have you had any disputes with people in your building?"

"Um . . ."

"Try and think about it. Maybe there was something you didn't even feel like it was that big a deal . . ."

"Oh." He rubbed his temples for what felt like a full minute. "Oh, wait. Oh, *man*."

"Yes?"

"About six months ago, I had a party. Remember, Alena?"

"Loud party," Alena said. "*Bilo je plesa*. Much dancing."

"Yeah," Blake said. "Somebody called the cops, but I don't know who."

"Interesting," I said.

Bethany gave me flat eyes. "You really think someone would do all of this over one noisy party?"

"That night of lost sleep could have cost someone a job, or made them miss an important event or even get in an accident," I said.

"Shit," Blake said. "Holy shit."

"Frankly, it's hard to imagine someone who doesn't live in this building getting past lobby security. Not that it couldn't be done . . ." I made a mental note to speak to the head of security in the morning and ask to see CCTV footage. They didn't always like to comply with private investigators—especially in snooty buildings like this one—but I could be pretty darn convincing when I wanted to be.

"Maybe it's one of the guards," Blake said.

"Probably best not to speculate," Bethany said. "Right, Sunny?"

I stayed focused on Blake. "Could you have left your door unlocked?"

"No. It locks automatically."

"Does security have extra keys?"

He nodded.

I looked at Bethany. "As speculations go," I said, "it isn't a bad one."

Grasping the table for support, I struggled out of the beanbag chair and stood up. Rosie stood up, too. I took another biscuit out of my purse and gave it to her.

"That guard downstairs," I said. "Is he here every night?"

"Most weeknights," Blake said.

"Was he here last night?"

Blake said he didn't remember, and looked at Alena.

"Yes," she said.

"Do you know his name?"

She nodded. "Eddie."

"He's kind of a dick," Blake said.

"Yes," Alena said.

I slipped the photo back into the manila envelope and attached Rosie's leash. "I believe it's time Eddie and I had a little chat."

SEVEN

One thing I'd learned over the years: Certain men—the ones often described as "kind of a dick"—responded better to questioning when faced with a direct physical threat. Fortunately, I had one of those at the top of my contacts list.

Spike arrived at Blake's apartment building within fifteen minutes of my call, and Rosie and I met him just outside the front door. As always, we were very happy to see him. After greeting both of us, Spike stepped back, gazed up at the building, and let out a whistle. "This is where that kid with the punchable face lives?"

I nodded.

"Not bad," he said.

"If you like that kind of thing."

"I do."

"Maybe you and Sam should take a look at this place. Get yourselves a sweet one-bedroom with a view of the Charles..." Sam was the host of *Good Morning Boston* and a genuinely nice, funny guy. He and Spike had been seeing each other for fourteen months, and for at least twelve of those months, I'd been trying to convince my best friend to make more of a commitment. I'd even offered to pay $40 to the Universal Life Church so I could become a minister and officiate their wedding, which may have been a little pushy. I couldn't help it, though. Spike was genuinely happy with Sam. He had a shot at making that happiness eternal. I didn't want to see him blow that chance the way I had.

"You never quit, do you?" he said.

"Sorry. I can't control it."

Spike sighed heavily. "So what am I doing with this doorman? Black eye? Busted nose? You want some judo moves?"

"For now, I just want you to stand there and be large."

"You're no fun."

"I said 'for now.' It could change."

The three of us strode back into the lobby, Spike, Rosie, and me. Eddie looked as though he'd grown since the last time I spoke to him, his barrel chest straining against the buttons of his rent-a-cop uniform as he tapped away on his phone. I realized he was the same height as Spike, as well as the same physical type, which Spike himself called "hard fat" and other people called "terrifying." Good quality for a security guard, and the polar opposite of this sleek, flimsy building.

When we got within a foot of Eddie, he finally looked up from his phone. A deep mechanical voice said, "Tasty." Candy Crush. I'd always hated that game.

"You forget something?" he said.

"Actually," I said, "I enjoyed our previous conversation so much, I decided to come back for more."

"No, you didn't."

"Sharp guy."

His beady gaze traveled from me to Spike and back again. "What do you want?" he said.

"I'm a private investigator," I said. "My client is Blake James."

"Yeah? And?"

I removed the manila envelope from my purse and slipped out the picture and held it up for Eddie to see. "You recognize this photo?"

He barely glanced at it. "No."

"It was taken by someone without Mr. James's knowledge, then placed in his apartment to scare him," I said. "Both times on your watch. Which strikes me as strange, considering how seriously you take your job."

He shrugged.

"You really don't know anything about it?"

"Nope."

"And you aren't alarmed? You're not going to investigate?"

He shrugged again. "Nothing *Mr. James* does or gets done to him *alarms* me. He doesn't even pay rent."

"He doesn't?"

"Nope," he said. "Management lets him live here in exchange for taking pictures of himself. So far as I care, he took that picture. Or one of his porno friends. You could have taken it."

"Me?"

"Sure."

"What do you mean, 'one of his porno friends'?"

"I'm done talking." He stole a purposeful glance down my shirt. "Unless you want to . . . you know. Speak in body language, if you catch my drift. I might remember some stuff." He grinned.

I looked at Spike, who was glaring at Eddie as though he'd like to rip his head off. If it weren't for the security cameras, I may have let him. "No, thanks," I said. "I'll just talk to your boss about it."

"You think you're gonna do that?"

"I do."

"Yeah?"

"Or . . . Oh, this is an even better idea. I have a good friend, Tom Gorman. The *Globe* columnist? I bet he'd love a story about a luxury building that's so unsafe, famous Instagrammers are getting terrorized in their own apartments . . ."

Eddie stared at me for what felt like a full minute. "Am I supposed to be scared?"

Spike said, "This guy asks a lot of dumb questions."

Eddie looked at Spike. "Who the fuck are you?"

"See what I mean, Sunny?"

"Yep."

"You think you can take me, asshole?"

"Wow, they keep coming," Spike said.

I nodded. "It's like a dumb-question monsoon."

"Wish I'd brought my umbrella."

Eddie's gaze stayed locked with Spike's for so long, I half expected him to bring up body language. Instead, he stepped around the desk, balled up his fist, and took a swing at Spike's face. Bad idea. Spike grabbed his arm before it connected. "You don't want to punch a guest, unprovoked, in front of these security cameras, do you?" Spike said. "Let's shake hands instead."

I picked up Rosie and moved out of the way.

Spike shook Eddie's hand vigorously and smiled, grasping the crook of his arm with his left. As far as the security cameras were concerned, it was a classic handshake. But from where I was standing, I couldn't help but notice how tightly Spike gripped Eddie's arm, just above the elbow, the whiteness of his fingers as they dug into his flesh.

Eddie's eyes went big. He let out a yelp.

"This is called a pressure point, Eddie," Spike said between his teeth. "Ever do jujitsu?"

Eddie's eyes got even bigger.

"I'll take that for a no," Spike said. "Here's the deal. I keep doing this, it's going to hurt a lot more. A minute or so of it, you'll need a splint. More than that, we're talking permanent damage."

Eddie's face flushed. His breath came out in shallow gasps.

Spike leaned in closer. "I could really fuck up your tennis game."

A tear slipped down Eddie's cheek. Then another. He murmured something I couldn't hear.

"Was that, 'let go'?" Spike said. "You'll have to enunciate better, Eddie."

"He'll let go," I said, "if you tell us who took that picture."

Eddie shook his head.

Spike tightened his grip.

"Would security footage tell us different?" I said. "How about the sign-in sheet from last night?"

"You really want to make this permanent?" Spike said.

Eddie gritted his teeth. Forced out the words. "I . . . know who took the pic . . . I'll tell you."

"You going to answer me truthfully?"

"Yes."

"Promise?"

"Yes. Let go. Yes. I promise. I swear."

Spike loosened his grip. Eddie took a breath.

"Fuck," Eddie said. "Who the hell are you?"

"No more dumb questions," Spike said. "Unless you want another handshake."

"He knows where you work," I said. "If you lie to us, he can find out where you live."

"You . . . You can't . . ."

"I have connections on the police force," Spike said.

"Yeah? Who?"

"Me," I said. "I used to be a cop, dumbass. I know every-body."

Eddie rubbed his arm.

"Eddie," I said. "Who took the picture?"

Eddie took a deep breath, then let it out slowly, his massive body trembling, his weepy stare plastered to Spike's face. "I did," he said. "I took it."

EIGHT

As big and aggressive as Eddie had seemed on the surface, he was very easily broken. And so it didn't take much longer for Spike and me to find out that 1) he used a security key to get into Blake's apartment the previous night. 2) He printed out the picture and slipped it under Blake's door a couple hours ago. And 3) He did both of those things because he was paid to do it.

"I really needed the money," said this new, cowed Eddie, who was so different from the Eddie of ten minutes ago, it was as though Spike had rewired him with that pressure-point maneuver. "My mom lives with me and she has arthritis real bad," new Eddie said. "Medicare won't pay for her health aide anymore and I've got debts of my own. I can't support her and me on what this job pays. This guy shows up a couple days ago. He gives me a whole bunch of cash. Says he's not gonna hurt nobody. He just wants to send a message."

I glanced at Spike. "So you did it."

"Yeah."

"For your mom."

"Yeah."

"What did the guy look like?" Spike said.

"Just like . . . a guy. A little shorter than me. Bald-headed. Nice suit."

"I'm taking it he didn't give you his name," I said.

"No."

"And he paid you in cash."

"Yes."

"Did he tell you what the message was supposed to be?"

"No." Eddie stared at the floor. "I figure Blake James must have fucked with the wrong people. The guy seemed . . . you know."

"What?"

"Connected."

"How so?"

"He had these face tattoos. Teardrops. Three of them."

"Right or left eye?" I said.

"Left," he said. "What fuckin' difference does it make?"

"Left eye means he killed someone in prison. Three teardrops means he killed three people in prison," I said. "Nice work letting him terrorize someone you're hired to protect."

Eddie visibly shuddered. "Can I get back to work now?"

"I don't care what you do," I said.

Spike was already on his way to the elevator. I set Rosie down on the floor, and we both followed him.

Eddie was whining at me to "please don't say nothing to my boss" about what he told us. "Please. I need this job. I won't do nothing like that again."

I didn't turn around. Didn't say anything until Spike, Rosie, and I were in the elevator and on our way to the twenty-fifth floor. "What do you think he meant by 'porno friends'?" I said.

"I was going to ask you the same thing," Spike said.

Back in the apartment, Blake and Bethany were watching Jillian Michaels on his cinema-size flat screen. "See the way she engages with the camera?" Bethany was saying to Blake as she let us in. "That's what the fans want."

But once the door closed behind us, she turned off the TV. "That was fast," she said.

"Where's Alena?" I asked.

Bethany explained that Alena had gone back up to her own place to get some sleep. She had an early shoot in the morning for a "plant-based dietary supplement" she no doubt hated as much as she hated Gonzo.

Blake said, "Did you guys find out anything from Eddie?"

I recounted our entire conversation, save for the part where Spike put Eddie in a Vulcan death grip. I wasn't sure they'd approve.

Blake and Bethany listened intently, Bethany with her chin resting prettily on the crook of her index finger, Blake with his jaw dropped open, like a kid at story hour.

"What the fuck?" Blake said once I was done. "Leave me a message? What message? I don't get it."

Bethany said nothing. It struck me that she hadn't said anything for a very long time—not since I'd informed them that Eddie had been paid off by a bald guy who he'd said seemed "connected."

"Usually, when the Mob wants to give you a message," Spike said, "it's because you owe 'em."

"I don't owe anybody."

"You sure?" Spike said.

"What? Yeah. Of course I'm sure."

Blake looked at Bethany. She was examining her nails. "Blake doesn't owe anyone anything," she said. "He's self-supporting."

"Okay, good," I said. "Because Eddie said one other thing that kind of . . . gave me pause. Not because I'm a prude. But because you never mentioned it to me, Blake, and if I'm going to protect you, we can't keep things from each other."

Blake's blue eyes widened. "Huh?"

"He mentioned something about your 'porno friends.' Are you involved in porn?"

"Are you kidding me? No!"

"I know. Eddie's an idiot." I moved over to the director's chair, ran my hand over the ring light, which was a large, circular movie lamp on an adjustable metal pole, with a camera mount at the center of the circle. "Had to ask, though."

Blake shifted on the couch. The leather squeaked. Bethany lifted her head.

As I've mentioned, I was not the most tech-savvy person of my generation, nor did I have much of an interest in social media or any of its permutations. But that didn't mean I was completely out of it. You're a private investigator long enough, you learn things you might never have known otherwise. "I worked with a client once," I said. "Erin Flint. Big movie star for about five minutes back in late 'aughts. Ever hear of her?"

"No," Blake said.

"I have," said Bethany. "Isn't she retired?"

"From action movies, yes. But ever since the pandemic, she's been making a mint." I looked directly at Blake. "On OnlyFans."

Blake's cheeks reddened.

Spike said, "Oh, ho."

I suppressed a smile.

"Blake," I said. "Do you have an OnlyFans?"

His eyes dropped to his hands. "No."

"Of course he doesn't," Bethany said.

"There's nothing to be ashamed of," I said. "Sex work is work. And OnlyFans is a great business model. You produce your own porn. Subscribers pay you directly. No middleman other than the site itself. You don't do anything you aren't comfortable with. No pimp. No exploitative director . . . And for somebody as sought-after as Blake, I mean . . . An Instagram superstar can earn a lot of money on that platform."

"He *doesn't make porn*," Bethany said.

Spike and I stared at her. Rosie whimpered.

Bethany cleared her throat. "I didn't mean to raise my voice," she said. "I just know for a fact that Blake doesn't do that. That ring light is for The Shred Shed." She gave Blake a warm smile. "Don't feel bad, sweetie. Obviously the doorman is jealous."

Blake said nothing.

I said, "There goes my theory, then."

"What's your theory?" Blake said.

"I was thinking that the bald guy works for one of the crime bosses, and that crime boss might want to scare you into turning over a cut of your OnlyFans profits."

"That's ridiculous," Bethany said.

"Oh, I don't think so," Spike said. "That actress what's-her-name had an OnlyFans. Made a million bucks in a day without even taking her clothes off." Spike smirked at me. "Straight men. Am I right?"

"Tell me about it," I said.

"Anyhoo, if I were Desmond Burke or Jackie DeMarco, I'd want a cut of those profits," Spike said. "And if I knew Blake well enough, I'd try and scare that cut out of him."

"Same," I said. "But we're obviously barking up the wrong tree, so . . ."

"Say I did have an OnlyFans," Blake said. "Why would the Mafia think I owed them a cut?"

Bethany turned to him. "What are you talking about?" she said. "Why are you even pursuing this conversation?"

Blake eyed my mostly untouched scotch on the coffee table. "You mind?" he asked.

I shook my head. He picked up the glass, drank from it, and winced. "I don't have an OnlyFans, I swear," he said.

"Of course, you don't," Bethany said.

"But I did have one. About six months ago."

I bit back an "Oh, ho."

"I only had it for two weeks. But I made a shit-ton of cash. These guys are right."

Bethany drained the rest of her own scotch, staring daggers at Blake. When she spoke, her voice was very quiet. "Why didn't you tell me?"

"Because I wanted to have something for myself. Without you judging me or directing me or . . ."

"Blake, I am very disappointed in you."

"It wasn't even real porn," Blake said. "I put on a speedo and did chores around the apartment. Subscribers would ask me to, like . . . vacuum or clean my oven or whatevs. It's like a kink for some people, I guess." He gulped down more scotch. "Pretty wild how much they were willing to pay."

I walked over to the bar, poured short glasses for Spike and me, the two of us watching Blake and Bethany's conversation like tennis fans at a match.

"Anyway, what's it to you?" Blake was saying. "I don't have the OnlyFans anymore. No harm done."

"How much did you make?" Bethany said.

"Like nine hundred K."

"How much of it do you still have?"

He opened his mouth, then closed it again. "I'm not . . .

I'm not giving you any of it, if that's what you're thinking. I made it on my own. It's my money."

"You need to listen to me, Blake."

"No way. It's mine."

"I'm not asking you out of greed."

"What are you asking me out of, then?"

She cleared her throat. "Concern."

"You don't need to get all freaked out about the pics," he said. "I never showed my dick. My image is still clean."

"I don't care about your image."

"Then what are you worried about?" He grinned. "The Mafia?"

She picked up the glass, then slammed it down on the coffee table. *"Yes, Blake. I am extremely fucking worried about the fucking Mafia."*

Blake's grin disappeared.

I looked at Spike. He mouthed a *Wow* at me.

"Shit," Blake whispered.

I took my glass and walked over to the couch. I stood over Blake and Bethany, the two of them gaping at each other as though the couch, the floor, the coffee table, everything they knew to be real had suddenly exploded into bits, leaving them frozen, with nothing left to do but wait for that inevitable moment when they disintegrated, too.

"All right, Bethany," I said. "I'm going to need you to tell me everything."

NINE

"Seed money." That's how Bethany described the significant investment a certain "forward-thinking individual" had made in her business four years ago, when she first moved to Boston. She'd met said individual through a mutual friend in L.A. whom she declined to name. And since that friend's name wasn't all that important to the story, I didn't press her for it. I also didn't bother asking her why she didn't go to more traditional sources for a loan—family, a bank, a credit union. None of that changed what we had to work with— which was, quite frankly, a mess.

Bethany's company, Insta-Fame Inc., was born thanks mostly to this one investor. In exchange for that initial "spon-sorship"—which was apparently enough to pay for a top-flight

Web designer, the down payment on a chic Newbury Street office, plastic surgery for Bethany, Alena, and several other clients, hair, wardrobe, targeted advertising, a splashy opening-night party, and countless other necessary start-up expenses— Bethany had been giving him a cut of her biggest clients' earnings ever since. This was where Blake's brief flirtation with OnlyFans came in. Not knowing anything about it, Bethany of course hadn't sent the investor a cut. If our theory was correct, the investor believed Bethany had withheld the money intentionally, and was attempting to scare it out of her—with a series of threats to her most prized client that were clear but untraceable.

It was a big *if*, though, and I told Bethany so. "Keep in mind," I said, "we're basing this entire idea on the word of one person. Eddie, who also happens to be a total asshat."

"No, no," she said. "It all makes more sense than you could begin to imagine, Sunny."

"It does?"

"I've only had one direct conversation with this investor," she said. "It was early on and over a burner phone. He told me that if I tried to cheat him out of his share, he'd find out. And he'd make it known."

I looked at Blake. His face was nearly as white as his tank top. "How come you didn't tell me about this deal?" he said.

"I didn't want you to worry."

"Does Alena know?"

She shook her head. "I tell you guys everything that's

important," she said. "But this isn't. Not really. It's just . . . my problem now." She smiled at Blake and gave his hand a squeeze.

"I don't want you to have this kind of problem," he said. "I don't want you to have any problems." And again I got the strange feeling that there was something going on between Blake and Bethany—something too big to fit within the boundaries of manager and client.

"I can make it go away," Bethany said.

"You can?"

"I'll just need a third of that OnlyFans money. I'll wire it to the investor. And then things will be back to normal." She grinned at Spike. "We still on for tomorrow lunch?"

"You bet."

"Ready to make Spike's into a worldwide destination?"

"I'd settle for Massachusetts-wide."

"That's too easy, doll. I like a challenge," she said. "By the by, I have a little surprise for you tomorrow afternoon."

Blake raised my glass to his lips and drained the rest of it. His hand trembled. "You okay?" I asked him.

He shook his head.

Rosie trotted up to him and sniffed his foot. He scooped her into his arms.

"Bethany?" I said. "What's the name of the investor?"

"Why do you ask?"

"Because," I said, "I might know him. And I might be able to help."

"Law-abiding former cop like you? I don't think so."

Clearly, Bethany knew me about as well as I knew her. "I used to be married to Desmond Burke's son," I said.

Her eyebrows shot up. "No. Really?"

I nodded.

"Well, for your sake, I hope you're on good terms. Are you?"

"He's not involved in the family business," I said. Which was about as much of an answer as I could give her at the moment. I tried to remember the last time Richie had stopped by, even to visit Rosie. I couldn't. "Time marches on. No matter how much you try to hold it down, people grow, they change, they move forward. They move away." I realized I was talking more to myself than to anyone in the room, and I could feel Spike frowning at me. I cleared my throat.

"Business deals like the one you made, Bethany," I said. "They're the only things I can think of that really are till death do us part.'"

Bethany exhaled hard. "Moon Monaghan," she said. "That's the investor's name."

I winced. "A sweetie pie."

"You know him."

"I've met him."

"Is he going to kill us?" Blake said.

"Not if Bethany honors her deal," I said.

"I'll need a third of that OnlyFans money, hon."

Blake looked as though he'd just swallowed his own tongue. "I . . . uh . . . I . . ."

"I can try and talk to him," I said. "Buy you a little more time if you need it. But until you pay up, I should probably keep close to Blake."

Bethany said she agreed, and told me she'd make it worth our while. "In the meantime, it's late," she said. "I'm going to go home and get some rest, and I want you to do the same, Blake. You've got your TV meeting bright and early."

Spike said he'd walk Bethany to her car, adding that he'd come back up and stay the night, too, if I wanted.

"If you don't have plans," I said, "I could use the company. And the backup."

"You guys can both stay in my guest room." Blake put on a half-hearted smile. "It'll be like a sleepover. I've got bunk beds."

Spike raised his eyebrows at me.

"I call top," I said.

"Now, there's a sentence I don't hear very often," Spike said.

After Spike and Bethany left, Blake said he was going to make some more chamomile tea and asked if I wanted any. "I also just realized you don't have any clothes to sleep in," he said. "I can get you guys T-shirts, but I don't think I have any that would fit Spike." He moved toward the hallway.

"Don't worry about it," I said.

"And I know bunk beds are kind of weird. It's just something I never had as a kid, so I thought it would be fun."

"Spike and I are going to sleep in shifts," I said. "And we'll both probably keep our clothes on anyway, so there's no need."

"You sure?"

I nodded. "I will take that tea, though."

"Okay . . ." he said. "Okay."

Blake drew in a sharp breath, then let it out, his eyes aimed at the closed door, his whole body on edge. I picked up the empty scotch glasses to take to the kitchen. As he lifted the mugs from the coffee table, one slipped from his hand to the floor. It didn't break, but he acted as though it had. "Oh, shit," he said. "Shit. I'm an idiot. Shit."

"Blake?"

"Yeah?"

"What's going on?"

He picked up the mug. "You ever try online gambling?"

"No."

"It's really fun," he said.

"I'm sure it is," I said. "Until it isn't," I watched him. "Right?"

Blake said nothing. He cradled the mug in his hands as though it were an injured baby bird.

"You don't have a third of that OnlyFans money, do you?"

He shook his head. "Not even close."

I nodded. My pulse was racing, but I made sure not to show it. I even managed to force a smile. "I kinda figured," I said.

"What are we going to do?"

I looked at my phone. Richie's number gaped at me from my contact list. My finger hovered over it. But I chose Richie's dad's number instead.

TEN

Desmond Burke answered his phone after one ring. It had been months since we'd spoken, but he didn't act that way. "Is your father all right?" he asked. No preamble. No *Why are you calling?* Not even a hello. I found it surprising and also touching—yet another reminder of how much time had passed and how all of us had changed, Desmond and my father especially. They'd grown to care for each other against their better judgment, against their equally strong wills, as slow and inevitable a process as the erosion of cliffs.

"He's fine, Desmond," I said. "Sorry to call you so late, but I had a question for you."

"You want to know why, ask him yourself."

"Excuse me?"

"Richie."

I winced. I could feel my cheeks flushing. I heard the *ding* of the elevator, the faucet running behind the kitchen door as Blake made tea. Rosie snored at my feet. Life went on around me, no one in this luxury apartment the least bit concerned with what was happening inside my head. I tried to focus on that. "This isn't about Richie," I said. "This is more of a business question."

"Ah."

"I have a client who may have gotten on the wrong side of Moon Monaghan. Unintentionally."

Desmond chuckled. "Moon Monaghan doesn't care about intentions."

"I know," I said. "I was hoping maybe he's mellowed a little over the years."

"Moon doesn't mellow," he said. "His cruelty is one of the absolutes."

"That's . . . unfortunate."

Blake came out of the kitchen with two steaming mugs and set one of them down at the bar where I was sitting. Rosie woke up and followed Blake to the couch. He put his mug down on the coffee table and immediately started playing with her. I wasn't sure I'd ever seen anyone over the age of five take such an active interest in my dog. I was glad for that. With Blake distracted, I pressed on, as quietly and calmly as I could.

"There's money owed," I said. "My client didn't realize it was owed until very recently, but she's good for it. She runs a thriving business."

"What type?"

"Internet."

"Porn?"

"No. Influencing."

"Pish."

"It's like advertising."

"I know what it is," Desmond said. "Pish."

"Anyway, Moon's deeply invested in the business."

"Always looking for that next big thing is Moon," he said. "Fancies himself some sort of Hollywood player."

Desmond was right. My last run-in with Moon Monaghan happened years ago, when my client was Erin Flint. Back then, he was trying to be a movie mogul and taking full, disgusting advantage of that position. Oh, and he also had a few people killed. "He set a new standard for bad behavior in the entertainment industry," I said.

"I try not to judge," Desmond said.

"My client, though—Bethany Rose. She didn't withhold the funds on purpose. One of her associates brought in some money that she was unaware of until recently." And apparently, so was Moon. It dawned on me that Moon had likely discovered Blake's OnlyFans while stalking Erin on that very same site. The thought made my skin crawl. "Bethany fully intends to give Moon his share. But she needs some time. You think you can put in a good word for me? Maybe arrange a meeting between us?"

Desmond exhaled into the phone.

I glanced at Blake. He was standing in front of the window with Rosie in his arms, pointing out the Swan Boats to her as though he expected her to answer. "I don't think they allow doggies on the boats, but I can check. Would you like that, Rosie? We can have a picnic!"

I lowered my voice to a whisper. "Moon is threatening to eliminate the source of that money, Desmond, if you know what I'm saying."

"I do."

"If I could just talk him into waiting a couple weeks, he could be paid back, and this very, very steady income source could keep providing. There's even a TV deal in the works. Moon could be back in show business. It would be win-win."

Desmond didn't say anything for several seconds, but I knew enough to wait. Like his son, Desmond Burke wasn't intimidated by long pauses, and saw no need to fill them. "I'll see what I can do," he said.

My shoulders relaxed. "Thank you."

"I would like something in exchange, though."

"Good girl," Blake was saying to Rosie. "You have any more of those treats, Sunny? She looks hungry to me."

I grabbed another biscuit out of my purse and tossed it to Blake, who caught it with one hand. I was glad to keep him occupied, though I really didn't like to give Rosie this many treats in one night. I could practically hear my vet scolding me over it. "What can I do for you, Desmond?" I said.

"Talk to Richie."

My jaw tightened. I heard the door opening, Spike telling me he was back and going on about how "mint" Bethany's car was. "Sweet, sweet S-class convertible," he said.

I held a finger up and mouthed "One minute" as Blake greeted him.

"I thought you were just going to ask for a cut," I told Desmond.

Another long pause that was awkward only for me.

"He's the one who's leaving town," I said.

"So?"

"So," I said, "shouldn't he be the one calling me?"

"I've never known you to stand on ceremony, Sunny," he said. "Especially when it concerns something important."

"Has Richie told *you* why he's leaving?"

"Not really," he said. "He did let me know that he's found a taker on the saloon."

My jaw dropped. "How could he . . . How could he just . . . He sold the saloon?"

"I was surprised about that, too."

I could feel Spike watching me. Blake, too, though he might not have caught the importance.

I sighed. "I'll call him, Desmond."

"Thank you," he said, his Irish brogue sneaking out. *Tank* instead of *thank*. "I'll talk to Moon then."

He ended the call.

I knew Spike had heard Richie's name and wanted to

know what was going on, but I wasn't on that page. Not yet. I stayed where I was for a long moment, the phone pressed to my ear, trying to look as though I was still engaged in conversation so that my friend wouldn't ask me any questions.

After close to a minute, I said, "Okay, goodbye, Desmond," to no one and put the phone down. I drank some of the tea Blake had left for me. It burned the back of my throat and tasted overly cloying. I assumed Blake had put some type of trendy "natural" sweetener in it. Agave syrup or birch tree sap or crushed beetles. Whatever. It was terrible. "I just talked to someone who knows Moon Monaghan," I told Blake. "We're trying to fix things for you."

"Oh, good." Rosie was sound asleep in his arms, the love between them clearly mutual. He kissed the top of her head and set her down on the couch with great tenderness.

"So," Blake said, "they're not gonna, like . . . kill me, right?"

"I don't think so."

"Whew." He yawned loudly, like a little boy.

My chest tightened. I was hired to protect him, and I would. I knew that. I'd shoot Moon's people if I had to. Hell, in many ways I preferred that option to negotiating with them. But it still made me angry, not at Blake but at Bethany. Putting an innocent kid in this position—a kid who so clearly trusts you—just to finance a snake-oil-selling business. If a portion of all the money he made hawking shitty energy drinks or nutritional supplements or even images of his own body was going to a crime syndicate, Blake at least deserved to know that ahead of time, didn't he? At the very least, that knowledge might have given him some pause about venturing into the world of online gambling.

"I always wanted a dog," he said. "I never got to have animals growing up."

I frowned at him. "Didn't you grow up on a farm?"

"Yeah. I did." He stretched elaborately. "Anyways . . . Wow. I'm tired. I've gotta get some sleep. You guys are probably tired, too, right?" He showed Spike and me where the guest room was and said it had its own bathroom, "with clean towels and toothbrushes and everything."

"Thanks, Blake," I said.

"If you guys need anything, let me know," he said. "Feel free to raid the fridge. It's mostly keto stuff, but the lamb jerky's pretty awesome."

After Blake went off to bed, I turned to Spike. "Who grows up on a farm and doesn't have animals?"

"Could have been a vegetable farm."

"I guess."

"Acres and acres of alfalfa."

"Or corn."

"Or corn. Yeah."

"Hey, you think Eddie's fit to work the rest of the night?"

Spike shrugged. "He wasn't at his desk."

"I hope we didn't go too hard on him."

"Who cares?"

There was not much I could say to that. I didn't care much

myself. "Listen, if you want to sleep," I said. "I'm happy to take the first shift."

"Richie's leaving town, huh?"

And here we go . . . I swallowed hard. I felt like crying, but I didn't. "That's what it looks like."

"Fuck that."

"He has his reasons, I guess?"

"Sam and I broke up."

I stared at him. "Shit. Seriously?"

"Yep," he said. "Anyway . . . I bet you can get him to stay. Richie. Not Sam. That ship has sailed."

"I'm really sorry."

"Don't be," he said. "It wasn't working for a while."

"But . . . I like Sam."

"I like Richie. Always have."

"You know, Spike," I said. "We could probably learn a thing or two from Blake and Alena."

He snorted. "How to be young and rich?" he said. "I don't think that can be taught."

I walked to the couch and picked up Rosie. "How to appreciate what you have while it's still there."

Spike gave me a look. "Since when did you get so philosophical?"

"Comes with age," I said.

"Well, cut it out."

Spike scratched Rosie's ears. I put my head on his shoulder. "You're not going anywhere, are you?" I asked him.

His shook his head, his beard tickling my scalp. "You know me," he said. "I'm a lingerer."

My phone rang. I handed Rosie to Spike and went to the bar to pick it up. It was Desmond. "Moon will talk to you," he said.

ELEVEN

Blake's meeting with the TV producers was early, at eight-thirty a.m. Not a bad time under normal circumstances, but quite a challenge after a night of sleeping in shifts in a strange apartment. Plus, I had to squeeze in a seven a.m. trip to my loft in order to feed and walk Rosie, shower, and change into something that felt appropriately unobtrusive.

I settled on a black linen skirt, a white T-shirt, and black Chloé Lauren ballet flats, paired with gold hoop earrings and a gold chain. Because of the summer heat, I decided to forgo the speed holster/jacket combo I'd planned on originally, and carry the gun in my purse instead. I was going for casual but professional. And when I checked myself out in the full-length mirror, I felt like I'd achieved it. Kind of. Make no mistake, I was exhausted and stressed out. But considering the fact that I was running on coffee, adrenaline, and Blake's lamb jerky, I looked okay.

The production company was an affiliate of a European megacorporation that had dozens of reality TV shows currently airing, and its offices were at 101 Seaport Boulevard—a seventeen-story glass jewel box that had made headlines a few years back as Boston's most expensive office building per square foot. I'd been looking forward to getting a peek inside the place. The producers were renting offices on the top floor, and I was guessing the view was even more spectacular than Blake's. But as it turned out, I had to leave Blake and Spike outside the building before Bethany even showed up, so that I could haul ass to Cambridge to be on time for my nine a.m. get-together with Moon Monaghan.

Why Moon wanted to meet up in Cambridge, at that hour of the morning, was a mystery to me. The time and place seemed very out of character for a louche night owl like him. But maybe that was the point—keeping me (or whomever else might be tracking his movements) off-balance. His choice of a meeting spot seemed to support that theory: a lone bench across from the Charles, overlooking a not-very-busy stretch of Memorial Drive. Desmond had gotten one of his younger associates to text me a Google map with a pin in it ("I can't be bothered to learn this high-tech shit," he'd said), and it had turned out to be a twenty-minute walk from the T stop. Twenty minutes of torture. As I sort of mentioned earlier but might not have made entirely clear, we were in the midst of a heat wave. The sky was cloudless, the temperature already close to ninety. By the time I found this random park bench, the effects of both the coffee and my morning shower had long ago worn off, and I felt a little like Clint Eastwood in *The Good, the Bad and the Ugly*, after Eli Wallach had been dragging him through the desert for weeks. I hadn't even spoken to Moon yet, and already I was resentful. Couldn't he have chosen somewhere with air-conditioning?

Moon, however, seemed perfectly content on that bench, cosplaying an elderly tourist in a Hawaiian shirt, khaki pants, and mirrored sunglasses, his face half hidden behind a book called *A Bird Watcher's Guide to North American Waterfowl*.

I spied on him for a few moments before approaching. Moon Monaghan had never been the virile specimen he believed himself to be, but he'd aged considerably since the last time I'd seen him, his shoulders slumped, his cheeks sunken, his comb-over gone wispy and dyed a strange coppery shade that brought out the sallowness of his skin. When I sat down next to him, though, he put the book down, lowered his mirrored shades, and regarded me with snakelike eyes that were as coldly alert as ever. "Sunny Randall," he said.

"Moon Monaghan."

"You haven't changed much," he said.

"You neither."

He snorted. "I look like shit." He pushed his glasses back in place. "You must really want something outta me."

"You're a good judge of character, Moon."

"So I've been told." He pointed at a car stopped directly

across from us on the expressway, its hazard lights on. "Looks like that poor guy could use some help, huh?" He grinned.

I followed his gaze. The driver wore a black baseball cap and mirrored glasses like Moon's. Moon waved at him. He waved back. Then he raised a semiautomatic, a silencer attached to the barrel, and aimed it directly at my head.

"I don't want to cause trouble," I said.

"Wise choice."

"Actually," I said, "I want to appeal to your business sense, which I've always thought of as excellent."

A few cars sped by. Baseball Cap lowered the gun as they passed, then raised it again.

"Go on," Moon said.

I did. I told him about Blake, what a rising star he was and how he was meeting with big-deal TV producers as we spoke, how he was Bethany's highest-earning client and he was only going to rake in more money and what a huge mistake it would be to take him out of the picture—from a purely profit-driven perspective. I told him how Bethany had never even known about Blake's side gig and that Blake had been unaware of her deal with Moon, and so the problem was simply one of communication. The whole time, I spoke calmly, making sure to smile as though Moon and I were the oldest and dearest of friends. But my mind was reeling. From where Baseball Cap was parked, he could blow my head off in about as much time as it would take for me to undo the clasp of my purse. Pointless of me to have bothered bringing my .38.

Another car whizzed by. Again Baseball Cap lowered the

gun, then raised it back into place. "There's a hitch here, kiddo," said Moon—the only person I'd ever met who could make the word *kiddo* sound like a slur.

"What's that?"

"Whatever you want to say about what the problem was—"

"Lack of communication."

"Whatever. Bottom line is, your client didn't hold up her end of the deal."

"And for that you're going to get rid of your gravy train?"

"I got other gravy trains," he said. "And they don't try and take advantage of my generous nature."

"She wasn't *trying*. She didn't *know*."

"You still with that small-town cop?"

"Huh?"

"What's-his-name from Podunk? Stone. You still with him?"

"Jesse Stone. From Paradise. And he was an L.A. cop before he was a small-town cop," I said. "But to answer your question, no."

He leered at me. "That mean you're single?"

I exhaled. This wasn't going the way I wanted it to. I glanced at the car again. "Let me ask you something, Moon."

"Yeah?"

"Why didn't you get rid of Erin Flint?"

"Huh?"

"Buddy Bollen was her manager and he screwed you over big-time. But you and your people never touched a hair on her pretty head. Why?"

"Because."

"It would have been stupid, right?" I said. "No Erin, no movies. No chance of getting the money you were owed. Back end or otherwise."

"Yeah. So . . ."

"So . . . If you're owed a whole bunch of golden eggs, you don't want to send a message to the farmer by shooting the goose. You knew that with Erin."

"I was banging Erin," Moon said. He grinned. I cringed.

"Bethany is good for that OnlyFans money. And a lot more on top of that, so long as Blake is safe," I said. "You know she's good for it. She just needs a little time to get it together."

A few more cars passed. I didn't bother looking at Baseball Cap. In this heat, turning my head seemed like too much of an expense of energy. The sun beat down on my scalp, and I could tell that Moon, too, was feeling it. Sweat beaded on his upper lip. He fanned himself with his bird book. Took a handkerchief out of the pocket of his Hawaiian shirt and mopped his forehead with it, then turned it over and did the rest of his face. "Her real name ain't Bethany Rose, you know," he said.

"What?"

"It's Betsy," he said. "Betsy Rosanski. And she ain't no angel, either."

"How did you find that out?"

"I got an in-house research department."

Moon stood up and stretched, the buttons straining on his Hawaiian shirt. "Two weeks," he said.

I started to thank him when I heard the whistle of the silencer, the bullet tearing into the back of the bench. For several seconds, I couldn't move, couldn't speak. I smelled burnt wood, and turned. The bullet hole was in the top plank, no more than three inches from where I was sitting. Smoke rose from it. I opened my mouth, then closed it again.

Moon smiled so wide, I could see the gold teeth in the back of his mouth. "Don't worry, sweetheart," he said. "If I wanted him to hit you, he would have."

He started to laugh and didn't stop. Baseball Cap tore away from the curb and sped off, the car's tires shrieking.

A few minutes later, another car pulled up directly in front of us—a shiny black SUV with tinted windows. Moon tucked the book under his arm, strolled up to it, opened the back door, and slid in, laughing like a lunatic the entire time.

After he left, I got a closer look at the bullet hole. It was a little more than six inches from where my heart had been. So if I'd leaned to the right—to escape a bee or more likely to put some distance between Moon and me—I'd have been killed. In an instant. At a point in my life when I was still making believe I could fix everything in the future. What I'd said to Moon about Bethany (Betsy, whatever her name was) could have easily applied to me. *She just needs a little time to get it together.*

Of course, needing something and getting it were two entirely different things. And as much as I tried to control time, to lasso it and make it stand still, I couldn't. Nobody could. Loved ones aged and weakened and grew up and moved and left you sitting on a park bench next to a bullet hole, longing for what you used to take for granted.

I took my phone out of my purse and checked the time. It was close to ten-thirty. The production meeting included screen tests and was slated to last all morning. I texted Bethany: Moon says two more weeks.

She replied quickly: OK thx.

My morning was now officially free. I found myself going into my contacts again, my finger hovering over Richie's number. Again.

This time, though, I tapped "call."

Richie picked up right away. "Sunny?" He sounded surprised but not unhappy.

"Hey, stranger," I said. "Can I take you to breakfast?"

TWELVE

Richie said that he could meet me at eleven-thirty, and suggested the Russell House Tavern. He knew I loved the place. We'd spent a lot of good times there, when we were dating, when we were married, and in the years after, when we were in and out of various romantic entanglements—his involving a marriage and the birth of his son, Richard, then a divorce and shared custody, mine far shallower than that, save possibly for Jesse—but still, on one level or another, hoping we might find our way back to each other. In time. When we were both ready.

Or was that just me?

I got to the restaurant fifteen minutes early, grabbed us a high-top near the bar, and ordered a cup of coffee while I waited. What I really wanted was a Bloody Mary. It could have been my very recent brush with death, the memories the Russell House stirred, or its proximity to my shrink Susan Silverman's office. Or it could have just been due to the indisputable fact that, Spike's excluded, Russell House made the best Bloody Marys in the greater Boston area. But since I'd barely eaten this morning and I was still technically on the clock, I withstood the temptation.

I'd just taken my first sip of coffee when I felt someone approaching. For some instinctual reason, I knew it was Richie. His voice confirmed it—so familiar at this point that it was almost a part of me. He said my name. I looked up from my cup and there he was, in faded jeans and a blue-and-white striped button-down shirt that brought out the best in him more than I ever did. "You're early," he said.

"So are you."

"You look amazing."

"So do you."

Richie sat down across from me and gazed into my eyes. "I'm glad you called, Sunny," he said. "I've been thinking about you a lot."

My throat tightened. "Me too."

He asked what was going on in my world, and I told him about Spike and his restaurant and Bethany and Blake and Alena and everything that had happened in the past three days, all the way through my conversation with Moon. I stopped talking only once, when a waiter approached and we ordered brunch—orange juice and the farmstand omelet for

Richie, iced water, and the extra-dirty Caesar salad for me—and then I picked up where I left off.

I wasn't usually this big a talker, especially with Richie. But for the first time, the silence between us didn't feel comfortable. I needed to fill it, to say anything but what was really on my mind.

"So you want my two cents?" Richie said, once I was done.

"I wouldn't mind them."

"This woman. Bethany? Betsy? I'd keep a close eye on her."

"I know," I said. "Even if she just had one name, it's a special kind of person who gets her nest egg from Moon Monaghan."

"Then again, Lee Farrell recommended her, and he's an honest cop."

"Lee only knows her through his niece." I gave him a look. "Remember Emily Barnes?"

"Oh. Well, in that case . . ."

"Yep," I said. "I don't trust Bethany as far as I could throw her. Which . . . well, she's tiny, so that's actually pretty far."

Richie laughed.

"On the other hand, she's damn good at her job," I said. "She's already improved Spike's business. He brought in more money two nights ago than he has in the past year. And now he's all excited about going to lunch with her and finding out about her five-point plan."

"Interesting."

"And yet she lied to me about her name, she's a social

media professional who avoids social media, and for someone who's spent that much money on her appearance, she seems to hate having her picture taken."

"Hey, doesn't your new boyfriend work at *The Globe*?" Richie said it with a forced casualness. "Maybe you can get him to do some research on her. Find out about her past without getting the cops involved."

I took a sip of my coffee and regarded him for a long moment. "He's not my boyfriend."

"No?"

I shook my head. "In fact, I'm not seeing him anymore."

"Oh." His tone was maddeningly neutral. I wanted to scream, or slam my hands down on the table or at the very least order that Bloody Mary. Where was the Richie I knew and loved? Forget loved. Where was the Richie I knew?

I heard myself say, "Why are you leaving me?"

I hadn't intended to say it yet. But by the same token, I wasn't sorry I had. It was going to come out one way or another. Richie and I sat across from each other at this high-top, just like we had so many times over the years, a lifetime spent in this restaurant, holding hands, laughing at the same jokes, trying to remember the lyrics of the songs playing over the speaker system. The waiter showed up with our food and I found myself thinking, *What if this is the last time I'll ever see him . . .*

I ordered a Bloody Mary. So did Richie.

When the waiter left, Richie said, "You don't remember, do you?"

"Remember what?"

"The last time we were together."

"Of course I remember," I said. And I did. But also, I didn't. It was an afternoon that bled into an evening. He had a large group at the saloon—a teacher's retirement party—and so he couldn't pick Richard up from soccer practice and it was his day. He called and asked if I could do it for him, and I did. I'd done it plenty of times. I picked Richard up and dropped him off at his mom's, and by the time I got to the saloon, the teacher's party was winding down and it was dark outside. He poured me a beer and poured himself one, too, and we sat at a corner table and talked.

"I asked you how long you thought we could go on like this," he said. "You remember your answer?"

"Forever?"

He nodded. "Like planets orbiting each other."

"I said that?"

"Yeah."

"Wow," I said. "I must have had a few too many beers." I smiled.

He didn't smile back.

"I didn't mean it literally," I said. "We're not planets. Nothing lasts forever."

"Love does."

I looked at him.

"I love you, Sunny. That's not going to ever change."

"I love you, too."

"I know you do. And you also love things just the way they

are. So as long as we stay here, in the same town, we'll just keep orbiting each other. We'll never move forward."

I felt a lump in my throat. "What's wrong with that?"

"People need to move forward, or else they die."

"That's sharks, Richie."

The waiter arrived with our Bloody Marys. I took the garnish out, set it on my napkin, and proceeded to drain half my drink in one gulp. "Sharks, not people. It's fucking murderous, pea-brained sharks who die if they don't move forward."

He put his hand on mine. It burned.

"Sunny," he said. "I've got to make some changes in my life. I need to move on. Start a new chapter. And with you around, I don't stand a chance of even turning a page."

"What about Richard? He loves his school."

"He's starting private school in the fall. A great place his mother found."

"Where?"

"New Jersey."

That did it. A tear seeped down my cheek. Then another. Richie handed me a napkin. Always so considerate, even when he was breaking my heart. I wiped my tears, then breathed into the napkin for a moment, getting myself together. I wasn't going to cry in public, not to mention at the Russell House Tavern like some college freshman getting dumped by the boy she met at orientation. "New Jersey," I said. "Jesus."

"There's other reasons to move," he said. "Business has

been bad at the saloon. I've been struggling since the pandemic. I was lucky to get the offer I did and now I can think about where I want to go next, career-wise."

"You love that place."

"I'm tired, Sunny," he said. "I don't love being tired."

He drank. I drank. I knew I wouldn't cry anymore, but I wanted to.

"Maybe you were right before," I said.

"About what?"

"Us getting together again. Giving it another go. Maybe we should try that."

"No. You were right. Neither one of us has changed enough. We'd just make the same mistakes all over again."

"I said that?"

He nodded.

"I say a lot of stupid things."

He brushed a lock of hair out of my eye, stroked my cheek. "You're the smartest person I know."

I swallowed hard. Looked at my untouched food. "When do you leave?"

"A little less than a week," he said.

"Did you buy a house?"

He shook his head. "I'm renting."

"So there's hope."

"There's always hope," he said. "Also, you don't need to act like I'm going off to war. Jersey's not that far, you know."

I finished my drink. "Stop saying 'Jersey.'"

"I got a job managing a bar in Asbury Park," he said. "It's

got big windows overlooking the boardwalk. Springsteen played there once. If you come visit, you can drink for free."

"Maybe I will."

I stood up. Richie stood up, too. I threw my arms around his neck and pulled him close and the two of us stayed like that, life buzzing around us, Bob Dylan singing *"Lay Lady Lay"* over the speakers, a group of Harvard types at a table nearby, talking loudly about Heideggerian phenomenology. A few old guys at the bar arguing local politics. He wasn't going to find a place like this in Asbury Park. He wasn't going to find a life as good as this one. He couldn't. There wasn't any life as good as this one. Richie cupped my face in his hands and kissed me very softly. One of the old guys yelled at us to get a room, or maybe it was one of the Harvard types. It felt like our first date and our last date, and I didn't want it to end.

My phone rang. I pulled away and whispered to Richie that I had to answer it. I was still on the clock. "Of course," he said.

I saw Spike's name on the screen and cleared my throat before answering. "Meeting over?"

"We're taking a fifteen-minute break," Spike said, "but we should be all done in about an hour."

"How'd it go?"

"Good. Seems like *The Shred Shed* is getting the green light."

"That's great," I said. "We can all go out and celebrate after your business lunch."

"I'd love to do both of those things," he said, "but we're gonna need to find Bethany first."

My eyes widened. I looked at Richie as though he'd heard. "What do you mean?"

"She never showed up at the meeting," Spike said.

THIRTEEN

If there was a logical reason for Bethany Rose to bag out on her star client's meeting with top-notch reality TV producers, I wasn't aware of it. And when I met Spike and Blake outside 101 Seaport Boulevard, where I'd left them four hours earlier assuming Bethany was on her way, the two of them were clearly as in the dark as I was.

"Look at this," Blake said, showing me his phone. After one brief text from Bethany at eight-thirty a.m. (At my office. See you at the meeting!) the screen was striped with Blake's unanswered texts to her, the last one of which was simply Helllloooooooooo???????

"I'm taking it she usually replies right away," I said.

He nodded.

"I texted her, too," said Spike.

"And?"

"Nothing."

"Okay, well, I did hear from her," I said.

"You did?" Blake said.

"About an hour into your meeting." I showed them the exchange from ten a.m.

Moon says two more weeks.

OK thx.

"That's good news about Moon," Spike said.

"Unless Bethany's skipped town," I said. "Then it isn't."

I probably shouldn't have said that out loud. Blake had already established the fact that he was unnaturally attached to his manager, and now he had a look to him I didn't like, as if he was this close to collapsing on the sidewalk and assuming the fetal position.

"How much did you make on OnlyFans again?" Spike said to him. "Can you get a third of it together in two weeks?"

Blake said nothing. He didn't even move.

"I know you weren't the one who made the deal," I said. "But guys like Moon Monaghan can be sticklers when it comes to debts."

He stayed frozen, his mouth dropped open, his gaze plastered to the text exchange on my screen. It was as though someone had pushed Blake's pause button.

"There's no need to panic yet," Spike said. "Something

could have happened with another client. An emergency meeting. Something."

"He's right," I said.

Finally, Blake spoke. "She doesn't do that."

I exchanged a glance with Spike. "Doesn't do what?" I said.

He tapped his finger on the screen, on *thx*. "That."

"Abbreviate?"

"Yeah. She doesn't do it with 'thank you.' WTF and OMG are fine, but she says if you can't be bothered to type out a full 'thank you' to someone who's shown you a kindness, you have no class."

The fine points of text etiquette. "She could have been in a hurry," I said. "Just this one time."

"It isn't her," Blake said, his voice shaking. "I know her."

"Take it easy, dude," Spike said. "It's just a text."

"It isn't her. Someone else has her phone. Something . . . happened to her."

I looked at Blake. Truthfully, I was less worried about Bethany at this point than I was about him having a full-blown panic attack in the middle of Seaport Boulevard. I put a hand on his shoulder and spoke as soothingly as I could. "What do you say we drop by her office, since that's where you last heard from her?"

He nodded.

"Did you want to call a friend? Alena, maybe? See if she can meet us there?"

He nodded again.

I got us an Uber. While we waited, Blake called Alena, stepping away from Spike and me and speaking in a voice so low I could catch only a few words. "... scared, Lanie," I heard him say. "... don't think I can live without her."

"Is Alena going to meet us?" I asked, once he was through.

"I hope so," he said. "I just got her voicemail." Blake sounded calmer, if not any happier. It seemed as if the simple act of calling his girlfriend and hearing her prerecorded voice had grounded him. It made me think about Richie, how he used to have that effect on me and probably still did, if I was going to be honest. *I'll be just a road trip away,* he had told me back at the Russell House Tavern, just before I'd left, adding, *and I'll probably be the one doing the driving.* Richie, who had never been much of a talker, but nearly always said the right thing.

The Uber arrived and took us to Bethany's office at 200 Newbury. None of us said anything on the way there.

I'd been to this building, but only to Niketown on the first floor, to buy running shoes. So as classically elegant as the brick façade was, the place reminded me of failed New Year's resolutions.

Insta-Fame's office suite was two floors above the store, on a turret. And it truly reflected the style of the woman in charge.

There were big rounded windows, ivory planked floors, and a blue velvet couch and hot-pink velvet chairs in the waiting area, puffy and fun-looking and flattering to all skin types. An enormous flat screen hung on the far wall, broadcasting images of colorful fish. Another smaller one in the corner displayed footage of a crackling fire. The whole place seemed designed for taking the perfect selfie.

I approached the front desk. The receptionist wore a billowy chiffon dress in a seafoam shade that complemented the furniture, along with big Chanel logo earrings and a Bluetooth. She was insanely photogenic, like a young Naomi Campbell, her hair styled in a choppy bob that someone with less perfect features never would have been able to pull off. I asked if Bethany was in and she replied in an icy British accent, "Is she expecting you?"

"Well, no, but I work for her and—"

"If she isn't expecting you, I must ask you to leave."

"Hi, Daphne," Blake said.

The receptionist's gaze fluttered away from me and landed on him. Her expression brightened. "Blake!" She stood up to give him a hug. Her height matched his. "How are you, pet? How was the big meeting?"

"It was good," he said. "This is Sunny. She's my bodyguard."

Daphne turned to me. I barely reached her shoulders. "Oh, right," she said. "Bethany's told me about you. Sorry to be such a bitch, but we get so many wannabes in here. Partly because of Bethany's reputation, but also just because of the company name."

"Who doesn't want Insta-Fame?" I said.

"Exactly." She gave me a movie-star smile. "Anyway, I've learned to be something of a bodyguard myself."

She turned to Spike. "You must be the restaurateur, then?"

He told her he was and shook her hand.

"Daph," Blake said, "do you know where Bethany is?"

Daphne frowned. "I assumed she was still with you."

"Still?" I said.

Daphne looked at me. "Blake called Bethany this morning and said he was missing his lucky scarf. She had to drive home to get it, and then she went straight to the meeting." She looked at Blake. "So then I'm taking it she left? I haven't talked to her since this morning, when she was here."

Blake gaped at her. "I don't have a lucky scarf," he said.

"You didn't call her this morning? On her cell phone?"

"No."

"Right, then," she said. "Someone did. And Bethany told me it was you."

I turned to Blake. He was on pause again. "Do you know where Bethany lives?" I asked Daphne.

She gave us her address—in Sudbury.

I tapped it into my phone. Blake unpaused himself and told us he knew how to get there. Spike headed toward the door and Blake and I followed. "We can take my car," I said.

And that's what we did. My loft wasn't that far. We could have gotten there in fifteen minutes on foot, but thanks to Uber, we were there in two. Within five more minutes we were in my car, embarking on what would turn out to be a forty-minute drive to this peaceful historic suburb, but what would seem a lot longer thanks to Blake's nervous energy. He sat in the passenger seat, his knee bouncing wildly, not speaking at all except to shout directions at me like a human GPS. Spike said nothing, though he did sigh and groan a lot—mainly due to my cramped backseat, which was unfit for most adult humans, let alone those of such imposing size as my dear friend. It went on like this for around thirty minutes until I finally got the bright idea to turn on the radio. "How about the Rolling Stones station?" I said. I knew Spike, at least, shared my affection for the band, and Blake didn't protest, so I turned to channel 27. We listened to a string of those peppy, early hits, "Satisfaction" and "Get Off of My Cloud" and "Ruby Tuesday" and "19th Nervous Breakdown"—a song that seemed especially appropriate, given the tension in the passenger seat. The mood lifted a little—at least, for me it did. Spike and I sang along, and I found myself thinking about Spike's now ex-love, Sam. He loved the Rolling Stones, too. I remembered another road trip I'd taken to the Cape—Sam and Spike in the front seat of a rented SUV, Jesse Stone and me in the back—Sam belting out "Miss You" at the top of his lungs, completely and adorably off-key.

I wondered if Spike was remembering that day, too. I tried to catch his eye in the rearview mirror. But then "You Can't Always Get What You Want" came on and Blake moaned.

"What?" I said.

"This is her favorite song."

"Bethany's?"

He nodded. "She knows every word."

I found it hard to imagine. Polished, poised, pulled-together Bethany loving a soulful, messy song like that one.

"She used to sing it to me," Blake said.

I turned and stared at him.

"Really?" Spike said.

"When?" I said.

"I should have told her," Blake said.

"What?"

"About OnlyFans," he said. "I should have told her and let her take her cut."

"I'm sure she's fine, Blake," I said.

He didn't reply. He was focused on the road, or the song, or whatever was going on inside his head.

He didn't speak again until midway through "Shattered," when he told me to take my next right on a tree-lined street called Pratts Mill Road. I recognized the street name from when Daphne gave me Bethany's address, but I almost wanted to ask if there was some mistake.

We passed a couple grade school–aged kids riding bikes, an elderly woman walking a schnauzer. A boy sitting next to a girl on a porch swing, sneakered feet dangling. It was like driving through a Norman Rockwell painting.

"That's it." Blake pointed to a modest yellow split-level with a two-car garage, a small, cared-for lawn, a line of bright red geraniums on either side of the front door. A tetherball swung from a pole in the yard. The mailbox was shaped like a duck.

"That's Bethany's house?" I said.

"Are you sure?" Spike said.

It didn't look like a house where a single person would live, let alone a single person like Bethany Rose. The only thing that looked remotely like something Bethany might own was the red Mini Cooper in the driveway.

I pulled up in front of the house and parked.

Blake opened his window. "Lanie!" he yelled.

The driver's-side door of the Mini Cooper flew open, and Alena emerged, dressed in the world's most uncomfortable-looking athleisure wear—a tight black T-shirt and long black leggings with fluorescent-green stripes down the sides, heavy socks, and running shoes. It was as though she'd gone out of her way to find an outfit that was completely wrong for this oppressive heat. Clearly she'd gotten Blake's call and hopped into her Mini Cooper, still wearing her clothes from this morning's shoot for the plant-based nutritional supplement.

Alena slammed the door shut and rushed down the driveway, each step tumbling into the next.

Her face at first looked red and sweat-slicked, which surprised me. I never would have thought her capable of sweating. But as she got closer and threw her arms around Blake, I saw that it was not sweat. It was something more shocking than that. Alena Jade was crying.

FOURTEEN

For the first time today, I was afraid that something really had happened to Bethany. But once Alena pulled herself away from Blake and caught her breath, she told us, in her thick accent, that she didn't know where Bethany was. She hadn't even been in the house. "I forget the key," she explained.

I didn't bother asking her why she had a key to her manager's house. But I did ask why she was so upset.

Alena explained that she had rung Bethany's doorbell, texted and called Bethany's phone, and circled her house, pounding on walls and doors and windows. "No answer," she said. "No nothing. It is not like her. She always answers texts like . . ." She snapped her fingers.

"Does she normally park in the driveway or the garage?" Spike asked.

"Garage." Blake and Alena said it in unison.

"Okay, so either she's here or she left," I said. "In a neighborhood like this, I'd assume that if there were some sort of . . . violent incident at her house, someone would have already called the police."

"Something's happened to her," Blake said. "She wouldn't just leave on her own without letting us know. Also, Lanie, she texted Sunny and she said, 'thx.'"

"Oh my God."

"Do you have a key, Blake?" It felt like a stupid question, and it was.

Blake pulled a ring of keys out of his pocket and charged toward the front door, the three of us trailing behind him. I didn't believe we were heading into anything dangerous, but I was still technically his bodyguard, which meant my gun and I should be entering this house before him. And as fast as Blake was moving, that was easier said than done. I had to break into a full-on sprint to get to the front door when he did. Once he unlocked it, I told him to step back. I slipped my gun out of my purse and went in ahead of him. Spike took my side. "Hello?" I shouted. "Bethany?"

No answer.

The shades were drawn, but someone had turned on a light, revealing a living room that was . . . shocking. Sparsely furnished and generic, it was even more off-brand for chic, vibrant Bethany than the house's exterior. There was a beige pile rug, a beige couch stacked with brown corduroy pillows, a pair of rust-colored chairs, and a pine coffee table—a living room set that looked like the cover art for a 1996 Ikea catalog. A framed poster hung on the wall: a black-and-white photo of the Eiffel Tower that read—you guessed it—EIFFEL TOWER in white letters. No fire or water features. No screens at all. A bouquet of dried flowers in a beige ceramic vase on the coffee table. No bookshelves or books, which actually *was* on-brand for Bethany. Still, the room was so devoid of personality it was almost frightening.

"Do you hear that?" Spike said.

We all froze. The hum of a man's voice seeped out of the next room. I put a finger over my lips and moved slowly toward the door, gun raised. "Hello?" I said. The man kept talking. I inched closer, the hairs on the back of my neck bristling. When we were just outside the door, I was close enough to make out words.

". . . tell you how to cool off in style," the voice said. It was cheerful and very familiar.

I pushed open the door and called out "Hello!" again.

To nobody. To the TV. The voice was on TV and it was Sam's voice. We were in Bethany's kitchen—an airy space with polished wood counters, a stainless-steel fridge, and a gas stove that looked brand-new. Sam was plugging tomorrow's *Good Morning Boston* on a small TV mounted over the breakfast bar. "All that and so much more," Sam said. "Plus the weather! Will we ever get a relief from this heat? Whew!" He looked happy. Of course, everybody on morning shows looked happy. I grabbed the remote off the counter and switched the TV off. We all stayed still for a few moments, catching our breath.

"Wow," I said. It was intended for Spike, but he didn't seem to care about seeing his ex on TV. He was standing on the other side of the breakfast bar, carefully examining a gun.

"Where did you get that?" I said.

"Junk drawer."

"Jeez."

It was a sizable firearm. A .45, it looked like, with a magazine extension attached. I couldn't imagine Bethany working with it, or even lifting it. It probably weighed as much as she did. And it definitely belonged in a safe, not a junk drawer. "I was hoping for a knife or scissors, but I struck gold," Spike said. He checked the magazine. "Loaded," he said.

I looked at Blake and Alena. "Did Bethany ever mention anything about needing to protect herself?"

They both shook their heads.

Blake looked petrified. "Why?"

"It's just that this is a serious weapon," I said. "I mean . . . for a kitchen in Sudbury."

"I'm going to check upstairs," Spike said. He took the gun with him.

I gestured to a door at the far end of the kitchen. "Garage?" I asked, because I heard noises coming from it. A rustling sound. Something or someone moving around in there.

"Yes," Alena said. "Garage."

"Bethany?" I called out. "Are you in the garage?"

More rustling. I put Blake and Alena behind me and moved toward the door, my own gun grasped in both hands. My arms were steady, my expression calm. It always was when I held a gun, the cold, clinical part of my brain taking the wheel. But I was nervous now. There was no avoiding it. Something wasn't right. Why was the TV on? Why was that gun loaded? What the hell was going on in the garage? My heart pounded so hard, I felt like Blake and Alena could hear it.

I pushed open the door. "Bethany?" I shouted. "Are you in here?"

There was a light switch next to the door. I flicked it on. A fat orange cat bounded toward me.

"Mr. Francis!" Blake said. "How did you get stuck in the garage?"

I let out my breath. Other than Mr. Francis, the garage was empty. No people. No cars. Bethany wasn't here. Well, her car wasn't, anyway.

Alena scooped the cat into her arms. He was wearing a collar with the Gucci logo on it and looked rattled but well cared for.

"Indoor cat," Alena said. "Poor thing."

Before closing the door, I looked around. Save for a few cardboard boxes, the space was immaculate.

"Are you hungry, Mr. Francis?" Blake said.

I heard heavy footsteps approaching, and Spike came in through the kitchen door. "Nobody's upstairs," he said.

I was more relieved than I thought I'd be. "So she left, but without her gun," I said. "And she didn't bother turning off the TV or making sure her cat was inside."

"Maybe somebody should try texting her again," Spike said.

Blake and Alena were petting Mr. Francis, who was on the counter, devouring the contents of a hot-pink bowl. All three of us reached for our phones. I texted.

We are at your house. Where are you?

No answer. No bubbles to show she was typing.

"Did you hear that?" Blake said.

I looked at him.

"I'm texting her now." He thumbed away at his phone. "Listen."

From somewhere in the house, I heard a faint *ding*.

"I am calling her," Alena said.

We all heard the ringtone. We followed the sound of it back into the living room, up the stairs, down a narrow hall, and into a bedroom, where we found Bethany's bejeweled phone on the floor next to a neatly made king-size bed with a fluffy white down comforter. I picked up the phone. We all looked at each other.

"I'm taking it," I said, "that it isn't like her to go anywhere without her phone."

Alena shook her head.

"Either one of you know her code? We could check her texts . . ."

They both said they didn't know it, which surprised me.

"I'm freaking out," Blake said.

"We cannot call the police," Alena told him.

I looked at her. Technically, Alena was right. You can't report a grown woman missing because she happens to blow off a few morning meetings. It was the way she said it that got me. The cautionary tone.

"Police scare me," Alena said. "From my childhood in Bosnia."

Police scared Bethany, too. That was pretty obvious. "It's too early to get cops involved anyway," I said. "But we could canvass the area."

"What?"

"We could talk to some of the neighbors," I said. "See if they might have seen anything suspicious. Maybe one of them talked to her before she left."

Everyone seemed to think that was a good idea.

I put Bethany's phone on her nightstand and told them I'd meet them outside. I said I needed to make a phone call, but what I really wanted was to take a closer look at something I'd noticed under the bed when I picked up the phone. A shoebox. From Payless. Talk about off-brand.

Once everybody left, I slipped the box out from under the bed and lifted the lid. There wasn't much inside—a string of fake pearls, a child's drawing of a blue blob, surrounded by stick figures. A driver's license for Betsy Lynn Rosanski with an address listed in Reseda, California, and a birth date that would make her close to fifty-eight years old. Remnants of a previous life.

A million years ago, when Bethany, Blake, and I were having breakfast at The Blue Hut, she'd shown me her driver's license as proof that her real name was, in fact, Bethany Rose. It hadn't struck me as the most iron-clad evidence even then, but I'd been willing to let it go. What I'd noticed most had been how she kept her thumb over the birth date on the license, and how flattering the photo had been, the flawless makeup, the *Mona Lisa* smile, not a hair out of place, as though she'd hired a glam squad for her trip to the DMV.

Betsy's photograph wasn't like that. And at first glance, she looked nothing like Bethany. I gazed at the frizzy brown hair, the wide nose, the pale skin, the dowdy cowl-neck sweater. After several seconds, I could see not so much a resemblance as the *potential* for one. It could have been a "before" picture from one of those extreme plastic surgery shows, where the contestants shed their natural features the way snakes shed skins.

The other thing I couldn't reconcile with the Bethany I knew was the expression on Betsy's face. There was something about the set of her features, the look in her eyes, a lost quality that seemed completely foreign to Bethany Rose. It made you feel sorry for her, without even knowing her. I put the license back and went through the rest of the box. I took out a gold cross on a chain, a pink plastic kid's ring, a lock of light brown hair tied up in a red ribbon.

Who are you, Betsy Rosanski?

The last item I took out of the box partially answered that question. It was a stamped pass for the premiere of *Woman Warrior* starring Erin Flint—the movie Moon had invested in, back in the day. I shook my head. *In-house research department, my ass.* Bethany and Moon had a history. What kind, I didn't know. But she didn't just happen upon this crime boss when she was starting up her business and looking for investors.

I pulled my phone out of my pocket and took a picture of the driver's license. Then I put everything back in the shoebox, replaced the lid, shoved it back under the bed, and got out of the house, as fast as possible.

Once I was outside, I saw Spike knocking on the door of the Tudor house to the left of Bethany's, Blake and Alena talking to the boy and girl on the porch swing in front of the Cape Cod across the street.

I took the brick two-story on Bethany's right. When I rang the doorbell, the schnauzer walker answered. She was very small, and eyed me through the crack in the door. "Who are you?" she said. I could hear her dog barking.

I put on what I hoped was a disarming smile. "Sunny Randall," I said. "What a cute dog you have. I love schnauzers. I have a small dog myself."

"What kind?"

"Miniature bull terrier. Her name's Rosie." I found a

picture of Rosie on my phone and held it up. She stuck her head out a little farther to see it. Her expression warmed. "Oh, she's cute," she said.

"She likes to think so."

"Mine's Happy," she said. "That would be his name. Not his disposition."

I laughed.

She opened the door a little wider. "I'm not interested in buying anything," she said. "And I'm not converting to your religion."

"Fortunately, I'm not here for either," I said. "I'm an employee of Bethany Rose."

"Who?"

"The woman who lives next door."

"With the Mercedes convertible?"

I remembered Spike expounding on Bethany's mint S-class. "Yes," I said.

"Nice ride."

"It is," I said. "I'm taking it you don't know Bethany that well, ma'am?"

"Glenda," she said. "Call me Glenda. I hate 'ma'am.'"

"God, me too."

"It's awful at any age, isn't it?" Glenda said. "Why is it that 'sir' feels so respectful and 'ma'am' feels . . . I don't know . . ."

"Dismissive?"

"Exactly."

"I'd almost rather be called babe or chickiepoo."

Glenda laughed.

"So, outside of the car . . ."

"I don't know her at all," she said. "She keeps to herself. She doesn't have a dog. She does have visitors sometimes. That Mini Cooper looks familiar."

"That belongs to one of her clients."

"Yes, well. She's been here for more than a year, but we've never spoken other than an occasional hello."

I nodded. "You don't remember seeing anything unusual at her house this morning?"

"Why do you ask?"

"She was supposed to be at a meeting, and she never showed up."

"Oh, dear."

"I'm worried. It isn't like her."

"Actually, I did notice her leaving this morning," she said. "The only reason why I did is that she peeled out of that driveway in such a hurry."

"When was this?"

"Right after Happy's breakfast, so around ten-thirty," she said. "I heard tires, and by the time I got to the window, she was already up the street." She looked at me. "Maybe she was late for the meeting and trying to make it on time. I hope she didn't get into an accident."

"Did you notice anything else? Was she with anyone?"

"You know, that was the other strange thing. I couldn't tell."

"Why was that strange?"

"Unless it's raining, she always drives with the top down," the woman said. "Very glamorous for this neighborhood."

"Very."

"But when she left this morning, it was up."

"Hmm."

"Why do you suppose she'd do that?"

I gave her the only reason I could think of. "To hide?"

She nodded slowly. "That sounds about right."

Happy started barking. "I should get back inside," the woman said. "It was lovely talking to you. Take care of that cute dog."

"Yes, ma'am."

She gave me a look.

"Kidding."

"Good one."

I gave Glenda my number and asked her to call me if she found out anything about Bethany, and she assured me that she would. She went back into her house. Someone called out my name, and I turned to see Blake and Alena running toward me.

I left Glenda's porch and met them on the street as Spike strolled up. "What's going on?" I said. "Did you guys find out anything?"

"Nothing. They did not see her," Alena said. "But Kimmy said she would look in on Mr. Francis tomorrow if Bethany still hasn't returned."

"I'm sure she'll be back by then," I said.

"Blakey, what is wrong?"

"I thought you told me two weeks," Blake said to me. He looked as though he was going to cry.

"What?"

"Are you okay?" Spike said.

"You said two weeks, Sunny. We had two weeks to get the money together. But they're still doing it."

"Who?" Alena said.

"The Mafia, Lanie. The fucking Mafia."

"The Mafia? Why? What money?"

Blake didn't answer. He showed me his phone. There was a text on the screen, from a restricted number. And it had come in one minute ago.

You reap what you sow, it read.

FIFTEEN

Terrified by the text as he may have been, Blake still had a lot of explaining to do. Not only did he have to inform his girlfriend that a significant portion of her earnings was going to a crime boss she'd never met, he also needed to tell her that without her knowledge, he'd sold his body virtually for more than half a month.

I wasn't sure which one of them to feel sorrier for. Though Alena's shock and disgust were compelling ("What other betrayals are you not revealing to me?") I settled on Blake, based on his rattled nerves and terrible delivery. He was stressing to Alena that, despite some impressive offers, he'd never "whipped out the lightsaber" for any of his clients, when I finally interrupted him.

"I don't mean to cut your apology short, Blake, but if we're going to make sense of that text, I need to get out of here and try and meet with Moon again. Quickly." I remembered that shoebox, the stamped pass from the movie premiere. "He may even be able to help us find Bethany."

Spike agreed to guard Blake in my absence, even though it meant squeezing into a Mini Cooper with an arguing couple, because that's the kind of friend he was.

As I started my car, I vowed never to take Spike for granted.

I programmed "home" into my car's GPS and got ready to call Desmond again. I didn't relish the idea, mainly because I knew he'd want to hear about my conversation with Richie, and I didn't feel like discussing that yet—especially not with Richie's father. Yet since Richie's father was the only person I knew whom Moon would listen to, I had no other choice. Life was full of situations like this one. At least, my life was. I probably needed to get out there and meet more people.

I started up the car and called Desmond on the Bluetooth. He didn't even allow me a shot at being evasive. "Did you talk some sense into him?" was how he answered the phone.

"I talked to him," I said. "The sense part was beyond my control."

I gave him a summary of my breakfast with Richie, minus the part where I cried. After I was through, I endured one of Desmond's patented long pauses.

"That's a bloody shame," he said at last.

"It is what it is," I said.

"New Jersey," he said. "Jesus Christ."

"My feelings exactly."

Desmond coughed, and I remembered the last time I saw him, how thin he'd looked. How he'd worn a cardigan sweater on a warm summer night and how, for the first time, I'd considered the possibility that he might not be around forever.

"Your father's very lucky," Desmond said. "Having a child smart enough to stick around."

"I don't know how smart I am," I said. "But I do know a good thing when I see it."

"Richie does, too," Desmond said. "He used to, at any rate."

I cleared my throat. "Actually, I'm not calling about Richie."

"No?"

"No," I said. "I'm calling about Moon Monaghan."

"Again?"

I gave Desmond an update on my meeting with Moon, and everything that had happened in the subsequent four hours. "The thing is," I said, "the guy I've been hired to protect is freaking out over this latest text. And I'm thinking my client may have bounced because Moon is still leaning on her, too. They both want to pay him back, but he's making it harder for that to happen with these threats."

"He told you they have two weeks," Desmond said.

"Yes."

"That doesn't sound like Moon. Threatening someone after he's reached an agreement with them."

"I can't believe I'm about to say these words, but I thought Moon Monaghan was smarter than that."

Desmond didn't speak for a long time. I knew it was

because he was thinking everything over. I focused on my driving, and waited. "What exactly is it that you are asking of me?" he said.

"Can you arrange another meeting between Moon and me?"

"I'm not sure of that," he said. "But I can tell you where he is at this exact moment."

It seemed Moon had a standing two-hour lunch at Durty Nelly's—an Irish pub on Blackstone Street in the North End. I'd been there before, with Richie once or twice and with his father years later. I was pretty sure my dad liked to go there, too, as it was a favorite among both cops and criminals. A unifying force, you might say. "Part of what Moon calls enjoying the fruits of his labor is inhaling a big pub meal on the daily," Desmond said. "He never used to eat lunch. Now he revels in it." Creature of habit that Moon Monaghan was, he would show up at Durty Nelly's at one p.m. every day, order two pints of Guinness and a turkey melt, and read the newspaper at the same table upstairs. "Used to be pastrami melts, but his cardiologist told him to cut it out," Desmond said.

"Say I were to drop by Durty Nelly's and plead my case," I said. "You think Moon would be receptive?"

"Absolutely not," Desmond said.

"I didn't think so."

"But I'm relatively certain that if I were to accompany you, we could get him to listen."

"You would really do that for me?"

"I wouldn't have said so otherwise."

I wasn't sure what had brought on this act of kindness. It might have been his son's decision to leave town or my father's relatively recent shooting or the fact that his brother, Felix—who had frequently done this type of favor for me—had died not too long ago. Or maybe I was reading too much into it, and Desmond just felt like getting out of the house.

"Thank you so much, Desmond."

"Pish."

After hanging up with him, I asked Siri for directions to Durty Nelly's and drove there as fast as I could without getting pulled over.

I parked my car a few blocks away from the pub and made it through the front door in time for Moon's second Guinness.

The first floor was small and very noisy. There was one bartender working the taps and another mixing drinks, the barstools taken up mostly by older, hard-looking men with classically Irish faces. Except for the collection of cloth police badges tacked up on the wall behind the bar, it was easy to see why Moon would feel so at home at Durty Nelly's that he'd want to dine here every day.

I spotted Desmond at the end of the bar. He wore dress pants and a plaid flannel shirt, his white hair neatly combed. Despite the heat, there wasn't a bead of sweat on him.

Desmond was as thin as he'd been the last time I'd seen him. Thinner, even, if that was possible. He sipped a cup of hot tea with the bag still in it. While he acted as though he was alone, there were two young men on either side of him, solidly constructed and with wary eyes, who seemed to be saying otherwise. They all glanced up as I entered, Desmond with that Burke calm, as though a bomb could've gone off and he'd have barely raised an eyebrow. He settled up his bill when he saw me and stood. The young men on either side of him followed his lead, but then he raised a hand and they sat back down.

"I'll only be a moment, lads," he said, and the two of us headed upstairs.

Frail as he looked, Desmond still carried himself with a seen-it-all confidence that I found reassuring. He feared nothing, which not only showed in the way he moved through the world but rubbed off on those around him. "It's good to see you," I told him as we walked.

"Always good to see family." He didn't look at me as he said it, but I smiled at him anyway.

Moon was sitting at a corner table with two other men. They were a good deal younger than him, with meaty builds. In spite of the brutal heat outside, both wore bulky jackets— something that could be explained only by the need to conceal firearms. One of them had thick ginger hair, the other a shaved head, and as Desmond and I approached their table, I made a point of looking at the bald guy's face. No teardrop tattoos. So it had to be some other thug of Moon's who'd paid off Eddie to take the picture.

"Twice in one day," Moon said when he saw me. He slapped on a shit-eating grin. "You must want my bod, huh, sweetheart?"

"Don't be stupid, Moon," Desmond said.

The grin dissolved fast. Moon gazed up at Desmond. So did his two henchmen. "Oh. Hello," Moon said.

"You boys mind giving us a little privacy?" Desmond said to Baldy and Ginger. "This won't take but a minute."

Like obedient children, the two of them got up and headed downstairs. In many ways, Desmond Burke was more reliably threatening than my .38.

Desmond and I took their vacated chairs. "What's this about?" Moon said.

"It's about my client," I said. "Obviously."

"I told you two weeks," he said. "No more negotiating."

I leveled my gaze at him. "She can't negotiate," I said. "Because she's disappeared."

Moon swallowed some of his Guinness. He looked at Desmond, then me. "Not my problem."

"You sure about that?" I said.

"'Course I'm sure."

"You and Betsy go back. Don't you, Moon?"

He shrugged.

"That's not an answer," Desmond said. He picked up Moon's steak knife and weighed it in his hands. "Is it, now?" He lifted his head, his gaze on Moon's face, direct and deadly.

Moon shifted in his seat.

"Answer the young lady," Desmond said.

"Betsy did some jobs for me back in L.A.," Moon said. "Never met her face-to-face. We just talked on the phone. She came out here with a business plan. Needed some start-up money. We had another phone conversation. We made a deal. End of story."

"Why are you so pissed at her, then?" I said.

"I'm not."

"If you're not pissed at her, and if you had nothing to do with her leaving, why are you still stalking Blake?"

"Huh?"

"I was there today, Moon. I was at her house and so was Blake. While we were looking for Bethany, he got another one of your little love notes. A text this time. Clever."

Moon's beady eyes narrowed. His gaze moved from Desmond's face to mine and back again, as though we'd suddenly started speaking a language he didn't know. "The fuck she talking about?" he asked Desmond.

"Her client. The influencer."

"Yeah, I get that part." Moon looked at me. "I didn't send nobody no text."

"Yes, you did. Or someone who works for you did." I leaned in closer. "Jesus, Moon. The text said the same thing as the direct messages."

"What direct messages?"

"'You reap what you sow.'"

He blinked at me. "What's that supposed to mean?"

Either Moon Monaghan was a world-class gaslighter or he really did have no idea what I was talking about. "The entire reason why I set up the meeting with you," I said, "was that you were threatening Bethany Rose's client, Blake James. Over the money owed from his OnlyFans."

Moon gaped at me. I looked at Desmond.

"Moon," Desmond said. "Did you pay off this kid's doorman to take a picture of him sleeping?"

"What? No, I didn't . . . The fuck is going on here?" he said. "Are you guys pulling some kind of prank?"

"I don't pull pranks," Desmond said.

"I know that, of course, but—"

"Neither do I," I said.

Moon took a swallow of his beer. He was starting to look angry. His cheeks were pink. "Listen, girlie," he said. "The only reason why I know Betsy owes that money is because you told me she does."

I coughed. "What, now?"

"I don't do social media. I don't do threatening texts. I don't take pictures of influencers when they're sleeping. What the fuck do you think I am? That bimbo from *Fatal Attraction*?" He turned to Desmond, a look in his eyes that was at once desperate and annoyed. "You know how I send messages to dickheads who don't honor deals, Mr. Burke," he said quietly. "You know I don't do it with my fuckin' *smartphone*."

"That is true," Desmond said.

My mouth felt dry. "Why . . ." I cleared my throat. "Why did you agree to meet with me?"

"Because Mr. Burke told me your client owed me for some gig her boy did but she didn't have the dough right now. He said you wanted to work out a deal for her."

I stared at him.

"I thought you wanted to get ahead of the problem. So I let you do that."

I thought back to this morning, to my conversation with him on the bench. I'd done most of the talking, assuring Moon that Bethany was good for the OnlyFans money, telling him that he had more of a chance of getting it quickly if her star client was safe. *You know she's good for it. She just needs a little time to get it together.*

Neither one of us had mentioned threatening DMs. Neither one of us had mentioned the picture of Blake passed out on his couch. Neither one of us had mentioned Eddie the security guard. "It wasn't you," I said slowly. "It isn't you."

"What isn't me?"

"Never mind." I got up. Desmond did, too.

"Two weeks," Moon said.

"Right. Whatever." I told Moon and Desmond I needed to go. Moon asked if Desmond wanted to stay for a pint on him and Desmond said thanks but no thanks, and when Moon continued to gawk at him nervously, Desmond told him no hard feelings, he just had things to attend to.

We both headed back downstairs, past all the tired-looking Irish guys, past Baldy and Ginger waiting patiently near the bar. The two young men who had been sitting next to Desmond rose together, keeping a respectful distance from us as we made our way out.

"If you don't mind my asking," Desmond said, once we were outside, "what on earth made you think that Moon was stalking your client online?"

"I assumed some things I shouldn't have," I said.

"Ah," he said. "Happens to the best of us."

"Not me."

"Me neither," he said. "But I was trying to make you feel better."

"Thanks."

"Hey, now. Don't beat yourself up," he said. It sounded kind of funny—that modern, touchy-feely phrase coming out of the mouth of the least touchy-feely person I'd ever met. "You've been going through things lately."

"I guess I have."

We said goodbye. For a few moments, I stood there alone on the sidewalk outside of Durty Nelly's, cars whizzing by, the midday sun pressing into my scalp, the back of my neck. Desmond was right. I had been going through things lately. And what bothered me most was the timing: Seeing the picture of Blake, questioning Eddie, getting Blake to spill about his OnlyFans and Bethany to confess about her deal with Moon and putting two and two together to make, well, five . . . All of that had happened on the same night I learned that Richie was leaving town.

Was losing him clouding my vision? Was it making me less thorough, more likely to jump to conclusions? Was it making me worse at my job?

I needed to talk to someone. I pulled my phone out of my purse, debating between calling my dad, my shrink, Richie . . . I quickly scratched that last idea.

Before calling anyone else, I needed to check in with Spike

and let him know what an unexpected dead end Moon had turned out to be. But then my phone rang and Spike's name popped up on my screen. I answered it fast. "I was just gonna call you," I said. "I got some news."

"Me too," Spike said. "And I need to go first."

I didn't like the way he said it, that hollow, serious tone to his voice. "What's up?" I said.

"So . . . that guard we questioned last night. Eddie."

"Yeah?"

"Someone stabbed him to death."

"*What?*"

"Yep. And apparently, you and I were the last known people to see him alive."

SIXTEEN

"S unny, make them stop," Alena said.

We were standing behind Blake's apartment building, the parking lot swarmed with squad cars, a fire truck, the medical examiner's van, and one pointless ambulance. Alena was still wearing her workout clothes, trying to stare down two male uniformed cops who stood several feet away from us, talking to a visibly shivering Blake. She was obviously feeling protective. I couldn't say I blamed her. Blake looked terrified, and I wasn't going to lie to her by saying I was sure that those two uniforms were good guys. I'd never met them. And though I'd been lucky enough to know a lot of truly decent people on the force (including and especially my own father), I also knew that being a police officer was like being a parent. Performing the job commendably was a never-ending struggle. Well-meaning people often fucked it up. And if you were an asshole to begin with, it brought out the worst in you.

The best I could do was tell Alena it would be over soon, which I did.

"You are sure?" she said.

"Don't worry," I said. "Blake was in his apartment when Eddie was killed, just like you were. They're doing what they did with you—and everyone in the building. Asking if he saw or heard anything unusual last night."

"Why is it taking so long, then?"

"Because Spike and I were in his apartment with him before the murder, after you'd gone back to your place. I imagine they've seen CCTV footage of us, talking to Eddie. They're asking him when we left his place and when we returned. What we said about Eddie. Whether we looked like we'd just committed murder. That kind of thing."

Alena nodded. I hoped that was enough talking for her, because I needed to collect my own thoughts. I kept trying to find Spike, but he was nowhere to be seen. According to Alena, he had been "taken into the lobby" by a detective in a suit.

"Was it a nice suit?" I'd asked.

She'd said it was a "very, very nice" suit, which gave me hope that the detective was Lee Farrell. Like his relative youth and sexual orientation, Lee's fashion sense made him stand out among his fellow Boston Homicide detectives. And I knew unequivocally that he was a good guy.

The uniforms finished with Blake and he joined us. "Aren't they supposed to give me a blanket or something?" he said.

Alena put her arms around him, and the two of them held each other tight. "Eddie was a dick," I heard Blake say, "but he didn't' deserve to die like that."

Apparently Eddie had been stabbed multiple times. The cops who questioned Alena had told her that—no doubt attempting to impress her with their insider knowledge.

"They think it was a personal thing," she said to Blake. "These policemen believe it was a crime of passion."

"They don't know," I said. The body had been discovered only a few hours ago, and not by those two rookies. They didn't know anything.

I scanned the parking lot. A pair of crime scene investigators were taking pictures of the entrance to the building, while more of them moved into and out of the lobby, studiously ignoring the group of residents who kept asking them what was going on, and when they could go back inside.

One of the tenants, a college-aged girl wearing sweats and a crop top, said, "My chinchilla's in there. I need to see my chinchilla and make sure she's okay."

I caught a cop rolling her eyes over the girl, but the request didn't strike me as unreasonable at all. Who else did the chinchilla have in the world?

It made me think of Rosie. Fortunately, I had a neighbor with a fourteen-year-old daughter named Cara, whom I paid to walk Rosie every day at three p.m. if I wasn't around. So I knew she'd get her walk today. But still, I missed her. I hated being apart from Rosie, even for a few hours. I figured Bethany's neighbor Glenda felt the same way about Happy. She'd even known exactly when she'd heard Bethany leave because it had happened *right after Happy's breakfast.*

Which, I remembered, had been at ten-thirty a.m.

A timeline started to form in my head: *Bethany arrives at work, well before her scheduled nine a.m. meeting with the TV producers. A call comes in on her cell phone while she's talking to Daphne, necessitating both a lie ("Blake needs his lucky scarf") and a fast drive home to Sudbury. Bethany's neighbor hears her car "peeling" out of the driveway at ten-thirty. She's obviously in a hurry. She leaves the TV on. A network. Morning shows. Did she turn it on for the news? She replies to my text, but she doesn't bring her phone. She puts the top of her convertible up . . .*

"Alena," I said. "Did those officers tell you when Eddie's body was discovered?"

"They say this morning. When I was at my shoot."

"Which was when?"

"From eight to noon," she said. "But I left early because I get the call from Blake about Bethany."

A noise behind me made me jump. Metal wheels on pavement. I turned around in time to see another group from the ME's office, gloved and in plastic coats, loading the building's dumpster onto a flatbed truck. I told Blake and Alena to stay where they were and approached one of the uniforms guarding the entrance of the building. "Can you tell me what's going on?" I asked. "Was the body found in that dumpster?"

"Please step back, ma'am."

I asked him who the lead detective was on the case.

"Are you a reporter?" He was very young. I glanced at the peach-fuzz mustache, the sprinkling of acne on his cheeks. I couldn't imagine him legally buying a six-pack at a 7-Eleven, even with the uniform on.

I told him that I was Phil Randall's daughter, but I just got a blank stare. "He was captain for thirty years," I said.

"Oh," said the uniform. "Sorry. Didn't know the name."

It made me wince. My dad was still a legend to most cops, but it was happening more and more, the newbies never having heard of him. It made me angry, but that was the way life worked. You reached a certain age and it kept erasing you with each passing year, whether or not you were around to see it happen. I told him my name and showed him my private investigator's license.

"Were you working for Mr. Voltaire?" he said.

"Who?"

"The deceased. Were you hired by—"

"Eddie's last name was Voltaire?"

"Yes, ma'am." His voice cracked.

I asked him if Spike was around. It sounded like *Is your mother around?* Same tone. Same energy. But then Spike emerged from the guard's office behind the front desk, thankfully eliminating the need for further conversation.

I smiled and gave Spike a little wave. He waved back. He wasn't smiling.

Lee Farrell came out next. He was indeed wearing a very, very nice suit. Cobalt windowpane, with a fitted white shirt, narrow black tie. I breathed a little sigh of relief when I saw him.

I walked up to the both of them, and Lee said, "It's about time you got here."

"Traffic," I said. "What the hell happened?"

Lee gestured for me to join the two of them, and the child in uniform went back to his job. We sat in the waiting area at the front of the lobby, Spike and I settling into two leather-cushioned chairs and Lee taking the couch. He pulled a silver pen and a small steno pad out of his jacket pocket and flipped through the pages, going over his notes.

Since no one had answered me, I asked what happened again, and Lee let Spike tell me everything. At nine-thirty a.m., a sanitation worker had found the body of Eddie Voltaire in the building's dumpster. He'd been stabbed thirteen times in the throat, chest, and abdomen. The official time of death was still unknown, but it was estimated to have been around two a.m.

I didn't want to admit that the cops questioning Alena were right, but thirteen times was definitely excessive—and that type of overkill is usually personal.

"That would have been like four hours after we talked to him," I said.

"You're making my job easy," Lee said.

"We've got no reason to make it hard," Spike said.

Lee nodded. "Can we just go over your conversation again? What exactly transpired between you guys and Eddie Voltaire?"

"We said some things he didn't like," I said, "but he defended to the death our right to say them."

Lee blinked at me.

"Voltaire," I said.

"I know. I get it," Lee said.

"Sorry," I said. "It's been a very long day."

Lee didn't even crack a smile. "I guess what I'm confused about is why Blake called you last night in the first place."

I realized that neither Spike nor I had explained the deal I'd made with Bethany. "Okay, so in exchange for Bethany upping Spike's social media profile, I agreed to look into some nasty DMs Blake had been receiving," I said.

"Like troll stuff?"

"Yeah," I said. "I was supposed to guard him, too, but to be honest, I don't think I believed the troll would try to make physical contact with Blake. Not until . . ."

"The picture."

"Right." I told Lee about arriving at Blake's apartment and calling Spike to help me question Eddie, and how surprised I was when Eddie admitted that he'd used a security key to get into Blake's place and taken the photo himself. "He told us he was paid to do it by a bald guy," I said. "With three teardrop tattoos on the left side of his face. He said the guy looked 'connected.' We assumed that meant he was mobbed up."

Lee glanced at Spike and said, "Your stories match."

"Why wouldn't they?"

"Sorry," Lee said. "It's been a very long day."

"I see what you did there," I said.

"How did Eddie seem," Lee said. "After you guys got through questioning him?"

"He seemed glad I let go of his arm," Spike said. "I shake hands, sometimes my grip's a little firm."

"Okay. What did you do next?"

"We went back upstairs to talk to Blake and Bethany and figure out who may have paid off Eddie to take the pic."

"Blake's girlfriend was no longer there?"

"She had a shoot in the morning, so by the time we finished talking to Eddie, Alena had gone back up to her own apartment to get some sleep."

"About how long did you talk to Blake and Bethany?"

Spike shrugged. "I don't know. Fifteen minutes. Then Sunny made a phone call and I walked Bethany out to her car."

Lee jotted something down in his notebook, then looked at Spike. "Did you see Eddie Voltaire on your way out?"

"Actually, I did," Spike said.

"You did?" I said. "You told me he wasn't at his desk."

"He wasn't." Spike looked at me, then at Lee. "He was outside the building, smoking a cigarette," he said. "It wasn't that memorable. And I wouldn't have even noticed him standing there if Bethany hadn't pointed him out."

"How did she point him out?" Lee said.

"She said pretty loudly that this building should screen their employees better," Spike said. "And then he muttered something. I asked him what the fuck he said, but he got real quiet . . . understandably."

Lee let out an irritated sigh. He and Spike respected each other, but they had very different ways of going about their business, and sometimes Lee got a little judgy about the way Spike went about his. Years ago, before they'd ever met, I fixed Lee and Spike up on a date. It wasn't the most well-thought-out plan I'd ever hatched, and it went about as well as you'd expect it to have gone.

"You guys happen to have any alternate numbers for Bethany?" Lee said. "I've got her office and her cell phone from Emily."

Spike and I looked at each other. "That's all we have, too," I said.

"Have either of you spoken to her about Eddie Voltaire's death?"

"No," I said. I nearly told Lee that Bethany had disappeared at around the same time that Eddie's body had been discovered, making it impossible for us to speak to her about anything. But then I spotted Blake and Alena through the plate-glass window, Alena's steady blue gaze on me. *We cannot call the police,* she had said—for reasons that I suspected had nothing to do with her childhood in Bosnia and everything to do with Bethany Rose. And so I stopped myself. Bethany was my client, after all. And odds were, the fact that she'd crossed paths with a murder victim hours before the crime wasn't material to the investigation.

Was it?

"Can I ask you something, Lee?" I said.

"Yeah?"

"You like anybody for this murder?"

"Too early."

"I don't mean anything definite," I said. "Just wondering if you have any personal theories about who might have done it."

"Could be any number of people," he said.

I exhaled. "Really?"

"He did seem like the kind of guy who has a lot of enemies," Spike said.

Lee nodded. "Plus, Eddie was a gambler. In debt up to his eyeballs."

I looked at Spike. "That makes more sense," I said, "about why he agreed to take the picture."

"More sense than what?" Lee said.

"He told us he needed the money to take care of his elderly mom," Spike said. "Said he lived with her."

Lee closed the notebook and put it into his pocket. We all stood up. "Eddie didn't live with his mom," he said. "He's got no next of kin."

"I had a feeling he might be lying about that," I said.

"You think it could have been the bald guy?" Spike said. "I mean . . . presuming he wasn't lying about him, too."

"Oh, he wasn't lying."

"How do you know?" I said.

"Voltaire called District D-4 a little before midnight. Told them the same story he told you guys—omitting the part where he accepted the offer and took the pic of Blake. He said he thought he was back."

"The bald guy with the tear tattoos," I said.

"Yep," Lee said.

"Why?"

"He claimed he heard someone in the guards' office. He heard footsteps. Someone moving things around."

My eyes widened. "Did the police show up?"

Lee shook his head. "He called back right away. Said it was a false alarm." He gave Spike a look. "He said a visitor had been 'mean and aggressive' with him a few hours earlier, and it'd gotten him all spooked."

Spike shrugged. "Some people don't get my sense of humor."

Lee smiled a little. "That's hard to believe."

"I know, right?"

Lee thanked us both for our time. He told us to call him if we thought of anything, and Spike headed back to the parking lot to check on Blake and Alena.

I was about to leave, too, but Lee stopped me. "You really want to know my gut feeling on this?"

I nodded.

"I feel like, if this really was over Eddie Voltaire's gambling debts, then the killer wanted to make it look like something else."

"Something else?"

"Something personal. Something dark. Psychotic."

"Because of the overkill?"

Lee's eyes met mine. His face went serious. "We found

something on the body, Sunny. We're not telling the press about it, so let's keep this between us," he said. "Okay?"

I nodded slowly.

"It's with the ME right now, but I took a picture." Lee slipped a phone out of the same pocket where he was carrying the notebook and tapped at it. "This was found," he said quietly, "in Voltaire's mouth."

He handed me the phone. A picture filled the screen. It was of a piece of paper, a computer printout, crinkled and bloodstained, but with the words still legible.

Be not deceived; God is not mocked: for whatsoever a man soweth, that shall he also reap.

Galatians 6:7

SEVENTEEN

I hadn't intended to tell Lee about Bethany's disappearance. I'd assumed I'd be long gone from this lobby by now, having provided him with all the information I'd needed to. But that was before the note. The note changed everything. It tied Eddie's murderer to Blake's stalker and, by association, to Bethany. Whether or not Bethany's going missing had anything to do with Eddie's death, she'd hired me to protect Blake. And barring the mother of all coincidences, he was now in more danger than any of us had imagined—especially if I didn't tell the cops what I knew.

So I did. First, though, I showed Lee the photos I'd taken of Bethany's folder of printouts—the direct messages and Instagram comments Blake had received. "From the troll," I said.

"Well . . . that's certainly interesting," he said.

"Unless 'You reap what you sow' is some meme we don't know about and everybody's saying it."

"Not likely."

"Agreed."

I texted him the photos.

"Did Blake or Bethany ever go to the police about this?"

I shook my head. "Bethany said the police wouldn't do anything about it."

"She's probably not wrong."

"I know," I said. "To tell the truth, before last night, I thought Blake was overreacting. A bunch of DMs and comments from fake addresses? Usually that's somebody who doesn't want to show themselves. They want to freak you out but they're not looking for a face-to-face confrontation."

"But then someone talks to his doorman. They pay him to take that picture. They know where he lives."

"And then today, around one-thirty, he gets a text from a restricted number. It says the same thing."

"'You reap what you sow.'"

"Right," I said. "So they know his phone number, too."

"I'm going to need to talk to Blake," Lee said.

"Me too, TBH." I told Lee how Blake had just learned he was in debt to Moon Monaghan, and about how we'd all assumed the comments and messages had been warnings from Moon's operation. "Turns out they weren't," I said. "But I haven't had a chance to tell Blake."

"'TBH'?"

"God, now I'm saying it without even realizing it."

I called Spike and told him to bring Blake and Alena into the building immediately and that Lee needed to talk to them. I heard Alena asking why, and I said to Spike, "Tell her it's important."

"You sure there isn't any other way to get hold of Bethany?" Lee asked, after I ended the call. "I had Emily contact her, too, but no luck so far."

"Yeah, well, that's because she left her phone in her house."

"Wait, what now?"

I filled him in on our trip to Sudbury and Bethany's abrupt departure.

"Busy morning you've had," Lee said.

I thought about the meetings with Moon. My breakfast with Richie. "You don't know the half of it," I said.

"Hopefully you'll be able to relax at some point."

"Hopefully," I said. "But considering what you just told me, my main concern is keeping *Blake* relaxed."

"He scares easy?"

"Oh, yes,"

Through the window, I watched Spike, Blake, and Alena making their way through the crowded parking lot to the building's entrance. Lee and I met them there, so they were able to forgo questioning from the kindergartener in uniform.

"What is this about?" Blake said. He looked more nervous than ever.

Alena's icy stare shifted from my face to Lee's. I knew what she was thinking. "I had to tell Detective Farrell," I said. "You'll see why."

Alena said nothing.

Once we got back to that relatively private spot in the corner of the lobby, Lee and I told them about the note that had been found in Eddie Voltaire's mouth.

"Wow," Spike said.

"Oh my God," Blake whispered. "Oh my God. Oh my God." I was glad he was sitting down.

"So is it that bald man?" Alena said. "Is he the one who has been leaving these messages for Blake? Is he the one who killed Eddie and put the Bible words in his mouth?"

"That's the million-dollar question," Lee said.

Blake, meanwhile, looked as though he was about to jump out of his own skin and hurl his skeleton through the plate-glass window.

"You okay, dude?" Spike said.

"Bruh," Blake said. "I am so literally not okay right now it isn't even fucking funny."

"Do not succumb to your fears," Alena said.

"That's easy for you to say!"

"Blake," I said, "are there any exercises you do before you tape Shred Shed?"

"Like . . . working out?"

"No." I tried my best to channel the soothing tones of Susan Silverman. "I'm wondering if there's anything you do to calm yourself. Yoga, meditation . . . anything?"

"Yeah."

"Can you tell me what it is you do?"

"I close my eyes and breathe in and out to the count of ten," he said. "And I imagine that the sun is setting, and it's beautiful and warm, and I'm in the Seven Seas with my family."

Alena gave him a sharp look. I wasn't sure why.

"Okay," I said. "Can you do that for me now? Close your eyes."

He did.

"Breathe in and out to the count of ten."

Blake inhaled deeply, then let it out.

"It's sunset, and it's warm and you're . . . where?"

"The Seven Seas," he said.

"It is from a story he likes," Alena said.

Blake nodded. A smile played at his lips.

"Good," I said. "Is it beautiful there?"

"I'm happy there."

"Your toes in the sand . . ."

"In the water."

"Your family's with you," I said. "They're telling you how much they love you. Can you hear them?"

Blake's lower lip trembled.

"Do you?"

He nodded.

"You feel better?"

"Yeah," he said. "A little."

We watched him open his eyes.

"You think you can answer a few questions for me now?" Lee said.

Blake took Alena's hand in his.

She looked at him and mouthed, *It's okay.*

"I'm ready," Blake said.

Lee pulled out his notebook. "You have any rivals, Blake?"

He shook his head.

"You sure?" he said. "I mean, you're young. Rich. You have a beautiful girlfriend. You flaunt all that stuff on Instagram. Nobody's jealous?"

"Nope."

I was starting to get impatient. "Blake, your entire livelihood is based on making people want what you have."

"They're not jealous. They're aspirational. Or I am. I never get that right."

"They're human," I said. "You've never gotten into a fight? A Twitter war? Nothing? You never got called a nasty name in your comments?"

"I mean, every so often, some dude will tell me to check my privilege, but it's not like . . . I haven't felt threatened. I mean, besides those messages. I swear."

"You beat anybody out for a sponsorship?" Lee asked.

"Probably? I don't know."

"What about Alena?" Lee said. "Anybody ever get weird with you about her?"

"No," Blake said.

"Well," Alena said.

Lee and I looked at her.

"I do not post very many pictures of me and Blake because some of my followers love me too much and they get, like . . ."

"Possessive?" I said.

"Yes."

"I didn't know that," Blake said.

"Because I don't tell you," Alena said. "You are so sensitive."

"Do they comment on the posts?" I said. "Send you direct messages?"

"I don't check direct messages, but I do see comments," Alena said. "They say things like, 'He doesn't deserve you. I would be so much better for you.' 'Run away with me.' 'Dump that loser.' Those kinds of things."

"Why haven't I seen—"

"Because I delete them, Blake. What do you think?"

"TBH, that fuckin' sucks, man," Blake said.

"You ever meet any of these guys face-to-face?" I asked.

Blake stared at Alena. We all stared at her. For a few moments, it felt as though she might never respond and we were all doomed to sit here, watching Alena's placid features, forever waiting for an answer.

"No, of course not," Alena said finally. She stood up, fists clenched at her sides. "You need to stop asking stupid questions and find this bald man."

"Unfortunately, Alena," I said, "you can't have the latter without the former."

"I do not understand."

"You don't have to understand," I said. "But you do need

to realize that in order to investigate a crime, you've got to ask a lot of stupid questions. It's just the way it works."

Alena's gaze dropped to the floor. "I . . . I am sorry," she said. "I am just nervous."

"I miss Bethany," Blake said.

"I do, too," Alena said.

"I'm sure she had good reason to go away for a few hours," I said. "She'll turn up soon. I know it."

"Are you really sure?" Blake said.

I wasn't, of course. But I told him I was, because Blake needed the type of protection that little white lies could provide. He also needed real protection, if I was going to be honest. "I think you guys should stay at my place," I said. "Just for a little while."

Blake closed his eyes. He took a deep breath and let it out.

"You okay?" I said.

He nodded.

"Rosie will be happy to see you."

"Oh, yay," he said. "I almost forgot about that dog!" He took his phone out of his pocket and messed with it. Then he handed it to me. His Instagram was on the screen—a picture of Blake sitting on his couch, cradling Rosie on his lap, posted at ten-forty-five p.m., when Spike and I were downstairs talking to Eddie. It was his most recent post.

"That's really cute, Blake."

Lee glanced at the picture. "Did Bethany take this?"

He nodded. "I have to post a certain amount of selfies in

my apartment per month," he said. "It pays for most of my rent. I always forget, but Bethany . . . she remembers." He took another deep breath and let it out slowly. Blinked away a tear. "This is the longest I've gone between posts in, like, fifty thousand years."

Blake had captioned the photo #Chillaxing with @RosieRandall, followed by two hearts, a dog emoji, and a few hashtags: #dogs #besties #blessed #doggo #BackBayLife. Already, there were more than two thousand likes on it. "Rosie's famous now," I said. I wasn't sure whether that was a good or a bad thing, but I settled on good. If any of Blake's more obsessive followers clicked on the tag and visited Rosie's account, I could keep tabs on them.

"I will take pics of you in the air, Blakie," Alena said, which confused me until I remembered that he had an event at five p.m. at an indoor trampoline place. "Don't worry."

"I want *her* to take the pictures," Blake said quietly. I knew he meant Bethany. She was supposed to escort him there, and maybe she would. It wasn't unheard of for someone to go missing and then return unexpectedly. When I was guarding Melanie Joan, she'd disappeared at one point for nearly twelve hours, and despite my growing sense of dread, it turned out she'd only wanted a little time to herself.

Lee handed everyone his card. He got Blake and Alena's numbers and said he'd be in touch. Then he headed out to the parking lot to talk to the medical examiner. Some of the squad cars were starting to leave the building. Residents began filing inside. Life was easing back into some semblance of normalcy.

Later, there would be a press conference and it would look well organized and imposing, Sergeant Frank Belson reading a carefully worded statement with Lee at his side and a line of officers behind them. Journalists would shout questions that would go unanswered. In the days following the press conference, news vans would show up, on-air reporters taping interviews with tenants, collecting sound bites about how scared they were to live here. The tension would escalate on this well-to-do block and people like Sam would discuss it on local TV, wringing the topic dry. It would either help or hinder the search for the killer. The case would either be solved quickly or drag on, or it would never be solved, becoming yet another piece of the grim folklore my beautiful city had been known to produce. But no matter what, all that attention would continue for weeks, or months, however long it took for some other big thing-to-be-afraid-of to come along. And even then, it would still rear its ugly head from time to time—a sentencing, an anniversary, another similar murder— stoking fears all over again. I'd been through it before, many times. And so I knew that this return to business-as-usual was too early, that it was only temporary. I knew that it was something to be cherished.

The girl with the pet chinchilla jogged past me to get to the elevator, and held the door open for a guy around Blake's age carrying a leather gym bag. "You hear anything?" he said as he slipped in. "Nope, but I'm glad it's over," Chinchilla girl said. Everyone in this building seemed young and sheltered and unused to fear.

"I would like to pack an overnight bag," Alena said. "Can you help me, Sunny?"

I thought it was interesting that she didn't want Blake to help her, but I said sure. Blake said he was going to get a few things from his apartment, and Spike joined him. We took two separate packed elevators and agreed to meet back in the lobby.

Alena's apartment was located on the end of a long hall. Like Blake's, it boasted floor-to-ceiling windows and a spectacular view. But unlike Blake, Alena seemed to appreciate colors. There was an electric-blue couch, stacked with yellow, pink, and white pillows, a stuffed purple bunny the size of a toddler that looked like it had been won at a county fair. There was a peach shag area rug and a coffee table made of pale green vinyl, like something out of Barbie's dream house. The star of the room, though, was a framed poster-size black-and-white photograph—Alena in a bikini, with her lips and the swimsuit tinted the same blue as the couch. There was an interesting look in her eyes, hard and cautionary, as though she was warning the camera not to come any closer.

"Blake took that with his phone," she said.

I turned around and looked at Alena. She was clutching the bunny to her chest. "Bethany had Blake's picture made into poster for my birthday. She hired artist to do Photoshop. You like?"

"Very much," I said. "It's really a cool piece of art."

She smiled a little.

I pointed to the bunny. "You taking that with you?"

"Is it okay?"

"Of course," I said.

"I know it seems weird, but he makes me feel safe."

"Not weird at all," I said, though it did actually seem a little weird. "We should get you packed quickly, though, so we can get out of here and meet up with the boys."

The layout of her apartment was the same as Blake's. I started for the bedroom but she didn't follow. "Sunny?"

"Yes?"

"If I tell you something, will you not judge me?"

I looked at her. I didn't know her well enough to judge her, and even if I did . . . "Who am I to judge anybody?" I said. It could have been my life's motto.

"The guys we talked about when we were in the lobby," she said. "The ones who send me messages. Who tell me to leave Blake for them."

"Yes?" I said.

"I did meet with one. Face-to-face."

"Okay."

"I didn't cheat. But I still feel guilty. I went to dinner with him a couple times."

"Why?"

"He was good-looking. Rich. He was . . . how do you say in English . . . A charmer. For a little bit, he made me happy. He even got me some work."

"No, I meant why do you feel guilty," I said. "You're not

married. You're young. You wanted to explore other options. And anyway, you didn't cheat."

"But I never told Blake."

"So tell him," I said. "Or don't tell him. It doesn't matter. From what I've seen, you guys are strong enough to weather a flirtation that didn't go anywhere."

"No, you don't understand," Alena said. "This man I'm talking about. I think he could have created those fake accounts and sent those messages to Blake. He could even have . . . made that happen to Eddie."

My eyes widened. "Do you really believe he's capable of that?"

"He has a lot of anger inside him," she said. "He knows bad people. He was very, very jealous of Blake. Maybe still is."

"Yeah?"

"Remember that loud party Blake spoke about?"

"Where somebody called the cops?"

She nodded. "The day before that party, I told him I don't want to have dinner with him anymore. He wouldn't stop calling me that night, and he was talking in a way like I've never heard him talk."

"How so? Did he make threats?"

"He said he wanted to hurt himself. He said he *would* hurt himself. He said he would hurt Blake. That he would take a knife to him."

"Wow. That's a lot."

"When the police showed up to shut down party, I

almost told them about him. That was how scared he was making me."

"But you didn't."

"No," she said. "He called back the next day. Said he'd had too much to drink and he was sorry. He didn't mean any of it. I've seen him a few times since then, just for business. And he's been fine. It seems like he's moved on. He even has a girlfriend. But you know . . ."

"What if he hasn't moved on?"

"Right."

"It's worth exploring," I said.

"He also knew that Blake was gone from his apartment during the time when Eddie left the photograph there." Alena let out a heavy sigh. Picked at a fingernail. "He knew ahead of time that the coast would be cleared."

"Who is he?" I said. "And how did he know?"

"He knew Blake would be with me, at his company's party," Alena said. "His name is Dylan Welch, and he is the CEO of Gonzo."

"The energy drink brand?"

"Yes."

I looked at her. "You hate Gonzo."

"Yes," Alena said. "Yes, I do."

EIGHTEEN

Alena and I met Blake and Spike back in the lobby. I gave them my address, and they hopped into Alena's Mini Cooper, which was parked about a block away across the street.

Spike said he'd go with me, but I was parked in the opposite direction, behind the building. Apparently, the press had learned about Eddie Voltaire's murder, and to get to my car, we had to pass a gauntlet of news vans. I heard someone shout out that they saw Spike and me with the lead detective, and a hailstorm of questions rained down on us—not just from the professional reporters, but from dozens of amateurs. Murder fans, I liked to call them. They'd been lurking around crime scenes since my days on the force, but now, thanks to those online message boards, their numbers had multiplied, and they'd grown much bolder.

"Did you guys know the victim?" someone shouted.

"Was the murder gang-related?"

"Is this the work of a serial killer?"

"Are the rumors true that it was devil worshipers?"

". . . ritualistic bloodletting . . ."

". . . the illuminati?"

"It was space aliens," Spike said.

"Very funny, dude," said one "reporter"—who was actually a teenage boy holding up an iPhone.

Spike stopped walking and stared him down. "Who said I was joking?"

The kid gulped visibly. "Whoa. Seriously?"

"That's deep background." Spike said it very quietly. "Anybody asks me, I'll deny it."

The kid and the amateurs around him were momentarily dumbstruck.

"Nice," I said to Spike, when we were out of their earshot.

"Can't wait to hear that podcast," Spike said.

I laughed.

I was glad to be alone with Spike for a change, to have that familiar rhythm back. I liked Blake and Alena, but there was something about them that I found exhausting. It could have been their youth or their look-at-me profession or their personalities (especially Blake's), all of which were antithetical to the things I craved: namely, peace and quiet, privacy, and the time and space to figure things out.

Spike seemed to sense this. "Can I drive?" He asked the question as though he simply missed being behind the wheel, but I knew it was for my sake. Spike was my best friend, and he could tell that after the past several hours, I wanted someone else to take charge of something—even if it was just my car and it was for only fifteen minutes.

I told him sure and we switched places. As he was turning the key, his phone dinged. He glanced at the screen. "Shit," he said.

"What?"

"Manager just texted. Flynn Tipton is going to be at the restaurant in an hour."

"Flynn who, now?"

"Ever hear of @You'veBeenServed?"

"No."

"That's because you don't cook or run a restaurant."

I gave him a light punch on the arm. "I cook. Sometimes."

"Well, @You'veBeenServed is Flynn's account. He's a super-famous Foodstagrammer," Spike said. "Do you remember back at Blake's apartment, when Bethany said she had a surprise for me?"

It felt like a lifetime ago. But yes, I remembered.

"Flynn was the surprise," Spike said. "She told me last night, after I walked her to her car. I immediately started freaking out, but Bethany assured me she'd be there, too, as she put it, to help keep everything chill."

I turned to him. "Maybe she will."

He started up the car and tore out of the lot, swerving around two drivers on the road and making it through the changing traffic light just as it turned red. Spike always drove like he was in the midst of a car chase, whether or not he was late for anything. Most people found it terrifying, but I was used to it. Kind of.

"It's weird, isn't it?" Spike said. "We've only known Bethany for a couple days, yet she disappears and it rocks our entire world. Or maybe I'm just taking everything too personally? I don't know."

"No, no. I get it. She's done a lot for Spike's already."

"So, so much. Since yesterday, she's had other clients tweeting and posting pictures. And apparently we've been packed all afternoon. The manager says there was a line outside during lunch hour. A lunch-hour line, Sunny. If Bethany Rose were a man, I'd propose."

"She'll come back," I said.

"I need her to," he said. "I need her there for this Tipton thing."

I watched him, but he didn't return my gaze. He was too busy riding the bumper of the SUV in front of us.

"I can meet the Foodstagrammer with you," I said. "I mean, if Bethany isn't back by then. Which . . . maybe she will be. With a perfectly good explanation. Remember Melanie Joan?"

"Well, her explanation sucked."

"True."

"Are you sure, though?" Spike said. "Don't you have to guard Ken and Barbie?"

"They have some trampoline thing to go to," I said. "I can drop them off, head over to Spike's, then meet them after it's over. It's supposed to last a couple hours. I'll even let Lee know they're going to be there."

Spike passed the SUV, narrowly missing a compact car that was headed the opposite way. Both blared their horns, but Spike was too far ahead to pay attention. I glanced at the speedometer. I shouldn't have. Everyone knew about Boston drivers, but Spike was next-level.

"So you never told me your news," Spike said.

"Huh?"

"When I called about Eddie, you said you had news."

"Oh, right," I said. "Moon Monaghan wasn't behind the picture of Blake or the online threats."

He nodded. "I figured," he said.

"You did?"

"Well, I did once I found out that Eddie's murder tied in with the threats," Spike said. "I don't know Monaghan, but themed messages shoved down victims' throats and multiple stabbings . . . It just seems a little *extra* for one of our local operations."

"I thought the same."

"I know the Burkes would never," he said. "Speaking of which . . ."

"Nope. Don't want to talk about it."

"Have you spoken to Richie?"

"You heard me," I said. "Also, you're going to make us flunk the Bechdel Test."

"This isn't a movie," Spike said, "And I'm a man." He

roared to the end of the street and swung into a right turn that nearly flipped my car.

"I had breakfast with Richie," I said, once I caught my breath. "After my first meeting with Moon."

"And?"

"And," I said. "He's still leaving."

Spike exhaled. "Fuck."

"I know."

We both sat in silence for a while. Spike reached a stoplight that he couldn't speed through. I decided to use the relative calm to take care of at least one piece of business. I pulled out my phone and started searching through my emails for Elaine Estallela from L.A.'s Robbery Homicide Division. Back when I was looking into the murder of Erin Flint's sister, Elaine was working for Jesse Stone's former boss, Captain Cronjager. Cronjager had since retired and Elaine had gone on to make full detective.

Elaine and I had kept in touch, mostly via email and texts and the occasional cocktail-hour Zoom, discussing just work stuff at first, but before long branching out into art and politics and whatever true crime series was in Netflix's top ten. Personal stuff, too. When Jesse and I broke up, Elaine provided a judgment-free shoulder to cry on.

Back in April, Elaine had flown out to visit her daughter Lyla, a sophomore at Tufts. During one of her last nights in town, I'd met the two of them for dinner, and after we dropped Lyla off at her dorm, Elaine and I had gone out bar hopping like we were college students ourselves. Since then, I couldn't think of her without feeling just a little bit hungover.

I found Elaine's latest email to me, tapped the reply button, and typed out a quick note.

Hey there! How's Johnny Walker treating you? 😉 Let's shoot for another get-together soon. I'm long overdue for a trip out west. I'll bring the Alka-Seltzer Plus . . .

In the meantime, I'm wondering if you might be able to look into the attached. Concerns a case I'm working on at the moment, and this lady has proven elusive.

xo, S

I attached the picture I'd taken of Betsy Rosanski's driver's license and hit "send" just as Spike peeled around another corner, which turned out to be my street. He arrived at my building moments later and parallel-parked a block and a half away.

We waited out in front of my building for Blake and Alena. The wait took several minutes, then several minutes more. After a while, I started to worry about the two of them. I'd tapped Alena's number to my phone and was about to hit the call button when the Mini passed us, Blake sticking his head out the window like a panicky golden retriever. "Where do we park?" he yelled. He didn't look happy.

I directed him to where my car was, and Alena passed it, parking farther down the end of the block, where we couldn't quite see them. Seconds later, they came running toward us. "Sunny!" Alena yelled. "Sunny, you must see!"

"See what?" I said. Though something told me what it would be, as soon as she reached my building and caught her breath and started thumbing her phone.

"You know how I tell you I never go into my direct messages?" she said.

I glanced at Spike. We both nodded.

"Look at this," said Alena.

I didn't need to. I knew what I'd see before she handed me her phone, her screen filled with direct messages from accounts she didn't follow, legions of men of all ages shooting their shot, the classier ones (if you could call them that) declaring their love for her with heart-eye and rose and diamond emojis, the sleazier dudes sending along eggplants and peaches and water droplets.

"You see it?" she said, tapping frantically at the screen. "You see, Sunny?"

I nodded.

Scattered throughout were direct messages from different accounts, all of them saying the same thing: You reap what you sow.

It was getting predictable.

There were three of these messages on her screen, but when I took the phone and scrolled down, I saw more and more and more.

"This is the first one," Alena said. She tapped a long red nail against the screen. It was from the same @AvengingAngel account that had messaged Blake. And it was sent two months ago.

"My birthday," she said.

Alena hadn't posted on her birthday. But Blake had. The picture of Alena blowing out the candles on a pink cupcake at the Loews Hotel. #NARS #Feelin'24 #Blessed.

I stared at Alena. The most disturbing thing about this message wasn't the words, to which I'd become all too accustomed. It was the video the sender had attached, of Alena and Blake sitting at a table at the Loews, Blake nodding at something Alena said, the uneaten pink cupcake between them. It was just a few seconds long, and it appeared to have been taken from a nearby table.

"Did you guys see anybody you knew when you were out to dinner that night?"

"Just Bethany," Blake said.

"She was with you?"

"No, she sent us over a bottle, but she had a meeting there that night," Blake said.

"Do you know who the meeting was with?" I asked.

"That guy from Gonzo, I think," he said. "Right, Lanie?"

NINETEEN

I started to say something, but Alena widened her eyes at me and put a finger to her lips. Blake and Spike didn't notice the gesture, but I did. And so I spoke carefully, directing my question to Blake. "What's his name?" I said. "This Gonzo guy."

"Dylan Welch," Blake said.

"What do you think of him?"

He glanced at Alena. "He's nice enough, even if Gonzo kinda sucks, right?"

"Sure," she said.

"So you don't think he could be behind these threatening messages?"

"No way," Blake said. "I mean . . . why? We've done a lot for his brand. He likes us."

I nodded. Alena stared at her sneakers.

Spike got another text from his manager, and told us he was heading off to his restaurant to help deal with the midday rush. I assured him I'd be there in time for the Foodstagrammer and accompanied Blake and Alena to my apartment, where Rosie greeted us enthusiastically. Blake got down on the floor and played with her for six solid minutes. Once he was finally back on his feet, I showed him and Alena to the guest room.

Blake went in and began to unpack. Alena squeezed my arm. "Thank you." She said it as though she was simply referring to my taking in the two of them and picking up the slack until Bethany returned, but of course I knew otherwise.

Alena went into the guest bathroom to take a shower, and I headed into my own bedroom, Rosie at my heels. I checked my watch. I had an hour before I needed to bring Blake and Alena to their trampoline event, so I changed out of my skirt and into my most comfortable pair of jeans, threw on a clean T-shirt, and curled up on top of my bed with Rosie, my phone, and my laptop. And after a quick check of my email, I got acquainted with Dylan Welch.

Much as I hated to use it myself, social media was my favorite way of getting to know those whom I was investigating. Scrolling through someone's Facebook, Twitter, Instagram, or what-have-you could provide more insight about who that person was—or at least how they saw themselves—than hours of direct questioning ever could.

Interestingly, I'd found that Facebook pages tended to be

the most revealing. I think it was the platform's familiarity, combined with its unlimited character count and confusing privacy settings. But for whatever reason, it encouraged over-sharing. And since it had been around for so long, Facebook provided not only a glimpse into people's psyches today, but where they stood ten and even fifteen years ago. If you were looking into someone Blake's age, for instance, you could click on their page and scroll all the way back to the mis-guided things they'd been doing—and posting about—in junior high.

Dylan's most recent Facebook post was a photo of himself aboard a yacht with a bunch of people his age—about twenty-four or twenty-five. Dylan was front and center in a blinding pair of madras shorts, red-framed Ray-Ban sunglasses, and a tight T-shirt with the Harvard logo on it, one hand flashing a gang sign, the other clamped on the waist of a brunette, who looked as though she was signaling to the photographer to call 911 (or maybe that was just me projecting).

I enlarged the picture and stared at him—the sun-kissed curls, the smug smirk, the vacation tan, the chunky Rolex riding his wrist as he made those ridiculous sideways scissor fingers.

He looked like the type of guy Spike tended to punch re-flexively. But on the other hand, looks weren't everything. Alena had called Dylan a "charmer"—and Alena did not seem like someone who was easily charmed.

I learned that Dylan's parents were named Bill and Lydia and that they owned a home in Nantucket, where his family had spent the Fourth of July and posed for a group shot. Everyone in the frame was tall and fair-haired and grinning broadly, save for the girl standing next to Dylan—the same unsmiling brunette he'd clutched to his side in the yacht picture. She was at least a foot shorter than everybody else. In this picture, Dylan's arm was around her neck, his fingers twisted in her hair. Dylan's status said that he was "in a relationship," but it didn't say with whom.

Not an insignificant amount of personal info right out of the gate. But when I looked more closely at the pics, I saw that like a lot of people under the age of thirty-five, Dylan had been neglecting his Facebook page for quite some time. The yacht shot had been posted three years ago. The Fourth of July party actually took place four years ago, and it had been Lydia who had posted about it. So much love under one roof, Lydia Welch had written in the caption. Happy Independence Day! She had then gone on to tag Dylan along with his relatives. Though the girl next to Dylan wasn't tagged—I assumed because she wasn't on Facebook or wasn't friends with Lydia—she was named in the caption. Teresa Leone. I typed the name into an email and sent it to myself as a reminder.

I scrolled back, through dozens and dozens of pictures friends and relatives had tagged him in and the very few that Dylan had posted himself—all of them glimpses into a life of enormous privilege.

I skimmed through gushy tributes to his alma maters Exeter and Harvard, photos snapped at debutante balls and glitzy rooftop parties, spring breaks spent in places like Turks and Caicos and the Amalfi Coast and snapshots taken from seats behind home plate at Sox games or courtside for the Celtics. I breezed past years of birthday wishes from people with familiar last names, old-money last names, time-traveling all the way back to Dylan's high school posts, one of which finally made me stop scrolling. It was a shot of him at seventeen, ruddy-cheeked and cherubic and passed out next to an infinity pool, empty beer bottles arranged around him. Someone had been kind enough to draw a smiley face in lipstick on Dylan's exposed belly. He looked like a vandalized Botticelli, only blackout drunk and in board shorts. The image had been posted by some so-called friend of his named Charles Pendergast.

HAPPY BIRTHDAY TO THE MAN, THE MYTH, THE LEGEND, Charles had written. PUSSY HOUNDZ 4-EVA!

I screenshot it and saved it into my photos, on both my phone and my computer. I didn't have cause to use it now, I figured. But it might come in handy in the future.

I shifted to Dylan's Twitter, which had only one hundred fifty followers. And though his tweets were more recent than his Facebook posts, they were mostly all retweets of tech articles. A few were about Welch Industries—a multimillion-dollar conglomerate run by his father. Career-wise, Dylan was clearly born somewhere between third base and home.

Predictably, Dylan's Twitter profile, which described him as a "Sagittarius and Entrepreneur," did not mention his father. I'd always found it interesting how the silver-spoon crowd was so often intent on appearing self-made, when showing some gratitude to their elders would make them appear more honest, which would ultimately be a better move, image-wise.

At any rate, I found a link to the website for Dylan's own company, DylWel Inc., which I clicked on. There, I read his bio, which said that after graduating from Harvard, Dylan had "put his out-of-the-box thinking to work," launching a dating app for sports fans called PlayTheField, before turning his attention to "high-octane soft drinks."

According to the bio, Dylan had contracted "a team of skilled nutritionists and scientists" to develop Gonzo—a "party beverage infused with antioxidants and electrolytes," which also happened to have the highest caffeine content per ounce of any energy drink on the market. ("It'll keep you going all night—and cancel your hangover in advance!")

He was asking for inquiries from drinking establishments, so I texted Spike, sent him a link to Dylan's site, and asked him to set up a meeting.

After about a minute I heard back: This drink looks like shit and he looks like a tool. But I'll do it for you.

"That's what you call a good friend." I scratched Rosie's ear. She stretched and snorted.

I texted Spike back: I owe you one. I'll be extra-charming with Flynn.

Bring the dog.

I gave his text the thumbs-up icon.

"You want to go to Spike's, Rosie?"

Her eyes were closed, her breathing heavy. I'd always envied Rosie's ability to fall asleep on a dime. It reminded me of an observation Richie once made: *Dogs never have trouble sleeping because their consciences are always clear.*

I now remembered that he had said it to me back when he was still married to Richard Jr.'s mother, Kathryn. He wasn't sleeping well back then. Neither was I.

"Focus," I told myself.

On Instagram, I found an account for Gonzo. It had seventy-five thousand followers, most of which were probably paid-for bots. The posts were giveaways, party announcements, or pictures of models holding cans of the stuff and smiling twitchily at the camera. Boring.

Dylan didn't have an Instagram of his own. At least not one that was under his name. For someone who appeared to rely on influencers for both publicity and a social life, it seemed odd how absent he was from this particular platform.

When I Googled Dylan Welch, though, I discovered two things about him: First, he still maintained a very active social life. And second, he had a type. In Google images, I found several pictures of him, some recent, some from five or six years ago, all taken at social gatherings, clubs, and fundraisers for local charities and political campaigns.

In nearly every one of them, he was getting cozy with a curvy brunette who was a lot shorter than him. Teresa Leone fell into that category, as did Alena, and another woman I noticed Dylan posing with at two separate events—one a "Let's Get This Summer Started" party for the PlayTheField dating app, the other the thirtieth birthday blowout for a popular local deejay. Both parties took place the previous year, and they were just a few days apart. But the reason those pictures in particular caught my eye was that I recognized the woman he was with.

It was that murdered influencer, Carlotta Espinoza. And from what I could remember, she'd died less than a month after the pictures were taken.

Coincidence? Probably. I'd followed the Espinoza case closely, and it seemed obvious from the start that it was her connection to politics—not Dylan Welch—that had done her in. Dylan had never even been questioned.

But still . . .

I thought back to the DMs and comments Blake had received from all those fake accounts. The printouts were on my desk, in the folder Bethany had given me. I grabbed the folder and brought it back to the bed and thumbed through the pages until I found what I was looking for: the profile picture of Carlotta Espinoza.

"How about that," I whispered. I held the picture up to my laptop screen, just to make sure I had it right.

I did. The fake account was called @JudgmentDay, and the image of Carlotta had been lifted from the picture she'd taken with Dylan Welch at the PlayTheField party—the hair, makeup, smile, earrings, and angle were all identical. And even though he'd been cropped out, you could still see the edge of Dylan Welch's arm.

Was that intentional? Was it some kind of hint?

Send me a picture of yourself without sending me a picture of yourself...

I texted Alena and asked her to come into my room alone. I need your help with something, I explained. Can you bring your phone?

Within the next few minutes, I heard a soft rap on my door, and then Alena's voice. "Sunny? You called for me?"

I opened the door, ushered Alena inside, and closed it behind her. She was freshly showered, her hair still damp. She'd changed into a form-fitting red dress and matching stiletto heels, but hadn't gotten around to doing her makeup yet. For the first time, I noticed she had a face tattoo—a small cross on her cheek that was usually covered by concealer.

"Is something wrong?" Alena said.

She looked slightly stricken, so I gave her a smile. "Sorry to be so mysterious with the text," I said. "I just wasn't sure whether Blake could see your phone."

Alena made an *o* with her lips and exhaled carefully, as if she was blowing out a candle.

"I wanted to see if I could take a look at those direct messages again."

"Of course," Alena said. She opened her message requests and handed me her phone.

I started to scroll through them, looking for the words *You Reap What You Sow.* Whenever I found the sentence, I'd look at the profile picture.

"So, I was wondering," I asked Alena. "Does Dylan Welch like to play games?"

"Like . . . poker?"

I shook my head. "More like mind games. Puzzles that kind of . . . mess with you."

"Like the Zodiac killer?"

I blinked at her. "Yeah," I said. "Exactly like that."

"Not that I know of."

I kept scrolling, past photos of cats and autumn trees and *Men's Health* covers and pieces of fruit—all random images. And then I found it. The fake account was called @JudgmentDay2. As though it was the sequel to the account that had messaged Blake.

The profile shot was the picture Alena had posted a few weeks earlier—the one taken with her so-called #BFFs aboard the yacht, only this one was just a close-up of Emily Barnes and the other girl. Alena had been cropped out of it, as had the cans of Gonzo in their hands. If you looked closely, though, the curve of her shoulder was visible.

I showed it to her. Her eyes widened.

"Was Dylan on the yacht with you that day?" I asked.

"It was his yacht," she said. "He took this picture."

I gave her back her phone, remembering Bethany in the shot Alena had posted, cowering in the background, covering her face.

"I am cut from it," Alena said.

"Dylan himself was cropped out of a different profile picture," I said, "on one of the accounts trolling Blake. It had almost the same name as this one: JudgmentDay, without the two at the end."

Alena chewed on her lip. "What does this mean?"

"I don't know," I said.

"Maybe Dylan does like puzzles," she said quietly.

"Maybe," I said. "Or maybe these messages are coming from someone entirely different, who found the pictures online."

She nodded.

"You told me Dylan has a girlfriend," I said.

"Yes."

"Did you ever meet her?"

"No," she said. "He just mentioned her a lot. An on-off relationship. A few weeks ago—I think maybe when we were taking pictures on his yacht—he told me they were back on. I was happy for him."

"Did he mention her name?"

"Teresa," he said. "He has known her since college."

I thanked Alena and she asked me if I needed anything more. I told her no, and she said she'd be ready soon—she just needed to do her makeup and put on some earrings.

"I hope this doesn't sound patronizing," I said, as Alena started to leave. "But how do you know about the Zodiac killer?"

"I watched the movie," she said. "I enjoy David Fincher."

After Alena was out of my room, I returned to Instagram and found an account for Teresa Leone, who was not an influencer but a normal person, with six hundred followers and a profile pic of her beagle. Teresa mostly posted shots of meals she cooked and views from mountaintops, but there were enough selfies in the mix to let me know that she was the same Teresa Leone from Dylan's Facebook page. In one shot, Teresa stood next to several other young women on the Harvard campus. 5th Reunion, she'd captioned it. #CrewTeam #Go-Crimson. There were no shots of Dylan at all.

I went into direct messages and typed one to her.

Hi, Teresa! You don't know me, but a friend suggested I contact you regarding Dylan Welch. Could you call me please?

I included my phone number and no further explanation.

I'd debated telling Teresa I was a private investigator looking into a stalker, or even giving her my real name. But I'd decided against doing either of those things because I was worried she might get scared off or, even worse, alert Dylan.

It seemed better to err on the side of vagueness.

I hoped my cute dog would come through for me, that someone with a beagle for an avatar might want to open up a message from the photogenic @RosieRandall and consider responding. But that was all it was—a hope. A line cast in murky water. There was no guaranteeing a bite.

TWENTY

Teresa bit. The call came in just after I'd dropped off Alena and Blake at Let's Bounce, where a publicist had greeted both of them with glasses of the party's signature drink, the "Jump for Julip." I was removing Rosie's leash and lifting her back into my car, reflecting on how good those drinks had looked and how I wouldn't have minded staying for one or two, even though I felt the same way about indoor trampoline places as I did about baseball or, for that matter, social media. *Not much I wouldn't do for a drink right now,* I was thinking. Because it was close to five p.m., on what was turning out to be the longest day in recorded history.

And then I heard my ringtone. I looked at my screen and saw an unfamiliar number with a New York City area code and answered after I started the car, so that the phone call came in over my Bluetooth.

"Who the hell are you?" said the caller, whose voice was high-pitched and breathy and at the same time seething with anger.

"Shouldn't I be asking you that?" I pulled out of the space and onto the road. According to the most recent text I'd received from Spike, neither Flynn Tipton nor Bethany had shown up yet. But Flynn had texted saying he was running just a few minutes late. Bethany was still on radio silence.

"Why did you message me about Dylan Welch?" the caller said.

Now I knew who she was.

"Teresa Leone." I cleared my throat. "Sorry, I just wasn't expecting—"

"Who are you? *Answer me.*"

Think fast . . . "Sunny. My name's Sunny Randall, and a good friend of mine may soon be going into business with your boyfriend, Dylan Welch," I said. It was difficult driving and cooking up half-truths at the same time, but I managed. "My friend. He owns a restaurant and is very interested in carrying Mr. Welch's energy drink, and we were told you might be able to provide some kind of insight as to the culture of DylWel. You know. As a company." I winced. *The culture of DylWel?* Had I really just said that?

Teresa didn't say anything for several seconds. I was starting to think she'd hung up on me, and I couldn't say that

I blamed her. I asked if she was still there, and then, finally, she spoke.

"Are you fucking kidding me?"

"What? No, I—"

"Did he put you up to this? Did he hire you?"

"No. Honestly. I don't know Dylan Welch. I've never met him."

"Why did you call him my boyfriend?"

"I . . . What?"

"Why. Did. You. Call. Him. *My boyfriend?*"

"Isn't he?" I said. "I was told that he was."

"Listen, Sandy—"

"Sunny."

"Whatever," she said. "If Dylan Welch comes anywhere near me, I'm ripping up that NDA, you got me? I don't care. I'll let the press know all about everything he said and did. I'll tank his business. I'll destroy his entire life. *So tell him to back the fuck off.*"

"There was an NDA?"

"I'm hanging up now."

"Wait. Please. I lied."

"Suuure . . ."

"No, really. I swear I don't know Dylan Welch. I'm not doing business with him and neither is my friend. The reason why I lied," I said, "was because I . . . I thought you might tell him."

"Tell him what?"

I exhaled. "I'm a private investigator, and I'm looking into him," I said. "He may be a serious threat to my client."

"Why should I believe that?"

"I can text you my credentials. Or . . . look me up online. Sunny Randall. I've actually been in the news a lot."

She sighed heavily. I heard the hum of voices in the background, then what sounded like someone tapping at a keyboard.

I said nothing. I kept driving. Traffic was horrible.

"Okay," she said finally. "I mean . . . if you really are Sunny Randall."

"I am. Trust me."

"What is going on with your client?"

"She's been getting hostile direct messages and comments on Instagram. A lot of them. Her boyfriend has, too. They feel as though they're being watched. Stalked. The doorman at their building was murdered last night. They are both influencers, and their manager, who was the person who retained me in the first place, has gone missing. And . . . I honestly don't know if Dylan Welch has anything to do with it or not, but all these things do seem to connect in some way, and if I can't put it all together, someone else may die."

"Oh," Teresa said. "Oh . . . wow. This is a lot."

"Can you help me?"

"Hold on. The doorman was murdered?"

"Yes."

Another pause. Someone shouted, "I have a latte for Tracy!"

"That's Teresa!" she called out. "One sec, Sunny."

She got my name right. That was progress.

I heard the faint murmur of Teresa talking to the barista, asking if there was an extra shot of espresso as she'd requested, then paying for her drink.

Traffic moved a little. I was finally able to make a right turn onto Storrow Drive. But it was even worse here. Bumper-to-bumper. That's what I got for trying to get anywhere during rush hour.

"The doorman," Teresa said. "Is that the same one from that building in the Back Bay?"

"Yes."

"Oh my God," she said. "I . . . I heard about that on the news."

"It was on the news in New York already?"

"What?"

"You have a New York area code."

"Oh . . . Oh, no. That's just my phone," she said. "I'm here. I live in Boston."

"Can you help me, Teresa?"

Her voice was low. Tremulous. "What do you want me to do?"

"I just want you to tell me about Dylan Welch. What your relationship was like. Why you got so angry when I mentioned his name."

My phone dinged. I checked out the screen and saw a text from Spike: Flynn Tipton is here. "Shit," I whispered.

"What?"

"Nothing. I just got a text. I . . . I have a meeting and—"

"Well, there you are!" she said. "I thought you'd never show."

"Teresa?"

I heard more voices. Teresa greeting someone. "It's been forever!" she said. "You look amazing. I got you a coffee! Latte with an extra shot. You still like those?"

"Hello, Teresa?" I said. "Are you still there?"

She came back to the phone, her voice curt and businesslike. "Listen, I'd like to help you, but I can't," she said. "Like I said, I signed papers."

My jaw tightened. "I can make sure it's completely confidential," I said. "I won't get you in trouble, I promise."

"Yeah, that's a no," she said. "Nice talking to you! Ta-ta!"

Teresa ended the call.

For a long moment, I glared at the phone as though I was hoping I could intimidate it into getting Teresa to reconsider. "'Ta-ta'?" I said. "Seriously?"

My foot slipped off the brake, and I almost hit the car in front of me. Traffic was at a standstill. It had clearly been like this for a very long time, the drivers on this street so hopeless, they'd given up on even honking their horns. The traffic light shifted from green to yellow to red, with no movement at all. Getting anywhere by automobile within the next two hours felt like more of an aspiration than a possibility.

I was still several blocks away from Spike's, but I knew it would be faster if I walked.

When I saw a spot along the sidewalk that was big enough to squeeze into, I put on my blinker and began inching toward it. It was good, at least, having something to aim for.

Annoyed as I was, I couldn't blame Teresa for not wanting to say more. She'd told me herself that she'd signed a nondisclosure agreement. Why risk the wrath of Welch Industries' legal team just to help out a stranger?

Still, though. It was disappointing.

Finally, I reached the space and pulled into it. I smiled. Susan Silverman told me once that I should seize joy wherever I could find it. Today, I supposed, it was going to have to be found in my superior parallel-parking skills.

I got out of the car, locked it up, attached Rosie to her leash, and started jogging in the direction of Spike's, my little dog gamely keeping pace. I hoped Tipton would take his time over there and that Spike wouldn't be overly annoyed with me when I arrived.

Once I was within five blocks of the restaurant, my phone buzzed. I slowed down to a fast walk and pulled it out of my shoulder bag. I fully expected a text from Spike, telling me Flynn Tipton had left already, and I was trying to think of what I could say, do, or buy for him that could possibly make up for my lateness.

When I saw what was on my screen, I stopped dead in the middle of the sidewalk, breathing hard. Rosie looked up at me. She was panting, too.

The text was not from Spike. It was from the New York number. Teresa Leone's number.

Let's talk in person, it read. When are you free?

TWENTY-ONE

Spike wasn't kidding about the uptick in business. When Rosie and I finally walked through the door, the restaurant was busier than I'd ever seen it at five-thirty on a weekday—or even at eight p.m. on a Saturday—with every seat at the bar taken and a wait for tables. It took me a little while to find Spike, but when I did, I smiled. He was sitting in a corner booth, a very handsome, bespectacled guy across from him who was either thoroughly enjoying Spike's company or faking it in a way that was Oscar-worthy.

They were both drinking glasses of red wine, with plates of bruschetta and charcuterie between them, and they were so completely entranced with each other that approaching them seemed rude. I tried waving, but the hostess, whose name was Mari, spotted me before Spike did. "Don't even bother, Sunny," she said. "He's got tunnel vision at the moment."

I gestured at the man sitting across from Spike, who was even better-looking at second glance. Like a young Cary Grant, only with lighter hair. "Is that Flynn Tipton?" I asked.

"Yep."

"I'd have tunnel vision, too."

"Right?" she said. "And thankfully, the feeling appears to be mutual."

"I guess Spike doesn't need my help entertaining the Food-stagrammer."

"I know he wants to see you, but you're probably going to have to get right up in his face for that to happen," Mari said. "Oh, that reminds me! Spike has a treat for Rosie in the kitchen. Wait here one sec." She sprinted away from her post and returned moments later with a steak bone in a plastic bag. She handed it to me.

Mari scratched Rosie behind the ear. "Lucky girl," she said.

Rosie stared at the bone in my hand the way Tipton was staring at Spike. I debated giving it to her, but that brought on mental images of what it would be like to try to separate Rosie from a juicy steak bone in the middle of a crowded restaurant. I shoved it into my purse instead. "Good things come to those who wait," I said.

I'd always hated that expression. I knew Rosie would've hated it, too, had she known what it meant.

I scooped her into my arms. "Time to get right up in Spike's face," I said.

"Good luck," Mari said.

As Rosie and I made our way toward Spike and Flynn's table, Sam sprung into my mind. I wondered what he was doing right now. If he'd found someone new. With everything going on in this case and in my life, I hadn't even had a chance to ask Spike why they'd broken up. I wondered if it was him or Sam who wanted out of the relationship, because splits were never mutual, no matter what people said. Even if the two people involved called it a "conscious uncoupling" and insisted that the end of the relationship had been both amicable and expected, there was always one of them left feeling just a little bit guilty and the other feeling ever-so-slightly blindsided and betrayed.

My guess was it had been Sam who'd called it a day. It could have been the best friend in me talking, but Spike was loyal to the core, and tended to stick with people or situations he cared about, no matter how much extra work or trouble they brought into his life. This restaurant was a good example. I probably was, too.

"Well, there you are!" Spike said, once I was within a foot of his table. He beamed at me. Spike did not beam often.

"Sorry. Traffic." I turned to the beautiful creature sitting across from him. "You must be Flynn Tipton," I said. "I'm Sunny Randall."

"I've heard so much about you," he said. "And this must be the adorable Rosie." On top of everything else, he had a British accent. God help Spike.

"That would be her." I set Rosie down. Flynn held a hand

out for her to sniff and she licked it. Rosie licked strangers about as often as Spike beamed. Over the speaker system, Heart's *"Magic Man"* was playing. It felt eerily appropriate.

I asked how everything was going, and Flynn told me that he'd already posted several pictures of the food, the wine, and Spike himself.

"How's engagement?" I asked.

Flynn glanced at his phone and looked up at me. "Quite good." He glanced at Spike, then winked. His eyes were a mesmerizing shade of green. "I can't say I'm surprised. The subject matter is quite compelling."

I don't know about Spike, but personally speaking, I swooned.

"Flynn also has a YouTube channel where he shows you how to do really cool things, like pulling together an afternoon tea at the last minute and making the perfect Eton mess," Spike said.

I gaped at him. "Who are you and what did you do with my meathead friend Spike?" I said.

He laughed. So did Flynn Tipton.

"Speaking of messes," I said. "Can we talk alone for just a minute?" I turned to Flynn. "It's about this case I've been working on."

"No worries at all. I'll wait right here," Flynn said. He began taking pictures of the charcuterie plate from different angles. I tried to pick up Rosie, but she was dead weight, preferring instead to sit at Flynn's feet and gaze up at him adoringly.

"You mind watching her for a few?" I asked. "She seems to really like it here."

"It would be my honor," Flynn said.

Spike and I headed through the crowd. I followed him past the restrooms, into his office. He closed the door and sat down at his desk. I took the chair across from his.

"So, I'm assuming," I said, "that I don't need to stay and help you endure the tedious company of the Food-stagrammer."

"Well, um . . . I mean . . ."

"I get it," I said. "Trust me."

"I'm not saying this is going to last, Sunny. But right now, in this particular moment, Flynn Tipton is just what the doctor ordered."

"And by 'the doctor' you mean . . ."

He grinned. "You know it."

"Spike."

"Yeah?"

"I'm really happy for you."

"Thanks," he said. He removed a flask from his desk, along with two tall shot glasses. "Tequila?"

"Please."

He poured out the shots and pushed mine toward me. "This is a very expensive *añejo*," he said. "It's meant to be sipped."

"Don't need to tell me twice." I took a sip. It was as smooth as honey and spread a warmth throughout my body that felt like inner peace.

Spike pounded his shot, then poured himself another. "Do as I say, not as I do."

I gave him a look. "Somebody's got first-date jitters. Or thrills, as it were."

He smiled a little. "Can you blame me?"

"No, I cannot," I said. "And I assume you'd talk about Sam with me if you wanted to?"

"You assume correctly." Spike took a sip from his glass, then leaned back in his seat. "So," he said. "You want to tell me why you're forcing me to meet with this energy-drink douchebag?"

I raised my glass to my lips. No wonder this tequila was expensive. It actually grew smoother with every swallow. "I think he might be our stalker," I said.

"Explain, please."

I told Spike about Alena's brief history with Dylan Welch—the furtive dinner dates, the mild flirtation, the guilt over Blake that caused her to break things off—and the disproportionate rage he'd expressed in response. "She nearly told the cops," I said. "And this is a young woman who definitely does not trust the police. About anything."

"Why didn't she tell them about him?" Spike said. "Or, for that matter, why didn't she tell you about him earlier?"

"Welch apologized. She figured he'd moved on," I said. "But I'm not so sure."

"Why not?"

"I spoke to his ex-girlfriend today," I said.

"And?"

"And . . . there's no love lost. I think she had a very negative experience with him."

"Okay."

"An NDA was signed."

"Wow. Why?"

"I don't know. Yet," I said. "I'll probably be able to give you more details later on, because I'm meeting her for drinks at Ned Devine's at seven."

He exhaled. "Do you need me to pick up Blake and Alena from their trampoline thingie?"

"Nah," I said. "Let's Bounce is really close to Ned Devine's, and I don't have to pick them up till eight-thirty."

"Let's Bounce." He rolled his eyes.

"I don't think that's a bad name for an indoor trampoline venue."

"Really?" he said. "When Jump on This is *right there*?"

I laughed. "Regardless, you're off the hook."

"Good," he said. "I mean, I'm with you, Sunny. You know that. But I kind of want to make tonight last, if you know what I'm saying."

"You don't need to explain," I said. "I've seen Flynn Tipton. I've spoken to him."

Spike grinned at me. "He is something."

"He is."

"And to think, just a couple hours ago, I was only worried about whether or not he'd post pictures of this place on his Instagram."

I raised my glass. "Here's to deeper engagement."

Spike clinked his shot glass against mine, and we both drank the rest of our tequila.

"We talked about Bethany," Spike said. "Flynn and I."

"Yeah?"

"He's worried," Spike said. "He's worked with her before. He says she's never missed a meeting. She's never even been late. Flynn says it's completely unlike her to just disappear."

"I bet he doesn't know she keeps a .45 in her junk drawer."

"True," Spike said, his expression darkening. "I hope she's okay."

"Me too."

We both started to get up, when Spike's phone made a whooshing sound. "Incoming email," he said. Spike turned on all his notifications during workdays. Sometimes I'd get together with him at his bar and he'd be dinging and whooshing nonstop. It was like having lunch with a human pinball machine. Spike looked at his phone. "Speak of the devil," he said.

"Huh?"

He stared at his screen for a long while. "It's from Dylan Welch," he said. "He apparently would like to meet with me as soon as possible."

"Dylan himself?"

"Yep."

"That's interesting," I said. "I assumed you'd hear from his assistant, or at least somebody lower on the totem pole."

Spike's gaze lifted from his phone.

"No offense, obviously," I said. "But it seems strange for a

CEO of even a small company to make a sales call like that." I looked at Spike. "You think he always meets with bar owners?"

He shook his head.

"So . . . why?"

"He says he's been wanting to meet with me. Ever since a few days ago, when he saw pictures of my restaurant on social media."

I stared at him. "On Blake and Alena's Instagrams."

Spike nodded slowly and gave me a meaningful look. "Welch said it must be kismet," he said.

I poured myself half a shot and downed it in a swallow. "I guess that's one word for it," I said.

TWENTY-TWO

When Teresa Leone had suggested over the phone that we meet at Ned Devine's, she'd been apologetic about it. "I know it's a little touristy," she'd said. "But I like it. It feels safe. And Dylan wouldn't be caught dead there."

I'd told her I didn't need any convincing. I loved Ned Devine's, which was located at the heart of Quincy Market, my favorite people-watching spot in the city and probably the world.

I didn't feel like dragging Rosie all the way back to where my car was parked, so I took her on the T. We actually found a car that wasn't too crowded, and I got to the pub fifteen minutes early.

It was a warm night, and there was quite a noisy scene going on inside Ned Devine's. So Rosie and I took a table outdoors. I ordered soft pretzels and cheddar cheese dip because I was starving, and a seltzer water with lime because I was still feeling the tequila shots I'd done at Spike's.

My order arrived quickly, along with a bowl of water for Rosie. As I waited for Teresa, I sipped my seltzer and ate the pretzels and checked my email on my phone.

There wasn't much there—just a friendly but brief response from Elaine, telling me she was in the midst of a crazy day but would look up Betsy Rosanski for me as soon as she got a free moment. The way she ended the email, though, gave me pause.

> BTW, were your ears burning yesterday? Jesse called—
> we're revisiting a case he worked when he was out here
> years ago. Your name came up, and suffice it to say, he
> still thinks about you A LOT. ☺

I reread that final sentence. I'd last seen Jesse Stone in the winter. At the time, Jesse had been "on a break" with Rita Fiore and my split with Tom Gorman had just happened. Jesse and I were both lonely and he looked great and, well, you know. It was what it was.

Actually, "what it was" had been pretty awesome. Jesse and I had always excelled at nonverbal communication. But in the morning, he'd been quiet. Moody. When I asked what was wrong, he'd said we shouldn't see each other anymore.

"Why?" I'd said.

"Because when I'm with you, I can't help but want you all to myself, and I know that can't ever happen."

I'd asked him why again, and he'd just said, "Richie."

I'd protested. But I got it now.

Here I was, sitting in a restaurant I'd been to probably twenty or thirty times with my ex-husband, before and after our marriage, all those memories crashing through my mind even as I attempted to think about Jesse. There was a dog curled up at my feet who was the same size and breed and temperament as the dog Richie and I had adopted together, the result of my visiting half a dozen miniature bull terrier rescues after the original Rosie had passed away. I'd chosen the closest match I could find to Rosie I that didn't involve cloning. And then I'd doubled down by giving her the same damn name.

All that work, trying to keep things the way they used to be.

Don't get me wrong. Rosie II was a great dog. I could take her anywhere. My friends all loved her. And at the moment, she was resting her chin on my foot, and you'd need to hold me at gunpoint in order to get me to move an inch—that was how much I adored her.

But it didn't change the fact that there was something deeply wrong with me. I'd been trying to put a name on it ever since I started therapy. And I was thinking now that Jesse Stone, of all people, had gotten it right: Richie. Richie was what was wrong with me. Richie was the reason I put so much energy into keeping everything the same in my life, from my dog, to my job, to the loft I lived in, which was the same layout and in the same building as the loft we'd rented during the latter part of our marriage.

All that work toward some unknown time in the future, when Richie and I would get back together and it would feel as though nothing had changed, as though we were still young, with our whole lives ahead of us.

Unless he made his own decision not to stop time. Which was exactly what he had done.

All that work . . . At least I'd gotten a good dog out of it.

Rosie lifted her head from my foot and peered up at me, as though she'd been able to read my thoughts. I ripped off a piece of my pretzel and fed it to her. "Who's your pal, Rosie?" I whispered.

"Sunny Randall?" I looked up and into the eyes of Teresa Leone.

She's like a ninja, I thought. I hadn't even noticed her approaching.

Teresa was a few years older than she'd been in the pictures I'd seen of her on Dylan Welch's Facebook page, and at first I thought it showed quite a bit. But at closer glance, I saw that the worldly cast to her features was more the result of makeup than aging. She'd obviously spent a lot of time and effort contouring and highlighting her cheeks and nose. Her eyes were outlined in smoky pencil. She'd gone for a red lip, her thick brows carefully arched, her hair pulled up into a sophisticated twist. In her conservative silk blouse, pencil skirt, and stiletto heels, she looked to me like a celebrity divorce lawyer—the kind the camera would always find and focus on at televised trials. In fact, she looked so impeccable at the end of a workday that I wondered if she'd made herself over just to see me—putting her best face forward, as it were.

I gave Teresa what I hoped was an encouraging smile. "I thought I'd have to be the one to recognize you," I said. "But here, you spotted me first."

"There was an article about you last year," she said, "in *Boston* magazine. I found it online and it had a picture. So."

"Right. I remember that piece."

"It was interesting. Your job sounds dangerous."

"Not most of the time," I said.

"Really?"

I nodded. "I mean, there are scary cases, and those are the ones that make headlines. But a lot of the job is digging up paperwork. Background checks. Stakeouts where you can't listen to podcasts or anything because you need your ears, and you can't even go to the bathroom for hours," I said. "To tell the truth, you'd probably find it pretty boring."

Teresa pulled out the chair across the table from mine and sat down. When the waiter approached, she ordered a vodka tonic. She was eyeing my pretzels so I offered her one. She took it. We both ate. I introduced Teresa to Rosie and let her feed my dog a small piece of pretzel. We talked about the weather. How brutal it had been. Whether we thought the heat wave would break soon. I asked her where she worked, not just for small talk but because I really was curious. She told me that she was an associate at a PR firm, and that her clients were mostly fashion designers. I asked if she got freebies and she said sometimes, and I told her she was lucky.

"Yeah," she said. "I guess I am."

Teresa didn't say Dylan Welch's name out loud until the waiter had brought her vodka tonic and she'd drained half the glass.

"I'm ready to talk about that asshole Dylan Welch" was what she said. And I understood why they called it liquid courage.

"I'm listening."

She took another swallow of her drink. I had some seltzer. Waited. She seemed very nervous, so I spoke instead. "My client says he's a charmer."

"Dylan?" Teresa exhaled. "He is. I mean. He can be, but that's not the real him. He changed after college."

"How so?"

She finished the rest of her drink, then called the waiter over and ordered another round. I'd had only a few sips of seltzer, but I let it happen. I also ordered a glass of pinot grigio.

"Back at Harvard, Dylan was idealistic. Creative. And he wasn't a snob. I mean . . . I was a scholarship kid, but he was still drawn to me," she said. "He said he found me fascinating."

I gave her a look.

"I know, I know. He's a guy."

"And you're cute," I said. "It isn't rocket science."

"Look, I was pretty naïve, but I felt like he really cared. At any rate, he said all the right things. He introduced me to his family. He met my mom and sisters and he was really polite. We talked about our dreams. I was an English major, and he read all my papers and critiqued them. He was a good listener."

I cringed slightly over the critiquing part, but I kept quiet about it. "He was sensitive," I said.

"Very."

"So, what happened?"

"He wanted to go to film school after we graduated, and I think things might have been different if he did. But his dad nixed that idea."

"How come?"

She chewed on a piece of ice. "I mean, Bill Welch isn't a bad guy—at least not by billionaire standards. Most of those dudes seem like Batman villains, don't they?"

"They do."

"Anyway, Mr. Welch said it was time for Dylan to start earning his keep. He wanted him to work for Welch Industries, but Dylan proposed starting up his own business," she said. "He came up with that dating app idea and a few others. So his dad said fine, but Dylan would have to find his own backing."

I looked at her. "Where did he find the backing?"

The waiter brought our drinks. Teresa set the straw down on her napkin and took a huge gulp from the glass. "Let's just say he didn't go on *Shark Tank*," Teresa said.

She was starting to slur her words. A lock of hair escaped

her updo. I made a mental note to get her safely into a cab, whether or not she'd driven here.

"You're gonna have to say more than that."

"He got involved with some bad people," she said. "Druggies. Gang members, even. Some of them had been in prison. And . . . you know . . . He picked up some of their habits."

She swallowed more of her drink. I pushed the rest of the pretzels toward her. She bit into one. Chewed. Swallowed. "It's interesting," she said. "If his dad hadn't tried to make Dylan more self-sufficient—which he probably thought was good parenting—Dylan wouldn't have turned into . . ."

"Into what?"

Teresa let out a long, shaky sigh. "Here's where all of this gets tricky," she said.

"The NDA?"

She nodded.

"Okay."

"I think I've come up with a solution, though."

She pulled her phone out of her bag and tapped the screen. "I saved some old texts from him." She set the phone in front of me. "If I get up and go to the bathroom, and I've had so much to drink that I just . . . like . . . leave my phone here," she said. "This nosy private eye could . . . like . . . read my screen."

"And there's nothing you could do about it."

"That's right," she said. "Disclosing information is one thing. But how can I prevent someone from eavesdropping at a busy tourist bar?"

I grinned at her. "You're a smart one," I said.

Teresa winked at me. "I went to Harvard," she said.

Then she left the table, unsteady on her high heels. I watched her head into the restaurant. The bathroom was up a steep flight of stairs, and I hoped she'd make it there okay. Maybe she wasn't as drunk as she looked.

Her phone was unlocked. I looked at her screen. A series of text messages, dated over a few days last year, all of them from Dylan.

Hey, babe. Tried calling. Where are you?

Helloooo??

You're not ghosting me, are you? LOL.

????????

This isn't funny.

Who the fuck do you think you are?

I'll ruin you, bitch.

I can make you go away. I know people who can do it.

YOU ARE DEAD.

I'M WATCHING YOU. I SEE YOU. YOU CAN'T FUCKING ESCAPE.
YOU WILL PAY FOR YOUR TREACHERY.

I swallowed hard, staring at the capital letters. That last phrase, which was another way of saying you reap what you sow.

Teresa returned to the table and I pushed the phone toward her. "Well," I said. "That got real ugly real fast."

"He sent me DMs on Instagram, too," she said. "But I deleted all of those." She slipped the phone back into her bag. "The thing was, it wasn't that surprising."

"Did he talk to you like this when you were dating?"

She bit her lip. "Not at first," she said.

"But . . . after he met the bad people."

"Some men," she said. "They can be perfectly nice. Charming. But they do a little coke, and it's Mr. Hyde time."

"Have you known other men like that?"

"No." She laughed a little. "I guess I was just trying to sound worldly."

"What brought on these texts?" I said.

"I told him I wanted to take a break," she said. "He wouldn't listen. He kept calling. One day he'd be love-bombing me, trying to woo me back, sending me flowers and gifts at work and leaving these adoring messages on my voicemail, the next he'd get threatening. Really scary. Finally, I just stopped answering my phone."

"Why did you want to take a break?" I said. "Was it the drugs?"

"Well, that," she said. "But what really did it was that I found out he'd been watching me through my webcam."

"What?"

"He put some kind of spyware in my computer. My phone. He was surveilling me. Like I said, coke can make you paranoid."

"Jesus. I'm so sorry, Teresa. That must have been terrifying."

"It was."

We both stayed quiet for several moments. I tried to imagine what it might feel like—the realization that you could never escape someone, even in your own home and with the door locked.

The waiter came by. I asked for the check.

"Teresa?"

"Yeah."

"Did he ever hurt you?"

"Physically?" she said. "No. But his friends would have done it. He made that clear. If his dad hadn't intervened, I . . . I don't really want to think about it."

His friends. I thought about the bald guy Eddie talked about. The tear tattoos on his face. Prison tattoos.

"Bill Welch got me to sign that NDA in exchange for Dylan going to rehab and never talking to me again," she said. "But that didn't mean he wouldn't start using again and go psycho on some other girl." The waiter came back with the check. I took it before she could see it, and put my credit card down. She thanked me.

I told her I was going to put her in an Uber. "I'm not really that drunk," she said. "The problem is, I can't walk in these shoes. I never dress like this. I basically put on a disguise to meet you here tonight. Just in case I was being followed."

"He's had you followed?"

She nodded. "For a while there, I'd almost gotten used to it."

"I'm sorry," I said. "It's got to be hard for you, my bringing all of this up again."

She shrugged. "I'll be fine. I just hope your client is okay."

I finished my glass of wine. "Me too," I said quietly.

I asked Teresa where the Uber should drop her off and opened the app on my phone. She gave me an address in Cambridge and I typed it in. The app told me a car would meet us at Union and State in five minutes. I made sure Rosie was hooked to her leash, then stood up. We walked Teresa there and waited with her and when the Uber showed up, I made sure to check the license plate before I let Teresa get in. "Stay safe," I told her. I meant it. Truly.

I'd been planning to take the T back to my car, but it was only a fifteen-minute walk if Rosie and I kept the pace up, and I really felt like I needed the fresh air.

I still had plenty of time before I needed to pick up Alena and Blake. But I couldn't stop thinking about what Teresa had said. *That didn't mean he wouldn't start using again and go psycho on some other girl . . .*

After walking several blocks, I texted Alena:

You guys having fun?

She answered quickly: Yes! Taking lots of pictures! She attached a short video of Blake on one of the trampolines, doing a backflip.

I smiled. Rosie yanked at the leash and coughed. "Jeez, hold your horses," I told her.

I typed another text to Alena.

Great! I will be there at 8:30. Wait inside the venue for me—not outside.

After I sent it, I thought for a few seconds and typed more: BTW, do you guys have your webcams covered up? Because if you don't, you should.

???

Just a safety thing. Nothing to worry about.

Rosie barked and pulled at the leash some more.

"Okay, okay." I unzipped my purse to slip my phone back in and felt something hard. I lifted it out. The steak bone. Rosie barked louder. "You're going to have to wait until we get home," I said. I dropped it back into my bag.

I was nearing Copp's Hill Terrace, the historic cemetery sprawling up the hill to my right, Langone Park to my left on lower ground. Life and death. Baseball fields and tombstones. I'd lived in Boston my whole life, and I still found its layout so unexpectedly poetic.

I would have stopped to reflect on the symbolism of it all, if it weren't for the car driving slowly beside me, speeding up and slowing down whenever I did.

I stared straight ahead and kept walking. I was not in the mood for this. Why were there so many losers in this world? I held my purse close to my side and felt the weight of my gun. I worked the zipper with my free hand. I heard a window rolling down, a man's voice saying something I couldn't quite hear. *He's going to either catcall me or try to mug me,* I thought. I wasn't going to put up with either option.

The car pulled to a stop. Its door slammed. I finally got my bag open and plunged my hand in, but the first thing I felt was not my .38, but my hairbrush.

Rosie was barking incessantly now.

I heard footsteps behind me. A man's voice. "Hey," he said. "Hey, you."

When I felt breath on the back of my neck, I knew it was time to stop walking.

I whirled around and took several steps back and saw him, not as a whole but the sum of his parts. The sun-kissed curls. The pasty-white face. The bloodshot eyes. The sweat-stained polo shirt.

"Dylan Welch," I said. "You piece of shit."

It was only then that I noticed he was holding a gun.

TWENTY-THREE

Y ou're in big trouble," Dylan Welch said.

If it weren't for the gun, I would have almost felt sorry for him. His pupils were pinpricks. His cheeks caved in, like the weak parts of an old mattress, and he gave off an oniony smell, as though he hadn't bathed in days. He was definitely off the wagon. (*Off the wagon. On a bender. Downward spiral.* Why did these phrases always sound like amusement park rides?)

Welch's hands were shaky holding the weapon. I doubted he could get off a decent shot if he tried, but as high and jittery as he obviously was, I wasn't going to risk things.

I kept my voice calm, quiet. "What do you want from me?"

"I want you," he said, "to keep away from my girl."

"Which girl?" I said.

He raised the gun. "Is that supposed to be funny?"

"No. It's an honest question."

"Don't patronize me or I'll blow your fuckin' head off."

"Okay, I—"

"What did you tell her about me?"

"Tell who?"

"This isn't *a fucking joke.*"

I took a breath. Let it out slowly. It was dawning on me that this was one of those damned-if-you-do-or-don't situations. Either Dylan Welch was going to shoot me or he wasn't. And it didn't matter what I said, because, Harvard degree or not, he was too stupid to listen to anyone—especially a woman.

May as well speak my mind.

"What I'm trying to say," I told him, "is that there's more than one girl out there who doesn't want anything to do with you. I know of two offhand. But I'm sure there are a lot more."

Rosie growled.

"You understand now?" I said.

My gaze stayed riveted on the barrel of Welch's gun. He probably thought he was aiming it at my heart, but it was directed more toward my shoulder. His hands kept quivering, and he still hadn't released the hammer. He wiped sweat out of his eyes and nearly dropped it.

Maybe tough talk was the way to go.

"You can add me to that list, too, by the way," I said. "In fact, I could probably throw a party for all the women who don't want anything to do with you, but I don't think I'd be able to afford the catering budget."

He was giving me his full attention now. His eyes were wide. His jaw slack. "What the actual fuck?" he said. Like the wordsmith that he was.

My shoulder bag was at my hip, and I kept fishing in it for my .38. My hand bumped against my phone. My makeup bag. A box of tampons. My rape whistle. Wallet. Water bottle. A spiral notebook. Ticket stubs. A bottle of perfume. Rosie's steak bone. I really needed to clean out my bag.

"How many Harvard grads does it take to change a lightbulb?" I asked.

"How many?"

My eyes widened. He had actually responded that way.

"Only one," I said. "The Harvard asshole holds the bulb, and the world revolves around him." I forced out a laugh. "Get it?"

Welch laughed, too, and I felt as if I'd landed in the middle of a fever dream.

"What is going on here, Dylan?" I said.

"You're a private eye."

"Yes, that's right."

"My dad hired you."

"What? No. No, he didn't."

"Fuck you. I know he did. Got you to talk to my girl and keep her away from me. It's all part of his plot to ruin my fuckin' life." He swatted at his face again. Licked his lips and let out a strange little giggle. "I'm onto him. I'm onto you. Don't even try to stab me in the back because I am fucking Teflon, bitch."

"What is that? A *Real Housewives* tagline?"

He lunged forward and growled, like a dog. Wow, was he tweaked. It was probably time to get serious. My stomach tightened. Sweat trickled down my rib cage. I kept my voice steady, my movements minimal. "Your father did not hire me," I said. "I don't know him. And I don't care whether you believe me or not. It's the truth."

He shut his eyes tight, then opened them.

"You know what's also the truth?"

He shook his head.

"If I go missing, there are a lot of people who will be looking for me," I said. "They'll find you. And you will go to jail."

"I won't. I'm fuckin'—"

"Please don't say 'Teflon' again," I said. "Here's the deal. I'm an ex-cop, and I maintain a close relationship with many on the force. Including Sergeant Frank Belson."

"You're lying."

I raised my eyebrows. "Am I?" I said quietly. "Why not try fucking around and finding out."

"I . . . I don't like getting messed with."

"You think cops like getting messed with, Dylan?" I said. "They're not happy about what happened to Eddie. But that's nothing compared to how they're going to feel if something happens to me." I glanced at his car—a sleek black

Lamborghini. "What's the plan, anyway? You shoot me and throw my body in the trunk of that penis substitute you got there? Dump me in the harbor without anybody noticing?"

Dylan shifted from foot to foot and sniffled, his whole body twitching as though he were trying to escape the oppression of his own skin. "S-Stop it."

"Or maybe you're going to make a statement. Like last time, right? Put me in a public place with a Bible verse in my mouth?"

He stopped twitching. "What?"

"It's not gonna work. If one of your friends did that to Eddie, the cops will know you were behind it. They have your name. I gave the cops your name, first and last. They know you. They know who your father is. They like you for Eddie. They're probably questioning your dad as we speak."

He swallowed hard. His throat moved visibly. I could tell he believed me now. I didn't like lying to anyone—even Dylan Welch. But I could create a good lie when I needed to. The secret: Start it out by telling the truth.

I leveled my eyes at him, my hand still traveling the confines of my shoulder bag. "You reap what you sow," I said. "Right, Dylan?"

He looked as though he might start crying. *"What are you talking about?"*

"Where's Bethany? Do your friends have her? If you tell the cops, they might go easier on you."

"Bethany who?"

I found my .38. Finally.

"Bethany who?" He said it again.

I yanked the gun out of my bag and got both hands around it fast, dropping both the bag and Rosie's leash in the process. "Great," I said.

"Fuck," Welch said.

"Don't move," I said.

And then everything started moving.

TWENTY-FOUR

The steak bone rolled out of my bag. Rosie made for it, scurrying between Welch's legs, the leash trailing behind her and somehow wrapping around his ankles. Welch's gun clattered on the sidewalk. I managed to kick it away after two tries, and at the same time the leash tightened. His feet slid out from under him. He landed on his back, his madras shorts smacking the sidewalk first, then his shoulders, then his head.

All of this happened in a matter of seconds.

After, I stood over Dylan Welch, my .38 aimed at his face, the two of us locked in a stunned, frozen silence, like two characters in a movie still.

Rosie chewed on the bone. The sound of it echoed.

"What the fuck?" Dylan said finally.

I released the safety. His eyes widened.

"Please." His voice came out in a thin squeak. "The gun . . . That gun I was holding. I just wanted to scare you. It's not even loaded."

I kept my .38 trained on him as I knelt down, picked his gun up off the sidewalk. I checked it. He was right. "Why did you want to scare me?" I said.

"Don't kill me," Dylan Welch said. His skin was grayish under the streetlight. My gaze went to the watery eyes, the sweat-slicked forehead. The quivering lip. A tear trickled down his cheek.

"Why were you following me?" I said.

"Because," he said. "Teresa."

"Seriously?"

"I still love her."

"That's your problem, not hers."

"Look," he said. "I'm not interfering in her life, but I hired somebody. They've been following her for days."

"I don't think you know what the word *interfering* means," I said.

He kept going. "Teresa was in Starbucks earlier today. She had a client meeting, but she was talking to you, and the person I hired told me everything you said. He saw the texts you both sent each other about where you were meeting. He saw her reading an article about you on her laptop."

I glared down at him. "Dylan," I said. "You really need to leave Teresa alone."

"You don't understand. I cleaned up. I mean . . . okay. Not

tonight. Not the past couple days. But I did. I went to rehab. For her. And I can do it again."

I took a breath. "If you still love Teresa," I said, "you'll do what she wants."

He sniffled.

I found myself thinking of Richie and me, of all things. "If someone you care about wants to leave you, you need to let them do it," I said. "You have to put their feelings first, or else they'll never come back. Not ever. Because they'll realize they're probably better off without you."

Welch closed his eyes. More tears spilled down his cheeks. I wasn't sure why I was bothering with the advice. He was a spoiled, paranoid, narcissistic stalker, and Teresa was never going to come back to him, no matter what tack he took. But I did feel like something within Dylan Welch had changed, around the time he smacked his head on the pavement. It was as though a window had opened just a crack. And at least temporarily, he was capable of listening, and telling the truth. "Dylan?"

"Yeah?"

"Have you been harassing Alena Jade and Blake James?"

"Huh? No. Of course not."

"You got angry when she called it quits."

"Yeah, because I knew it wasn't for real with her and Blake," he said. "They have no chemistry. I don't even think they've banged."

"That isn't for you to decide."

"I know, I know," he said. "She said she didn't want to

have dinner with me anymore, and I went out and got high and I said some shit I shouldn't have. But I apologized. I even stopped following Alena and took her out of my contacts."

"You did?"

"I mean, hell. I've dated a lot of cute girls. Tons of 'em. And Alena was one. But the only girl I've ever loved is Teresa. And I'm going to get her back."

I stared at him. "You reap what you sow," I said. "That isn't you?"

His head lolled back, and, if it was possible, his skin looked even paler. "I have no idea what you're talking about."

"Okay," I breathed. "Okay. One more question: If you aren't obsessed with Alena, why did you offer to make a personal sales call at Spike's?"

"Because it's the hottest place in town. It's all over Instagram," he said. "What does one thing have to do with the other?"

My shoulders relaxed. I believed him. He wasn't a killer. Just an asshole. And he wasn't harassing anyone other than his college girlfriend, the poor thing.

Dylan collapsed. I shined the flashlight from my phone on his face. There was blood on the sidewalk, in his hair. It must have happened when he hit his head, and it was a good bet he needed stitches. "I'm calling nine-one-one," I said.

"Whatever. Why?"

"You need medical attention," I said. "Detox, too, if you can get it."

I knelt down on the sidewalk. Rosie was chewing on the

steak bone contentedly. I grabbed my shoulder bag and pulled out my phone. As I did, I took a longer glance at Dylan's head. It didn't look great.

"Fuck detox," he said. "I'm not cleaning up until I get Teresa back."

"Dylan, you promised you'd keep away from her."

"You don't get it. I deserve her."

The window was closed. He was no longer listening.

I called 911 and as I told the dispatcher that there was a man with a head injury on the sidewalk right next to Copp's Hill Terrace, I kept thinking about Teresa, how she'd been forced to put on an entire disguise just to meet me for a drink. I wished there was something I could do . . .

The dispatcher told me an ambulance would be there in five minutes. I hung up with her and picked up my bag, un-tangled Rosie's leash from Dylan's legs, and told him to have a nice life.

But just as I was about to leave, I remembered his Facebook page and an idea came to me. A possible solution to Teresa's problem.

"You know what," I said. "I spoke to a friend of yours, Pendergast."

"Charlie? From high school?"

"Yep. He told me some interesting stories about you. Pussy Houndz with a z. Good times."

Dylan groaned. "He's full of shit. I haven't talked to him in like ten years."

I watched his face. Lying to this guy got easier and easier.

It was even kind of fun. "Charlie had images to back up what he said."

"Which pictures did you see?"

I thought for a moment. *Which pictures* . . . Only one had made it onto Dylan's Facebook history, and it hadn't been pretty. I could only imagine the ones that hadn't seen the light of day. "All of 'em," I said. "And I didn't just see them. I downloaded copies."

"Fuck."

"Yep."

"You want money? Is that it?"

"Nope," I said.

"What, then?"

"Listen to me," I said. "If Teresa tells me that you've bothered her in any way . . . I'm talking a text. A comment on her Instagram story. You try and buy her a drink at any bar anywhere. I'm going to share Charlie Pendergast's photos with your dad. With Gonzo's investors. And most definitely with my friend Tom Gorman. He's a columnist for *The Globe*, and he would love to do a piece on Bill Welch's son's out-of-control teenage years."

"This isn't fair."

"You reap what you sow, buddy," I said. He didn't respond. I heard a siren in the distance. "Sounds like your ride."

I started to walk away.

"It was consensual," Dylan said quietly.

I turned around. "What was?"

"You know. What Charlie has pictures of," he said. "The

girl was into it. She wanted me. She only got weird afterward."

I gaped at him. "Gross."

I wondered if Dylan could spot a bluff more easily when he wasn't coked up and bleeding from the head. If not, it was hard to believe that he had what it took to start one business, let alone two.

The siren was nearing. I needed to get out of there.

"Stay away from Teresa," I told him. "You've been warned."

TWENTY-FIVE

Rosie and I ran the rest of the way to my car, and by the time I took off for Let's Bounce, there was a lot less traffic, so we showed up only ten minutes late for Blake and Alena.

The place had mostly cleared out, except for a few teenage gymnast types who seemed intent on out-flipping one another. But my clients were keeping themselves busy. I spotted them right away, standing by the bar at the far end of the room, taking selfies with a few of the event's organizers.

I watched the two of them for a few moments. Much as I hated to admit it, Dylan Welch had been right when he said they didn't have much chemistry. In the time I'd known them, I'd seen a lot of affection between Blake and Alena—hand holding, warm glances, et cetera. But they never seemed remotely close to "get a room" territory, which was kind of surprising, considering their youth, how long they'd been dating, and how ridiculously good-looking they both were.

I picked up Rosie and walked the length of the room toward them, past a series of brightly colored trampolines, plus three cotton candy machines, a mechanical bull, another bar/dining area, and a small dance floor with a rotating disco ball. I wondered how much of this extraneous stuff was here for the event. Just looking at all of it made me even more exhausted than I was to begin with. A little nauseated, too, if I was going to be honest. Booze and trampolines did not seem like a wise combo. And don't even get me started on the mechanical bull.

Blake and Alena caught sight of me at the same time. They both waved.

Blake yelled out, "Hi, Rosie!" as though he expected her to answer.

Once I reached them, Alena said, "What happened to you?" and I realized I hadn't cleaned up after my altercation with Welch. I hadn't even bothered checking my reflection in my rearview on the ride over, which wasn't like me. I supposed I was more shaken than I'd thought.

I pulled my compact out of my bag and looked at myself. My hair was a sweaty mess. There was a smear of dirt on my face that must have happened when I was separating Rosie from the steak bone, and when I glanced down, I saw that there was a good-sized rip in my favorite Dior jeans, and my knee was bleeding. "That's perfect," I whispered.

Could have been a lot worse, considering the situation. But still.

I smoothed my hair. Pulled cleansing wipes out of my bag and went over my face with one, paying special attention to the smear on my cheek. Pulled out another and cleaned off my knee, which turned out to be a more serious cut than I'd thought. Reapplied my lipstick and examined my reflection. Not great, but better. One of the organizers, who introduced herself as Sandy, asked if I needed a Band-Aid, and when I said yes, she sprinted away, returning quickly with a professional-looking first-aid kit. Apparently, when you ran an indoor trampoline emporium, you had a lot of these on hand. I cleaned the wound with a peroxide wipe and bandaged it up.

"Did you fall, Sunny?" Blake said.

"Yes," I said. "I'm fine."

Alena just looked at me. I could tell she wasn't buying it.

I asked Blake if he could walk Rosie out and he practically jumped up and down saying yes.

I gave him Rosie's leash, and the two of them jogged out. Alena and I followed.

And Alena said it again. "What happened to you?"

I started to explain, but I still had an unsettling feeling. A sense that someone was watching. "I'll tell you all about it in the car," I said.

I did. But because she'd sworn me to secrecy about Dylan Welch, I was careful about it. Once we were on the way to my loft, I turned to Alena, who was sitting in the passenger's seat, and gave her a meaningful look. "Remember that potential suspect you told me about?" I said.

She glanced in the rearview mirror at Blake, who was

sitting in the back with Rosie in his lap, working his phone intently. "Yes," she said. "I remember."

"I had a little run-in with him tonight."

Her eyebrows shot up. "This is why you are a mess?"

"Yep," I said. "But I did find out something important."

"What?"

I checked on Blake. He was taking a selfie with Rosie.

"The potential suspect is not the one who's been stalking you guys."

"You are sure of this?"

"As sure as I am about anything, at this point."

"What potential suspect?" Blake said.

I exhaled hard.

"It doesn't matter," said Alena. "Just some follower who got a little . . . How do you say it, Sunny?"

"Creeptastic."

"Yes. He got creeptastic on me. But not for a long period of time."

Blake pushed the back of her seat. "Why didn't you tell me about him, Lainey?" he said. "I tell you about my weird followers."

"I didn't want you to worry. Especially with Bethany gone—"

"You need to stop protecting me," he said. "Stop treating me like . . . like I can't handle the truth without getting all emotional." His voice cracked.

"I know," Alena said.

"Who is this piece of shit? I want to kill him!"

"No offense, Blake," I said. "But you aren't doing much to prove your point here."

"Blakey," Alena said. "Sunny said it was not this follower who sent the messages and he did not do that to Eddie. His identity does not make a difference."

"It makes a difference to me. *Tell me who he is.*"

It was the first time I'd ever heard Blake raise his voice to Alena. Or to anybody, now that I thought about it. I glanced in the rearview. He was staring daggers at Alena. Bullets. Whatever text conversation he'd been engaged in was now a forgotten thing. His laser-blue eyes burned into the glass.

"Fine," Alena said. "It was Dylan from Gonzo. Are you happy now?"

Blake gasped audibly. We reached a stoplight and I turned to look at him. His eyes softened. His face seemed to crumble. "I've had beers with that guy."

"All I did was, I let him take me out to dinner," Alena said. "How do you say it? No biggie."

"How many times did you go out to dinner?"

"A couple," she said. "It was just to be friends, Blake. Nothing happened. Not even a kiss good night."

Blake said nothing.

"Believe me," Alena said. "Please."

Still no reply.

I really wanted to tell Blake to grow up and get over himself. I felt like reminding him that in the general scheme of things, Alena's decision not to inform him about a couple dinners with a sponsor was not that big a deal—especially when you weigh in the fact that Blake had never told her that just a few months ago, he'd raked in $900,000 on the down-low by making personalized fetish porn. But I'd said enough already.

"Did you guys eat enough at the event?" I said. "Should we order a pizza?"

"Does Bethany know?" Blake said, turning to Alena.

Alena shook her head.

"You should tell her, Lainey. You really should. As soon as she comes back."

Okay . . . What?

I cleared my throat. "Excuse me. I don't mean to interrupt," I said. "But why would Bethany need to know about Alena's personal life?"

Neither one of them answered me. We drove in silence for a little while. When I looked in the rearview mirror, Blake's eyes were closed, and he was breathing deeply, in and out.

Imagining himself in the water. The Seven Seas. Whatever that meant.

I looked at Alena. "Did I say something wrong?"

"No," she said. "He just misses Bethany, that is all. I think it is making us both a little bit crazy."

TWENTY-SIX

We ordered a pepperoni, sausage, and onion pie from Regina Pizzeria on the North End. It was delivered shortly after we got back to my place. I pulled out some plates and my cloth napkins, plus cutlery in case Blake and Alena wanted it, and the three of us ate it at my kitchen table. I wasn't that hungry, but I had one small slice to be polite and because Regina pizza is literally impossible to resist. Alena took a larger slice, but she carefully removed all the pepperoni and sausage from hers and gave it to Blake, who pulled the cheese, pepperoni, onion, and sausage off of three additional slices and ate all of it with a fork and knife, piling up the crusts at the side of his plate.

It honestly pained me to see a Regina pie desecrated like this, but what could I do? I doubted either Blake or Alena could remember how pleasurable it could be to eat like a normal person.

I poured water for all three of us and asked them if they wanted any wine, but Blake shook his head. "Carbs," he said.

"Of course," I said.

"I would like some wine, please," Alena said.

"Oh, good," I said. "I hate to drink alone."

I had a nice, dry rosé in my fridge, and I poured glasses for the two of us.

Alena held her glass up to the light and asked for the name of the wine. After I told her, she said, "It is a lovely color."

I told Alena that outside of whether it was white, red, or pink, I'd never thought much about the color of the wine I drank. But I understood why she'd said it when she pulled a selfie stick out of her purse and snapped several pics of herself, raising her glass so that it sparkled in the overhead lights.

"That's good, Lainey," Blake said. "It brings out your tan."

She took a small sip, then asked Blake to tell her which selfie he liked the most, and he put down his fork and knife and carefully examined the pictures on her phone, deliberating over two of them before choosing his favorite, which she then cropped, filtered, and posted. By the time they were done with this process, I'd finished my first glass and was halfway through another.

"It's a full-time job, isn't it?" I said. "Being an influencer."

"It is not so much a job as a mindset," Alena said. "You are selling not just the products, but yourself, your lifestyle."

"We have to be aspirational twenty-four/seven," Blake said. "Our followers expect that of us."

I looked at both of them, so obviously parroting words that were not their own, and for Alena, not even in her own language. The hold Bethany had on them was powerful—maybe more so in her absence.

There was an exposed brick wall in my kitchen, and Blake walked up to it, yanked down the neck of his T-shirt, and assumed the type of seductive pout that would make Zoolander proud. Turning slightly to his left, he snapped a series of selfies, his muscular arm raised so high, it looked uncomfortable. "I only posted one video from Let's Bounce," he said between snaps. "I need just a little more presence."

"Do you want me to take the photos, Blakey?"

"No." He said it quickly, and a little harshly, his device clutched in his hand like a battlefield flag—a thing he'd die before parting with. I wondered if there was something on Blake's phone that he didn't want Alena to see, and for a moment, I recalled him texting in the backseat of my car.

None of my business.

"I'm fine, Lainey," he said. "I mean . . . I'm all done with the pics anyways."

He went through his shots, prepped and posted one, then returned to the table. I told both of them that if they were going to take selfies at my place, to make sure they weren't with or around anything identifiable. "The stalker obviously watches your Instagrams," I explained. "And if there's anything that ties you to this place, or to me . . ."

They sighed in unison.

"We get it," Alena said.

"Can we change the subject, please?" Blake said.

I was happy to oblige. The two of them went back to sort of eating their pizza, and we talked about the trampoline event and the TV plans for *The Shred Shed* and whether being verified on Instagram was more or less of an achievement than scoring a blue check on Twitter. I asked if they'd streamed any good shows lately, and they told me about some reality dating series on Netflix that I'd purposely banned from my consciousness. We talked about music, and Alena said she was enjoying the most recent Beyoncé album. I agreed that the album was great, and so did Blake, who added that it was his workout jam. "That reminds me," Blake said to me, "do you have a home gym?"

"No. Sorry."

"That's okay," he said. "We passed an Equinox on our way here. I'll just jog there in the morning."

"What time?"

"Five-thirty or six," he said. "That's my usual."

I suppressed a groan. "Okay."

"Why?"

"Because I have to go with you," I said. "I'm your bodyguard."

"Oh," he said. "Right."

Blake settled into a moody silence. Alena joined him.

"We'll get this sorted out, and you can move back into your building." I said it as much for my own benefit as I did for theirs. My loft wasn't that big, and it was already starting to feel crowded. I got up and cleared the dishes. Alena helped. I told Blake he could feed one of his crusts to Rosie, and that seemed to lift his spirits.

"That's a good girl," he said to her. "Who's the best girl in the whole wide world?"

As he fed Rosie, I watched him. The phone never left his hand.

TWENTY-SEVEN

I started to rinse off the dishes and my own phone dinged. It had been a while since I'd received a text or a phone call, and the sound made my skin jump. I glanced at the screen. It was a text from Richie.

I set down the dish I was rinsing, picked up the phone, and read it carefully.

Just checking in. How are you?

I gazed at the screen, a million responses running through my mind, ranging from warm (*It's really good to hear from you!*) to accusatory (*Seriously? How do you think I am?*) to passive-aggressive (no reply whatsoever).

Then I remembered what I'd told Welch earlier, about

letting someone leave if you loved them. I settled on Hi with no punctuation. Richie texted back immediately:

Dad said he saw you today. He was worried about you.

I typed, I'm fine. You know what a drama queen Desmond can be. After rereading the text, I deleted the second sentence. Too sarcastic.

Instead, I tried, Your father doesn't want you to leave, either, you know. Which was true. But wow, did that ever sound needy. I deleted both sentences and started fresh.

I appreciate Desmond's concern, but I'm fine. Really. Please tell him that he doesn't need to worry about me.

Much better. I added a smiley-face emoji, just to make it clear how fine I truly was.

After I sent the text, I waited a full minute for a response from Richie. There was none. No pulsating bubbles, either, so I knew he wasn't even attempting. I rinsed the last dish and stuck it on the rack next to the sink.

"Is everything okay?" Alena said.

"All good," I said. "That was just my ex-husband, checking in."

"Your ex?"

"Yes," I said. "He's moving out of town, and I'm not happy about it."

"Why not?"

"Because," I said, "I love him."

She stared at me.

I hadn't meant to say that out loud.

"That sounds . . . How do you say it? Confusing."

"It is. Well, now it is. It didn't used to be. Not really."

As I hung up the dish towel, it occurred to me how rarely Richie and I had texted in the past—and how, when we did, we never used emojis. Perhaps that was because we'd never needed pictures to understand each other's feelings.

"Who's a good girl?" Blake said. He was down on the floor with Rosie, playing fetch with her favorite stuffy toy.

My phone dinged.

Rosie yelped.

Blake winged the stuffy toy into the living room. Rosie scurried after it, and he followed, shouting, "Go get it!" over and over.

Alena and I looked at each other. "He loves dogs," she said.

"I can see that. Why doesn't he have one?"

"Bethany doesn't think it's a good idea," she said.

I nodded slowly.

Alena shrugged. Obviously, even she understood how weird that sounded. "He may have to travel for *The Shred Shed*," she said. "Or for his other engagements. Bethany believes that if he is tied down, it could hurt his career."

"Still," I said. "That's a lot of personal involvement for a manager."

"She cares about us."

"All her clients?"

"Yes, of course. But, well . . . Blake and I are special to her."

"You're her top earners."

"True. And we are also her very first."

I looked at her. "You mean *you* are, right?"

"Pardon?"

"I'd thought you brought Blake to her after she was already established. At least, that's what Bethany told me."

"Yes, that is correct." She laughed. "Sometimes it feels as if Blakey and I have been together forever."

I smiled. Alena and Blake were the youngest "old married couple" I'd ever met. I nearly said that to her, but I was afraid she might take it the wrong way and get insulted. Instead I said, "You were her very first client?"

"Yes."

"So you must hold a special place in her heart."

"I believe that is true."

I thought of the shoebox under Bethany's bed, and what Moon Monaghan had said about her "doing some jobs" for him in L.A. I'd never mentioned anything about Betsy Rosanski to Blake and Alena—mainly because Bethany was the one who had hired me, and it wasn't my place to reveal any past secrets she might have been keeping from them. And while I wasn't about to do that now, with Bethany missing and unable to speak up for herself, I did wonder how far these two went back.

Alena moved over to my kitchen window and peered out.

"I love this time of night," she said. "The sky is purple velvet, and the streetlights glow like pearls."

I expected her to take more selfies, but she just stood there, enjoying the view.

"When I first met Bethany," she said, "I only had twenty-four hundred followers."

"That sounds like a lot."

"It is most definitely not."

"How did you meet her?"

"The way you'd expect."

"She direct-messaged you?"

"Yes," Alena said. "She asked me if I had representation and told me I had something special. Something she could spin into gold. She used those words. *Spin into gold.*" She turned to me, her eyes glistening. "To me, it sounded like a fairy tale."

"It does," I said. "It also sounds too good to be true."

"Not to me. Never to me. Bethany has a way of making anything feel possible."

"When she first DMed you, did you assume she had other clients?"

"Yes," Alena said. "But TBH, it did not matter to me whether she did. We chatted on the phone, then we met for coffee. By the time I signed with her, I had no doubt that she could make me famous."

"How long did it take?"

"After my makeover? It felt like overnight I was up to one

hundred thousand followers. But it was probably more like three or four weeks."

"That's fast."

"I am telling you. Bethany has a gift."

Alena's gaze floated around the room before landing on the kitchen counter. On her phone. "There it is," she said. "I must take advantage of this stunning background."

Alena plucked the phone off the counter, returned to the window, and attempted a selfie, raising the device over her head, then to her left and right. She seemed to be having trouble finding the right angle.

"Do you want me to take a picture?" I asked.

"That would be very helpful," she said.

She handed me the camera and posed in front of the window in her clinging red dress, with her back to me and her hands on her hips. She gazed coyly over her shoulder, eyes aimed straight at the lens. A classic red-carpet pose. I took three pictures of her and gave her back her phone.

She examined her screen carefully. "The second picture is perfect," she said, and immediately went to work, cropping and filtering and typing out a caption.

"I was wondering," I said as she tapped away at her phone. "Did Bethany ever tell you anything about her past?"

She kept tapping. "She had done some work in Hollywood," Alena said.

"What type of work?"

"Marketing. Public relations. She did some styling." She cleared her throat. "For photographers and ... um ... movies."

When she was through posting, she placed her phone back on the counter and smiled at me.

"That sounds pretty vague, Alena," I said.

"It does, doesn't it?"

"But you trusted Bethany enough to sign a deal with her right away?"

Alena shrugged. "I hadn't been in this country that long. I did not speak good English. I was naïve. Bethany was the first American person who seemed to care what happened to me. And when she spoke, it was like . . . poetry."

"Did she ever speak about her personal life?"

The smile disappeared. "No," she said. "Why do you ask?"

"She has no social media."

"I know that," Alena said. "So?"

"So . . . there isn't really a public way to get her attention. And if she has some ugliness in her past. Maybe an ex she *doesn't* love, for one reason or another."

"Yes?"

"These messages that you and Blake have been receiving could be someone's way of getting to Bethany. Especially if this person knows how close she is to the two of you."

Alena gaped at me. She said nothing for several seconds. I couldn't figure out whether she was thinking about what I'd just said or judging me for it. "Bethany never talks about her personal life," she said finally.

"You think there might be a reason for that?"

She chewed on her lip. "Maybe," she said.

My phone dinged again—a reminder that I hadn't heeded

the first ding. I turned away from Alena to check it: another text from Richie:

Nice emoji, it read, followed by an eye-roll emoji.

I smiled. I couldn't help it.

"From your ex again?" Alena said.

"Yep," I said. "As they say on social media, it's complicated."

"They say that?"

"They used to. Back in the day."

"Ah," she said. "Well, sometimes, complicated can be good."

I sighed. "Too good," I said.

And then my phone rang. My mother. It was my turn to roll my eyes.

TWENTY-EIGHT

While my mother and Elizabeth were kindred spirits, she and I were . . . well, whatever the opposite of kindred spirits was. She rarely called me, and when she did, it was almost always due to an emergency of her own invention. I excused myself, left the kitchen, and moved into my bedroom to take the call.

"Hi, Mom," I said.

As usual, she greeted me with an imperative sentence that included my dreaded first name and sounded as though the world would come to an end if it wasn't heeded immediately. "You need to talk to your father, Sonya."

"Why? What's going on?"

"I've told you he needs to rest, have I not? Have I mentioned his health issues?"

"Yes, Mom. You have." I was starting to worry. "Is Dad okay?"

She let out a dramatic sigh. "Do you care?"

"Of course I do."

"May I ask then why you keep getting him involved in your work?" she said. "Honestly, there is a reason why officers of the law are allowed to take early retirement, and I wish for his sake . . . *for the sake of your father's physical and mental health, Sonya,* I wish you would stop . . . *encouraging* him the way you always do."

Okay, so it wasn't anything to worry about. Just some run-of-the-mill, garden-variety emotional manipulation, as achieved by the master.

I sighed, too, though less dramatically than my mother, and thought back to my standing drinks date with Dad at The Street Bar. Our get-together had taken place the previous night, but it felt like at least a decade ago. "I didn't encourage Dad to do anything," I said. "All we did was have drinks. Like always."

"Did you not tell him about your current . . . I'm not sure of the jargon. Would you call it a gig?"

"I'm a private investigator, Mom," I said. "Not the lead singer in a cover band."

"Well, whatever it is, your father has been obsessing about it all day. I haven't been able to get him off the phone; he barely ate his dinner. And as I have mentioned to you, repeatedly, he needs to pay better attention to his diet."

I picked at a nail. "Obsessing?"

"Look, Sonya. Regardless of how little you may think I understand about you or that job of yours, I know for a fact you asked for his help with yet another one of your . . . your . . ."

"Gigs, Mom. Gigs is fine," I said. "And I swear I didn't ask him for any help."

My mother released another one of her signature sighs, this one nearly operatic. "Since when has that ever stopped your father? You give him a few details, he's like a dog with a bone. You know that, Sonya. *You know and you take advantage.*"

I tried to remember what details I'd given him about Blake, Alena, and Bethany. "I'm happy to talk to Dad," I said. "Can you put him on?"

"Promise me you'll get him to stop."

"I'll do my best."

"Phil!" she called out. "I'm on my phone with Sonya and I need you to speak to her."

Soon my dad was on the line and full of apologies. "I really should have just given you Dave's number," he said. "But once I talked to him, I figured, what harm could it do? And anyway, I have a lot more time than you do . . ."

"Okay, first of all, Dad," I said. "Who is Dave?"

"Dave Kolarszyk," he said. "That friend of mine I was telling you about last night. He's the police chief out in Bloomington, Indiana."

"Oh, right," I said. "You were going to give me his contact info so I could ask him about Blake Marshall."

"Blake Jameson Marshall," Dad said. "From Greendale, Indiana."

I could hear my mother's voice in the background, almost clearer than Dad's. "You don't sound like you're helping, Sonya!" she shouted. "Sounds more like you're making things worse!"

I ignored her. "You remembered his middle name," I said.

"I wrote it down as soon as I got home," he said. "Memory isn't what it used to be."

"You know, I rarely agree with Mom. But you are still technically recovering from a gunshot wound, and you have been told to avoid stress."

"Sunny, you know I love being retired," he said. "I love all the free time I get to spend with your mother."

"No one is believing you, Phil!" my mother said.

He went on as though she hadn't spoken at all. "But, well, you know as well as I do, I can't resist a great lead."

"I know, Dad, but—"

"And Dave gave me one. He said he thought there might have been some news involving someone named Blake Jameson Marshall several years back, but he wasn't sure what that news was. So I asked him if he knew anyone in Greendale, and sure enough, he did . . ."

"Sonya, do you want your father to wind up in the hospital again?" My mother again, her voice rising.

"Honey!" my dad called out to her. "Can you do me a big favor and make us a couple gin and tonics?"

I heard a muffled reply from my mother, and my dad told me, "I've bought us about three minutes."

"Okay, then. Let's hear it."

My dad spoke quickly. "So I know I was just going to give you names, but I called myself," he said. "I spoke to the sheriff of Greendale, whose name is Paul Rogers. He was expecting my call because Dave had told him about me."

"Great."

"I don't know how great it was," Dad said. "But it did feel like Paul wanted to talk to me more than I wanted to talk to him."

My father took a breath. I walked back into the kitchen, passing Blake and Alena, who were now sitting on my couch with Rosie nestled between them, watching an episode of a new cooking competition show called *Lovin' Oven*. I took in the sight of the three of them, the holiday glow of the TV screen reflected in Blake and Alena's blue eyes. Alena had that enormous stuffed purple bunny in her lap—the one she said made her feel safe. Blake was smiling. His face tended to do that when it was at rest.

"Wait one second, Dad." I grabbed the bottle of rosé out of the refrigerator, poured myself another glass, and took a swallow. "Okay," I said, once I'd closed the door, making sure I spoke very quietly. "Why did the sheriff of Greendale want to talk to you so badly?"

"It was the name," he said. "Blake Jameson Marshall."

"Like a movie cowboy," I said.

"A dead one."

I took a huge gulp of wine. "Excuse me?"

"Blake Jameson Marshall of Greendale, Indiana," Dad said. "He had a mother named Lisa and a sister named Rain, just like you said."

"Had?"

"He died twenty years ago, Sunny. When he was eighteen months old."

TWENTY-NINE

The real Blake Jameson Marshall had perished in a fire that had leveled his home. His father had died trying to save him—a tragedy that had made headlines in the sleepy town of Greendale twenty years ago, which was how my dad's friend in Indiana had remembered the name. Lisa and Rain Marshall had both survived the fire, and stayed in town long enough to rebuild and sell the farmhouse. They had then both moved out west, leaving those painful memories behind . . . along with the birth certificate of the baby in the family, which, for one reason or another, was snapped up at some point by the young man who was now sitting on my couch, watching *Lovin' Oven* with his girlfriend and my dog as though he had nothing to hide.

After I ended the call with my father, I opened the kitchen

door and stared at Blake, or rather at the guy I had known as Blake. *Who are you?*

Alena said something about one of the contestants being a good cook, and Blake pointed at the TV. "That's so not Todd's soufflé, it's what's-her-name's," Blake said. "Todd is one hundred percent lying to the judges and I am not here for it." Alena laid her head on his shoulder. I gazed at Blake's clear blue eyes, that innocent smile, that resting happy face of his, the gentleness of his hand as he petted Rosie.

Why were the simplest-seeming people always the most complicated beneath the surface?

I remembered breakfast at The Blue Hut, talking to Blake about his past, how he'd left the farm in order to pursue a modeling career in New York, but had made it only as far as Boston. I remembered thinking about how guileless he'd seemed—a sweet kid trapped in an Adonis body, a star by someone else's making, who wanted nothing more than the life he had—except, perhaps, for a dog of his own.

Bethany and Blake had shown me their driver's licenses, Bethany covering the age on hers but making sure the photograph was visible. And at the time—which had been pre-OnlyFans, pre–Moon Monaghan, pre–Betsy Rosanski—I'd no reason to doubt either one of them. I recalled our conversation once more—Blake talking about his life in Greendale, how boring it had been, how he'd longed to escape to the big city, telling the story as if it were his own. In my mind, I could see Bethany looking on, nodding her approval.

Were they both liars? Were they in on the lie together? Or

had she coached him, the same way she'd obviously taught him to be "aspirational, twenty-four/seven"?

In some ways, working as a private investigator was similar to working as a doctor—you were hired to look after someone, to take care of them, to solve potentially life-threatening problems for them—and all of those things became exponentially more difficult if they didn't tell you the truth about themselves to begin with.

"Blake," I said, "can I talk to you for a minute?"

He stood up. "Sure!"

I asked him to come into the kitchen, and he did, Rosie trailing behind him. I glanced at the phone, still clutched in his hand. He wasn't leaving it out there with Alena. I wasn't the only person he was hiding things from.

After Blake was in the kitchen with me, I tossed Rosie a biscuit and closed the door. "What's up?" Blake said. His gaze darted from my face to the closed door. He looked a little nervous.

"I was just wondering," I said. "When was the last time you spoke to your mom and sister?"

His facial expression changed three times over the course of five seconds. "Wait, who?"

"Your mom and sister. Lisa and Rain."

He gaped at me. "Right. Um . . . Sorry, that was just so random. Why?"

"I know you aren't on the best of terms with them—because of your leaving home and all."

"Yeah . . ."

"But I was thinking *I* could call them, ask if there's anybody from your past who might fit the profile of this stalker."

"I don't have their numbers."

"That's okay," I said. "I imagine it'd be pretty easy to track them down."

"That's . . . uh . . . probably not the best idea."

"Why not?" I said. "Again, I'd do all the talking. You don't have to say a word to them."

"Yeah, but . . . uh . . ."

"They might be able to shed some light on the subject, plus I'm sure they'd want to hear about any potential threats to your security. Don't you think?"

"No. I don't." He took a breath. Ran a hand through his hair. "They both said they never want to see me again. So."

"Why?"

"They were mad at me for leaving the farm. I was supposed to take it over after Dad died."

"How did he die again?"

"In a fire," he said.

"I thought it was a tractor accident."

"Oh. Yeah. Well, I was little back then. How am I supposed to remember? I don't even get why you're asking me this stuff when you seem to know half of it already."

Blake's voice was calm, smooth. But his movements told a different story.

Years ago, when I first started as a cop, a lot of my fellow officers swore by the Reid interrogation technique. It's not as universally accepted now as it was back then—and to be honest, I always thought a lot of it was bullshit. But in case you've never heard of it, one aspect of the Reid technique was the idea that certain visual tells—grooming oneself, fidgeting, looking up and to the left—were proof that a suspect was lying. It certainly wasn't true of everyone. But I did notice that as Blake responded to my questions, he exhibited so many of these tells, I could have used him in a Reid demonstration. And this was someone who was so consistently camera-ready that he normally never fidgeted.

At the moment, Blake was smoothing his hair in a way that almost felt compulsive, his gaze pinging back and forth between my face and that spot in his own brain where, according to Reid enthusiasts, lies were born. "I mean . . . Sorry, but I don't want to talk about . . . about Mom and Rain anymore," he said. "It brings back too many bad memories."

"Okay," I said. "I just didn't want to ignore people who might genuinely be able to help."

His phone dinged. He glanced at the screen and bit his lip. "Who's that from?"

"Nobody." He thumbed a text in quickly and shoved it into his back pocket. Then he wiped his forehead with the back of his hand. Sweating. Another tell.

"I won't call them," I said. "If it makes you that uncomfortable, I won't track down Lisa and Rain. Okay?"

His face relaxed into a smile. "Thank you," he said. "I hope you get it."

"I do, totally. Not everybody's up for family reunions."

He laughed a little. "Yeah."

"Is it okay, though," I said, "if I just ask you a few questions about your childhood?"

His features tensed up anew. "I guess."

"Did you like living on the farm when you were young?"

"I mean . . . As a kid? Sure."

"Do you ever miss it? Dream about it?"

"No. I left to pursue my destiny and I've never looked back." It sounded as though he was reading from a script.

"Okay," I said. "What did you grow there? On the farm?"

"Corn. Beets."

"Did you have cows, too?"

"Yeah."

"Chickens?"

"Uh-huh."

"You said you didn't have animals, though."

"Huh?"

"You said you never had any animals growing up, and that it made you sad."

His gaze shot up to the left side of his forehead again. "I meant pets," he said. "Not livestock."

"Blake."

"Yeah?"

"I'm going to ask you a question, okay? There's no wrong answer. No bad thing to say. I promise I won't judge you. But I need you to tell me the truth."

He scratched his cheek, smoothed his hair again. "I always tell the truth," he said.

"Okay, good," I said. "Then this should be easy."

"What is the question?"

I put a hand on his shoulder. He flinched.

"Who are you, Blake?" I said. "What's your real name?"

His jaw dropped open. "What are you talking about?"

"I've been trying to give you a chance to come clean on your own," I said. "I happen to know for a fact that you aren't Blake Jameson Marshall."

"Oh, man." He collapsed onto a kitchen chair and put his face in his hands.

"Like I said, I'm not judging. I genuinely want to help you, whoever you are."

"Please stop."

"People assume other identities for all sorts of reasons—lots of times because it's the only way they can escape from a very bad situation."

He lifted his chin and looked at me, his eyes hard and defiant. "I am who I say I am."

I met his gaze but said nothing.

"Alena knows me as Blake," he said. "Bethany knows me as Blake. All my friends, everyone who means anything to me, they all know me as Blake James. Five hundred thousand followers. I'm Blake James to them, too."

"How long have you been Blake James?"

"My entire fucking life."

"Blake?" Alena called out. "Are you okay?"

He stood up. His cheeks flushed bright red. "Did you hear

what she called me?" he said. "That smart girl out there who knows me better than anybody?"

"Yes."

"That's who I am," he said. "And if you don't believe that, then maybe I need to hire another bodyguard or private eye or whatever. Maybe I need to hire someone who *believes in me*."

"Blake?" Alena called out.

"I'm fine, Lainey!"

Blake pushed open the kitchen door and stormed out of the room. I stood there staring after him, at the door swinging in its frame.

That didn't go well.

Poor kid. It was all I could think. Whoever this guy was before Alena met him at the gym and brought him to Bethany, I'd scratched open an ugly wound with those questions, and I should have known better. I'd said it myself. People assumed other identities for all sorts of reasons, and for people Blake's age, it was very often the only means of survival.

Questioning him that aggressively was yet another rookie mistake of mine from the past forty-eight hours—the latest of many shockingly wrong turns I'd made since learning that Richie was leaving town.

"What's wrong?" I heard Alena say.

By the time I'd left the kitchen, Blake was back in the guest room, the door slammed behind him. Alena stood outside, softly rapping on the door.

"What did you say to him?" she asked.

"I tried to ask him about his past," I said.

She nodded and moved back to the couch. "It is late," she said. "He gets cranky when he is sleepy."

"How much do you know about him, Alena?"

"He is a really good person," she said. "He has a kind heart."

"Do you know where he came from?"

She gazed at me for a long while. "Yes." She said it as though she truly knew.

"I shouldn't have asked him," I said. "Should I?"

She took a deep breath, then let it out slowly. "He needs her," she said.

"Bethany?"

She nodded.

Alena lifted something from the couch—the stuffed purple bunny she'd brought from her apartment. She held it to her chest. "If we can find Bethany," Alena said, "she can give Blake permission to explain."

THIRTY

Blake opened the door to the guest room, and Alena slipped wordlessly inside, the stuffed purple bunny cradled in her arms.

Before he shut the door, I managed to blurt out an apology. "I didn't mean to treat you like a suspect," I said. "I was only trying to help. I'm sorry."

"I get it," Blake said. "I'm sorry I, like . . . exploded."

"I get it, too."

He stuck his hand out. "Friends?"

I shook it. "I'm going to put my energy into finding Bethany."

I started to say good night, but Blake didn't let go of my hand. He grasped it in both of his and stared into my eyes with a seriousness that surprised me. "I have a feeling she's going to come back, Sunny," he said. "You're not going to have to find her. She's going to come back on her own."

"I hope that's true."

"I know it is." He let go of my hand but didn't break eye contact.

"You do?"

"Sunny," he said. "Have you ever heard of positive manifestation?"

My first impulse was to roll my eyes. My second was to feel sorry for him. I made sure neither of those impulses showed in my face. "I think so," I said.

"It means, like, if you want something to happen really badly, you visualize it happening and you put that vision out into the universe, and then it comes to you," he said.

"Yeah, that's what I thought it meant."

"It works. It worked for the *Shred Shed* TV deal, and it worked for me getting five hundred thousand followers, and I've been doing it for Bethany coming back." He leaned in closer. "I know in my heart," he said, "that it's worked again."

I had no idea how to respond to that. I tried giving him a smile. "I'll tell you what," I said. "You keep positive-manifesting, and I'm going to try and look for her through more conventional channels, and between the two of us—"

"We'll find her," he said.

"Yes."

"It's gonna happen, Sunny," he said, his eyes sparkling. "You'll see I'm right."

The blind faith of this kid. That way he had of whole-heartedly believing in anything, whether it was the benefits of chamomile tea or his own phony identity or the idea that he could think Bethany into coming home. There was no doubt it had gotten him through a lot of tough times. But it also broke my heart a little. It just wasn't a sustainable way to look at the world. "Good night, Blake," I said.

"Good night," he said. "And thanks for taking care of me and Lainey." I gave Blake a quick, tight hug. He closed the guest room door.

It wasn't really that late—not even ten p.m. But I was happy that Blake and Alena had turned in so early. Much as I'd grown to care for the two of them, it was good to have them out of my living room. Not to mention that stuffed bunny, which (sorry, Alena) gave me the creeps.

I switched the TV off, grabbed my phone out of the kitchen, and returned to my own bedroom, grateful for the silence.

My laptop was on my nightstand. I powered it up and checked my email. Sure enough, Elaine had written me about Betsy Rosanski, sending her rap sheet as an attachment. I read her email first:

Hey, Sunny,

Here's what I found on your girl. As you'll see from the attached, she's done a little time, nothing really significant. Wire fraud. She passed some bad checks under another alias, Wanda Sinclaire. And she ran this scam with her sister, Linda, about twenty-five years ago, where they'd get guys drunk at this strip club near LAX, take them back to a hotel room, and roll them. She's been a little remiss about meeting with her parole officer. As you'll see at the end of the sheet, she was listed as a missing person seventeen years ago, and hasn't been heard from since. But I did manage to ask around about her.

Can you FaceTime me when you get this email? I'm getting tired of typing.

Xo,

E

Before I'd even read the sign-off, I'd grabbed my phone and told Siri to FaceTime Elaine. She picked up immediately, just as she was leaving work. It was still daylight out there—just seven p.m.—and Elaine wore big white-framed sunglasses and a bright yellow blouse, the mirrored glass of the police department headquarters glinting behind her like some backdrop from a futuristic movie. I didn't know that I'd ever seen anything so completely L.A. as Elaine's image on my screen at this moment.

"You're hurting my eyes," I told her.

"I'll take that as a compliment." Elaine grinned. Her teeth matched her sunglass frames. The last time I'd seen her, she'd shown off her new veneers.

"You should," I said. "Why does everybody look so vibrant and healthy out there?"

"The healing power of freeway driving."

"Road-rage therapy."

"Exactly. We should market it." She peered at her screen. "You look a little tired. You okay?"

"I had a run-in with a billionaire's douchebag son," I said. She gave me a thumbs-up. "Is he still conscious?"

"Barely."

"Attagirl."

"So what's up with Betsy Rosanski?"

"I kind of wanted to ask you the same question."

"Why?"

"Because as far as we're concerned, she's more famous as a victim than as a perp."

I squinted at her image. "If she's the same person I think she is, that's very surprising information."

"Good to hear," Elaine said. "A woman with a situation like hers, you assume the worst when she goes missing."

"A situation like hers?"

"Drug issues. Petty crimes that mostly involve pissing people off. A husband who's a world-class motherfucker."

I pulled my legs up under me and rested my back against the headboard. "Tell me more about the husband."

"He was a dealer—designer shit," she said. "But we couldn't get anything to stick to him because he was charged but never arrested. My guess is, he had friends in high places. But I was pretty green back then, so I don't know much."

I thought of Moon Monaghan, the ticket stub in the shoebox from Erin Flint's movie. Though Moon had become involved in the film industry via his cousin, a (since-deceased) lawyer by the name of Arlo Delaney, he was believed to have had a foothold in the L.A. drug trade. "You think Cronjager might know more?"

"I can ask him."

I exhaled. "Thank you."

"No problem. I talk to him a lot. He's bored since he retired." Elaine was walking down the sidewalk at a fast pace. She sounded out of breath.

"So, back to the husband. What's his deal?"

"Five domestic violence arrests while married to Betsy," she said.

I shuddered. "Great guy."

"Only one of the arrests stuck. He did close to a year. Came home, the cycle continued. Two more arrests. Lots of welfare checks on Betsy's record from that time period, but she never pressed charges. Numerous other arrests on his record—assault. Disorderly conduct. All showing that this guy has serious anger issues. Nothing sticks, though. Like I said, he's got friends in high places."

"Ugh."

"I know. Plus, in the middle of all this, Betsy goes missing. No one ever found a body, but you understand why her being alive is quite a pleasant surprise for me."

By now, Elaine had reached her car. She pressed her key fob. I heard the beep.

"Whatever happened to the husband?" I asked. "He still dealing drugs?"

She shook her head.

"Did he finally get arrested?"

"You're going to love this," she said. She slid into her car and started it up. The radio blasted twangy guitar. She shut it off fast. "So two years after she goes missing, Betsy's husband finally pisses off the wrong guy and gets himself shot in the head. The paramedics show up at his place, they rush him to the hospital. His life is miraculously saved. Meanwhile, the responding officers find his lab—hundreds of thousands of dollars in synthetic drugs. We get a warrant. He makes a full recovery—another miracle—but winds up getting fifteen years as soon as he's out of the hospital."

"Talk about a good news/bad news situation," I said.

"Right?"

"Is he still locked up?"

"Nope," she said. "He got out three years early. Made a name for himself behind bars giving sermons to the other inmates. Quoted from the scriptures at his parole hearing. Apparently this drug-dealing wife-beater had been a man of God all along."

I stared at my screen. My mouth felt dry. "The scriptures."

"Yeah, I call bullshit, too, but the parole board was impressed."

"What's his name?" I said. "The husband?"

"Gideon Walls," she said. "He also goes by 'the Preacher.'"

She peered at her screen. "You okay, Sunny? You look like you've seen a ghost."

"I'm fine," I said. "Just . . . you know. Processing."

She asked me if there was anything else I needed. I said no and thanked her and we signed off, everything she'd told me weighing on my mind, pulling at me, the way new facts so often do.

The Preacher. The Bible quotes in Eddie Voltaire's mouth. Eddie Voltaire, who had been paid off by a man with prison tattoos, and stabbed thirteen times. *You reap what you sow.*

Moments after we hung up, Elaine sent me a text: Walls's mug shot, in case you need. There was an image attached. I opened it and stared at the picture for a long time. The hollow cheeks. The taut mouth. The crazed blue eyes, the thick scar snaking out of his hairline and meeting his brow. No tear tattoos. No bald head. But that didn't mean anything. The mug shot had been taken fifteen years ago. People changed a lot in fifteen years. Betsy Rosanski certainly had.

On impulse, I checked Blake's Instagram, the picture of Rosie and him, posted the same night Eddie died. At this point, there were hundreds of comments—heart-eye and fire and dog emojis, followers praising his abs, his pecs, his smile, and just as many singing the praises of my adorable dog. No threatening comments. At least, not right away.

It wasn't until I was about forty comments in that I saw one from @AvengingAngel and my breath caught in my throat.

@RosieRandall CHECK YOUR DMS

I did. Rosie had several message requests, but the one

from @AvengingAngel was near the top. I opened it and read it, my heart pounding.

The companion of sinners will suffer great harm.

"Is that you, Preacher?" I whispered.

THIRTY-ONE

I composed an email to Lee Farrell, summarizing every-thing Elaine had told me and attaching the picture of Betsy Rosanski's driver's license, as well as her rap sheet, and the mug shot of her husband, which I'd emailed to myself and downloaded onto my laptop. For good measure, I sent along a screenshot of the DM I'd received from @Avenging Angel.

As you can see, the troll is still at it, I wrote. I think it might be Gideon "the Preacher" Walls who has been sending these notes, and Walls who killed Eddie. He may have been trying to get to Bethany through her clients—to scare her by scaring them. I know it's all speculation at this point, and I could be wrong. But it wouldn't hurt to find out where Walls was yesterday morning, if he is, in fact, findable.

I had sent all of the info to Spike before emailing Lee, because Spike needed to know all of this.

I then phoned Lee. When I got his voicemail, I left a message for him telling him to check his email and to call me if he had any questions. I also left Elaine's contact info, in case he wanted to talk to her, too.

After I hung up, I felt a lot less unsettled—as though, at this point in time, I'd done everything I could. And then Elaine texted me again.

Just got off the phone with Cronjager. His memory is incredible. Turns out that back when Betsy was around, Walls avoided doing time for dealing with the help of a certain lawyer. Two guesses which one.

I wrote back immediately: Arlo Delaney?

Bingo!

My suspicions about that ticket stub had proven correct. But really, talk about a small world. Arlo Delaney's murder had been one small part of the case that had brought Elaine and I together in the first place. A less-than-scrupulous L.A. lawyer, Arlo had also happened to be Moon Monaghan's cousin. He'd been deeply involved in Moon's brief foray into the movie business—until he made the fatal mistake of coming between Moon and his money. Arlo's killer was never caught, but the implications of his death were obvious.

So although I wasn't sure about specifics at this point, I did know one thing: While Moon may have had nothing to do with the threats against Blake and Alena, he definitely had something to do with their manager.

I closed my laptop and put my phone down. For a few moments, I found myself thinking of Betsy Rosanski—not the polished, chic Bethany Rose I'd spent time with, but the woman from the driver's license picture. If my theory was correct, this small and meek-looking petty criminal had somehow escaped the clutches of an abusive lunatic and made her way across the country, where she'd met up with a Bosnian refugee and a young runaway—both of them no doubt escaping abuses of their own—and saw in them a path to a glamorous new life. After securing financing from a gangster (whom she may or may not have met through her abusive ex's lawyer), Betsy Rosanski had gotten herself a makeover that rendered her unrecognizable, changed her name to Bethany Rose, and started a legit business that, ideally for her, had all the markings of a scam.

Instead of writing bad checks or rolling drunks with her sister, Linda, at airport-area strip clubs, Betsy was working out of a plush office and using her increasingly large stable of influencers to sell followers on the concept that they, too, could be living their best lives, if they only shelled out enough cash to eat at the same restaurants/wear the same clothes/slug

the same toxic energy swill/pseudoscientific plant-based nutritional supplement as Betsy's clients—all of whom gave her
a share of their earnings, along with the businesses who spon-
sored them. It was the ultimate con. And the best thing about
it was it was completely legal.

Did the Preacher want a cut? Or was it something else that
had led him to track down the woman who had left him all
those years ago and terrorize her two biggest moneymakers?
Was it something deeper, more personal, more dangerous?
"Where are you, Bethany?" I said. "Did you escape again—or
did he find you this time?"

My phone rang. I nearly jumped out of my skin.

I answered by reflex. I didn't even think to look at the
screen. "Hello?" My voice cracked. "Who is this?"

"I was going to text you again, but I was afraid you'd send
more emojis."

I smiled. "Richie."

"Also, I wanted to hear your voice. This texting thing is
bullshit."

"So is this leaving-town thing."

He said nothing.

"Can I see you?" I hadn't planned on saying that.

I didn't want to take it back, though. I heard silence on the
other end of the line, but I didn't care. "I know you're going
away. I know it's happening soon. I accept that. But I've . . .
I've had a day, Richie."

Still no response.

"I don't care if it's selfish, or unhealthy, or counterpro-

ductive to our moving on," I said. "I don't care what my therapist would say, or what your therapist would say, or if you
even have a therapist anymore. I have had a day, and I need to
see you. I need to be in the same room as you and breathe
the same air as you. It's essential, Richie. And I think you owe
me that."

I took a breath. Waited.

"Okay," Richie said.

I nearly thanked him, but that felt pathetic, so I held back.
"How soon can you get to my place?" I asked.

"Thirty seconds," Richie said. "Maybe a minute."

"What? Wait. Where are you?"

Richie laughed, the sound of it warm and a little awkward
and wonderfully familiar. "I'm right across the street, Sunny,"
he said. "I need to see you, too."

Less than thirty seconds later, my buzzer went off. I spoke
to Richie over the intercom and let him in.

He took the elevator up to my loft and I met him at the
door. He was wearing a clean white oxford and jeans, and he
had a slight five-o'clock shadow. *Just enough so I can feel it,* I'd
once said, back when we were married. *I like my men a little
scratchy.* I'd been joking at the time, but when I'd felt that
shadow against my skin, I realized I'd meant it. In our early
years together, it had become an unspoken sign between us.
When Richie wanted to get lucky, he skipped a shave. I wasn't
sure if he remembered that or if it was just a coincidence. I
hoped he remembered.

I hugged him. He smelled of pine.

Rosie jumped up on Richie and he scratched her behind both ears, then pulled a dog biscuit out of his shirt pocket, which she took from him happily, bringing it into a corner.

I raised an eyebrow. "Just happened to have a dog biscuit on you?"

Richie grinned.

I grinned back. "This visit was premeditated."

"I plead the fifth," he said. We watched Rosie devouring her biscuit. When it came to unexpected snacks, she was both delicate and thorough.

"We have to be quiet," I told Richie.

"Why?"

"I have guests," I said. "In the guest room."

He winked at me. "That never stopped us from making noise before."

My face warmed. "You want a drink? Wine?"

"Wine's good," he said.

I went into the kitchen and grabbed an unopened bottle of pinot noir out of the cupboard, along with two glasses and a corkscrew. When I returned, he was standing where I'd left him, right next to the couch.

Usually, Richie would make himself at home when he came over. I'd go into the kitchen to grab us a few beers, or make us a pot of coffee, and when I came back, I'd find him sitting on the couch with Rosie, watching a game on TV, or in my studio, admiring whatever canvas I'd stretched most recently.

Not this time, though. Granted, it had been at least six

months since he'd last been to my place, and obviously things had changed between us.

But there was something different in the way he was looking at me—an intensity to his gaze. I walked up to him. "So, I think it would be better if we hang out in the bed—"

He kissed me. Lifted me off my feet. I never finished the sentence.

THIRTY-TWO

At some point, early on, we made it into my bedroom and closed the door. I was glad about that. Though I was sure Alena knew enough to stay in the guest room once Richie and I stopped talking, I kept expecting Blake to stride into the living room, tap me on the shoulder, and ask if I had any keto-friendly snacks.

Once we were behind closed doors, though, those types of concerns fell by the wayside. All tension slipped away. It felt as though nothing else in the world existed but us and, for all intents and purposes, it didn't. I'd had a lot of good sex in my life, but with Richie, it was something different, something more. It was a glass of ice-cold beer after months in the desert. It was just what I needed and the last thing I needed, all rolled up into one.

After we finished, I lay in bed with him for a long time, my head on his chest, listening to his heartbeat. I used to do the same thing when we were newly married, in our cottage by the ocean. Interesting how, when some tiny aspect of a relationship stayed the same, it brought home how much everything else about it had changed. He was leaving in three days. I should have regretted sleeping with him tonight, if only for the way I knew I'd feel the first time I drove by his old apartment, or the saloon, or talked to Desmond and fully grasped it—the lack of Richie in my world.

But at this particular moment, I didn't regret a thing.

"Well," I said. "That was really something."

"Yeah," Richie said.

I ran my fingertips over his beard stubble, traced the softness of his lips.

"Can I ask you something?" he said.

"Yeah?"

"Why did you text me that stupid emoji?"

I laughed. "You know, I think maybe I was trying to provoke a response."

"Mission accomplished."

I grinned. "It was a very good response."

"My God, Sunny," he said. "I'm going to miss you so much."

He rolled onto his side and cupped my face in his hands. We kissed.

"Mission accomplished here, too, then," I said.

My plan had been to kick him out of my apartment right

after, but it didn't work out that way. Instead, we stayed in bed and talked, about our families and our shared memories, catching up on the past several months, then going back in time. We said everything we should have said during that sad breakfast at the Russell House Tavern, and probably a few things we shouldn't have said, too. Regardless, it felt good to say them.

Rosie scratched at the bedroom door. I let her in, and she jumped into bed with us and curled up between our feet, as though it was a situation she was used to. And then Richie and I started talking about the future.

"We can make this work," Richie said. "This long-distance thing."

I didn't protest. "I think we can" was what I said.

We envisioned a life lived together but apart, Richie in Jersey and me in Boston, taking long drives to see each other every other weekend. "I'll finally get Spotify," he said.

"I'll do audiobooks," I said. "Catch up on my reading."

"You'll fall in love with Jersey," he said.

"Let's not get ahead of ourselves."

"Okay, okay." Richie laughed. "But at least you'll give it a chance."

We talked some more, about how Rosie, who didn't like the feel of sand on her paws, would probably need those little rain booties to wear on the beach and how, with Zoom being what it is, it might be possible for me to do some of my work remotely from his place on the shore. Pluses and minuses. But all of it felt possible.

"You'd still have Boston as your home base," he said.

"And you'll be able to visit your family more often," I said. "Your dad will be happy."

I wrapped my arms around Richie and synched my breathing with his, and let it all slip away—this endless stress pit of a day, the relative strangers in my guest room, the ever-evolving backstory of Bethany Rose, and Gideon Walls the Bible-thumping psycho, and the thirteen stab wounds found in Eddie Voltaire.

Richie's breathing slowed. He was falling asleep. I gazed at his profile in the moonlight. *You're all I need,* I thought. Even though I knew it wasn't true.

I set my alarm for four-forty-five a.m. so I could squeeze in a shower before taking Blake to the gym. I wondered if Richie would be leaving then, too, or if he'd be long gone by the time I woke. He wasn't going to stay the entire night. I knew my ex-husband well enough to take that as a given.

It occurred to me that Richie and I might wind up spending more concentrated time together after his move than before. At least we wouldn't be in a position where one of us could sneak out and head home in the middle of the night.

Maybe we can really do this.

For the hell of it, I opened my laptop and looked up the distance between my place and Richie's new digs. I winced. "Wow," I said.

Richie stirred. Stretched. Still half asleep, he asked what I was doing.

I told him.

"How far is it?" Richie said.

"Four hundred and one miles," I said. "It's a six-and-a-half-hour drive."

"Ugh," he said.

"'Ugh' is right."

"We can make it work, though."

"We can and we will," I said.

Even though we both knew it wasn't true.

THIRTY-THREE

As expected, Richie was gone by the time my alarm went off, but there was a text from him on my phone.

See you soon, it read. Followed by three heart-eye unicorn emojis.

I smiled. Richie may have made a decision that was most likely going to destroy any chance of our ever getting back together, but at least he hadn't lost his sense of humor.

At any rate, it was time to think of other things. I decided to forgo the shower and threw on a pair of yoga pants, a T-shirt, and my cross-trainers and slipped my gun into my gym bag along with my wallet, toiletries, and a change of clothes. I had a membership at that Equinox. If I had to walk Blake there at this hour, I figured I may as well get in some me time on the elliptical. Considering how early he'd gone to bed and what an up-and-at-'em kind of guy he was, I expected Blake to be all dressed and waiting for me by the time I made it into the living room.

But instead of Blake, I got Alena.

"He was too tired," she said. "I think this is all getting to him. Bethany gone. The stalking. He is very sensitive, you know."

I nodded. "So . . . are we staying home?"

"I would very much like to go to the gym in Blake's place." She took a step back. "You see? I put on my Zumba clothes."

Alena smiled. She was picture-perfect, especially for this hour—the results of youth, quality beauty products, and plenty of sleep. Her hair was pulled back into a high ponytail, and she wore bicycle shorts, a skimpy crop-top, and platform-soled sneakers and carried a light nylon bag, all in an eye-catching pale pink. She was bound to get us gawked at on our way to the gym.

"Does Blake know to keep the door locked at all times, to not let anyone in?" I said. "And to call me immediately if anyone tries to enter the apartment?"

"Yes," she said. "But it probably would not hurt to text that to him."

I did. From behind the closed guest room door, Blake's phone dinged.

Alena and I headed out of my loft, down the few flights of stairs, out the door into what was already another brutally hot day. The sky was still pink from the sunrise, and the streets around my building were nearly empty, save a sanitation truck, whose driver predictably catcalled Alena. (Actually, he said, "Helloooo, sexy ladies!" But I knew he was including me only out of politeness.)

After we passed him, Alena turned to me and rolled her eyes. "Men," she said.

"You must get so tired of it," I said. "I mean, *I* get tired of it, and I'm not . . . well, you."

"Bethany says it is a . . . how do you say it? Occupational hazard."

"Meaning . . ."

"Meaning this body is my livelihood indoors, but when it comes to going out-of-doors, it can be a liability."

I looked at her. "You know, Alena," I said, "your English is really good."

She smiled. "Thank you," she said.

We picked up the pace, jogging side by side for the rest of the block. Waiting at the crosswalk, I turned to her. "Did you go to college?"

She shook her head.

"You ever think of going?" I said. "It isn't too late."

"I have thought of it, actually," she said. "I have been putting aside a little of my money every month." Her eyes widened. "Do not tell Bethany," she said.

I frowned. "Would she disapprove?"

She shrugged.

"You don't have to give up your livelihood, you know," I said. "You can take selfies in a dorm room."

"I suppose," she said. "But please do not tell her anyway."

I looked at her. Her face was unreadable.

"Anything in particular you'd like to study?" I asked.

She gave me a shy smile. "Art."

"No way," I said. "I studied art in college."

"I assumed," she said. "I saw your paintings. They are beautiful."

"Thanks," I said. "I paint to relax and work things out in my head, but I haven't been able to do either of those things for a while."

She nodded. "I hear you."

"What's your medium?"

"Photography," she said. "I have been told I have a good eye."

"You do."

A pickup truck rolled up to the crosswalk. Even though the light was green, it stopped right in front of us, the driver gawking out the window, his jaw slack. He looked at least thirty years older than Alena and wore a snap-back hat that said BUDWEISER on it. "Nice tits!" He said it almost like a greeting.

Alena turned to me. "Do you have your gun on you?"

"Yes," I said, "but if I shot every asshole in this town, I'd eliminate two-thirds of the population."

"I can dream, can I not?"

I laughed. "Occupational hazard. Remember."

Snap-back said it again, louder. *"Nice tits!"* As if we simply hadn't heard him the first time.

We both flipped him off, and he called us bitches.

The light changed. We jogged across the street and up the block. "I wonder how it feels to have a dick that tiny," I said.

"I hate most men," she said. "I really do."

I shrugged. "Be grateful you found yourself a good one."

She squinted at me for several seconds. "Oh. Yes. Blake," she said finally.

It made me feel a bit defensive of him. I wanted to ask her who she'd thought I was talking about, but instead I said, "Do you know what Blake called you last night?"

She looked at me.

"That smart girl who knows me better than anybody."

"That's nice."

"Not a word about the tits."

"I should hope not."

"He's a keeper, Alena," I said.

She started jogging faster, her sneakers pounding against the sidewalk. "The gym's right up there," she said. "I can see it."

"Is something wrong?" I said. "Are you and Blake okay?"

"We are fine," she said. "It's just . . ."

"Yeah?"

"Who is it that he keeps texting?"

I looked at her. Now it made sense. "You've noticed that, too."

"He hides the screen from me. Why? He never hides the screen before."

"He wouldn't cheat on you," I said. I honestly believed that.

The gym was a few doors down. Alena stopped jogging. She grasped her knees and breathed deeply, checking her pulse at the same time. "I'm not concerned about Blake cheating," she said between breaths.

"Then what?"

Alena straightened up. "I'm worried he is talking to some-one he shouldn't," she said. "Making a stupid deal. He owes those criminals a lot of money from the OnlyFans—which was another stupid thing he did and didn't tell me about. I have the money. I can pay them back. I have told him this. But he says it is his debt, not mine. He is stubborn."

"So . . . you think he might be borrowing money from someone else?"

"Or earning it. In a way he should not."

"Oh."

She sighed. "It is a full-time job, keeping Blake out of trouble."

"I could imagine," I said.

"No offense to you," Alena said, "but I don't think you could."

We went into the gym. Alena headed straight for the six-forty-five Zumba class, while I wandered around until I found a free elliptical. My favorite travel program happened to be playing on its tiny TV. I spent the next forty-five minutes working out on the machine, while daydreaming about restaurant-hopping through Tuscany with Stanley Tucci.

By the time I was done, I felt a lot more relaxed. I hit the shower, put on a clean T-shirt and yoga pants, and found

Alena showered and changed and taking selfies in front of a large lighted mirror. For someone who was always so well put-together, she took a surprisingly short time to get ready. "How was your class?" I asked.

"Great." She said it in the midst of snapping a picture, her lips stretched into a duckface. By reapplying her make-up, taking down her ponytail, and switching out both her lipstick color and bicycle shorts and crop-top combo (this time, all of it was lavender) she'd created an entirely new look. Influencing was a skill, I realized. There was no getting around it.

From her gym bag, she removed a bottle of something that called itself "Super Water" and took a few close-ups, nuzzling the product.

"How is that water super?" I asked.

"No idea," she said. "But they pay me well."

She blew a kiss at her phone as she took another shot. She changed the angle, and I remembered the cross on her cheek, now completely concealed. Lots of people her age had religious tattoos, but in Alena's case, it didn't seem in keeping with her practical nature—especially not a face tattoo, which was something she always needed to work to conceal, no matter what she wore. I wondered whether that tattoo had been the result of one drunken night or a decision she'd considered good at the time. It didn't matter.

You make one mistake, you have to deal with the consequences for years and years . . . At least it wasn't a pregnancy. Or a marriage . . .

"This is probably going to sound strange," I said. "But has Bethany ever spoken about an ex-husband?"

Alena shook her head.

She took a few more pictures with the water bottle, then put the selfie stick down. "Why do you ask?" she said. "Did you find something out?"

"Probably not," I said. "But you know what they say. Leave no stone unturned."

"What does that mean?"

"I don't know, actually."

"English is strange."

"Yes, it is."

"Is there some specific person you are thinking of?"

"Yeah," I said. "I'm wondering if she ever mentioned anyone to you by the name of Gideon Walls."

Alena gave me a look like I had just punched her in the stomach. "No."

The panic in her eyes said otherwise. "Are you sure?" I asked.

Her face relaxed slightly. She put on a smile, but the eyes didn't join in. "I think I would remember that name," she said. "It is a memorable name, no?"

"He also goes by the Preacher."

The fake smile dissolved. "No," she said. "I don't know anybody like that. She never talks about anybody. No social life. Only her work."

"Alena," I said. "I know it's hard to trust people after what you've probably been through, but I'm here to help. Honest. And the more you can tell me, the more I can help you."

"I understand that. But I have not heard of anybody like that from Bethany. She does not speak of her past."

I felt as if I'd just had this same conversation with Blake. This had to be the most tight-lipped group of people I'd ever worked with—which was really weird, considering their entire careers were based on letting strangers in on their so-called personal lives. It was frustrating. I was positive Bethany was the source of it all, and I couldn't help wishing that Blake's "positive manifestation" was more than just a bunch of New Age hooey, designed to make gullible people feel a sense of control. *If Blake could only wish Bethany back into our lives,* I thought, *then she could give the two of them permission to start telling me the truth.* "Well," I said, "if you think of anything . . ."

My phone rang. I looked at the screen. I didn't recognize the number, but I answered anyway.

"Sunny?" It was an older woman's voice. "I hope this isn't too early. But you told me to call if I saw or heard anything."

I recognized the voice now. "Glenda?" I said. "Happy's mom?"

She chuckled. "That's me," she said. "This is all probably unnecessary at this point. You do know your boss is back in the land of the living again, right?"

"What?"

"I heard her car pull in late last night and saw her taking

her trash can to the end of the driveway. I was going to go outside and say hi, but it felt kind of odd, seeing as it was very late and we've hardly ever spoken."

My jaw dropped open. I gaped at Alena. *Positive manifestation.* It was all I could think. "Bethany's back?"

Alena's eyes went huge. She let out a squeal.

"I thought for sure you'd know already," Glenda said.

"No, I . . . I didn't know at all."

"Maybe she wanted to surprise you? At any rate . . . spoiler alert. You're probably going to see her at work today."

"Is she still at her house?"

"Looks like it. About five, ten minutes ago, I let Happy out on my lawn to do his business, and I saw her moving her car from the driveway into her garage."

"Thank you, Glenda," I breathed. "Thank you, thank you so much for calling me."

"Anything for the owner of that sweet bull terrier," she said.

After I hung up, Alena started to jump up and down.

I quickly called Bethany's number. It went straight to voicemail. Battery dead. Or maybe she'd just turned it off. Either way, it was strange—for her to come home but contact no one about it. Still, though. *Still.*

I ended the call and looked at Alena.

"She didn't pick up?" she said.

I shook my head.

"There must be some problem with her phone."

"There must be." I took a breath. "I think we should drive to her house."

"Yes, of course."

"But I don't think we should tell Blake," I said. "Not until we know exactly how she is."

Alena nodded. If she asked questions, I would have said more, about how young and emotional and not-quite mature Blake was, and how, considering how close he was to Bethany, I felt that it was in all of our best interests to make sure she was all right before looping him in on her return.

But Alena asked no questions. I didn't need to explain further. "I get it," she said. "I know Blake. Can we go to Sudbury now?"

THIRTY-FOUR

Alena and I ran all the way to where my car was parked—
five blocks away from my apartment. Once we were inside
the car and we'd caught our breath, I took out my phone.

"Please do not call the police," Alena said.

I hadn't been planning on it. I doubted I could get anyone
from the BPD—even a close friend like Lee—to show up at
the home of a fifty-eight-year-old woman and interrogate her
about why she'd left her home in Sudbury for twelve to fifteen
hours.

But still, Alena's reaction brought up questions. "Why
not?" I asked.

"They make me uncomfortable."

"Well, me too, and I used to be one," I said. "Police are

supposed to make you feel uncomfortable. It's part of the job description."

"I told you," she said. "When I was a child in Bosnia—"

"I'm sorry, but I'm not fully buying that, Alena."

"What? Why?"

"Because you're tougher than that."

I looked at her. She said nothing.

"You traveled all the way across the world on your own," I said. "You made a life for yourself in a strange place where you had to learn a whole new language. You developed a look and a career where you have to constantly navigate your way around predatory types, and you've not only survived, you've become a huge success at it. You can't tell me that anything that happened to you as a kid is going to keep you from protecting yourself and the people you care about. I know better."

I didn't wait for a response. I just started my car and pulled out onto the road. I had to cope with a little more traffic than there was when we went to the gym, but the streets were still relatively clear. It was Saturday morning, after all, so there was no rush hour to worry about. If everything went well and we didn't run into any accidents, we could make it to Sudbury in a little more than half an hour.

"Bethany doesn't like police," Alena said quietly.

I nodded. "Okay. That makes more sense." It did. I'd seen her rap sheet. "Is it okay if I call Spike?"

"Yes. Of course."

I'd been planning to call Spike in the first place. Siri made the call for me and it came in over the Bluetooth. Spike picked up after a few rings. He sounded groggy.

"Late night?" I asked.

"Yep."

"You still with Flynn?"

"Yep."

"Then I'm sorry to have to ask you this."

"What is it?"

I told Spike everything Glenda had said, and let him know that Alena and I were on our way to Bethany's.

"Well, hey! This is great news," he said.

"I hope it is," I said. "But Glenda never spoke directly to Bethany—she just saw her out the window. And when we tried calling her, her phone seemed to be turned off."

"Say no more. I'm on my way."

I heard Flynn's muffled voice in the background, Spike telling him that Bethany had come back.

"Bring your firearm," I said. "Just in case."

"Will do. I, uh, got your email."

"So you understand."

"Yep."

After I hung up, we drove without saying anything for a few miles, but I could feel Alena watching me intently, as though she was trying to read my expression. "What did Spike mean," she said finally, "about getting your email?"

"Oh, well . . . I was just running a theory by him."

"Yes?"

"About that man I was telling you about. Gideon Walls."

I looked at her as I said it. She cringed visibly at the sound of the name.

"But you say you've never heard of him, so."

"How do you know this person is Bethany's ex-husband?"

"I don't know it. Not for sure."

"Oh. Okay, then."

I took a breath. If everything went the way I was hoping it would, we'd be seeing Bethany in twenty minutes, and I could question her directly about her past, without Alena ever needing to know about it.

But while waiting to talk to Bethany was what I normally would have done, I couldn't shake the feeling that Alena knew all too well who Gideon Walls was, and that she was holding back information that was potentially important. Like any relationship, though, this one required give-and-take in order to work. And so I couldn't expect Alena to be honest with me if I didn't open up myself.

"I spoke to a colleague in the Los Angeles area," I said. "Gideon Walls apparently has a connection with an ID I found—a driver's license—in Bethany's house."

She gaped at me. "You never told me this. You never showed me a driver's license."

"Because the ID was hidden under Bethany's bed. And if Bethany was hiding it from everyone, including you, I assumed that she must have had good reason to do so."

"Okay," she said. But she still sounded pissed.

"I don't know that it was Bethany's ID," I said. "The

woman in the picture didn't look like her. But I mean . . . as you know, she's had some work done. And I had heard from someone else that she legally changed her name."

"Someone else?"

"You don't want to know who," I said. "Trust me. He's a career criminal, not to mention a truly shitty individual."

Alena ran a hand through her hair. She put her head back on the seat and closed her eyes and said something I couldn't hear.

"What?"

"I said I may have heard that name before."

"Gideon Walls?"

"Yes."

"Was it Bethany who said it?"

"I don't know."

"Okay." I glanced at her. Her eyes were still closed, and she looked limp and deflated, as though her secrets had been the only thing keeping her upright. I wasn't going to press her. "Thank you for telling me."

"You believe this man is the one who is stalking us? Gideon Walls?" she said. "You believe he is the one who killed Eddie?"

I cleared my throat. "It's something I'm looking into."

"You don't need to."

"What?"

"You don't need to look into that. It will not pan out."

"Why?"

I could actually feel her tensing up in the seat next to me. "Because Gideon Walls is dead," she said quietly.

I stared at her. "How do you know that?"

"He died many years ago." She turned and stared at me. "I cannot tell you how I know."

We reached a stoplight and I saw the sign welcoming us to Sudbury. "I shouldn't have said it," she said. Tears welled up in her eyes. "I shouldn't have . . . have said anything."

"But, Alena," I said. "It isn't true."

"It is."

I shook my head. "It's impossible. Walls was arrested fifteen years ago. He spent thirteen years in prison. So if he did die, it had to have happened less than two—"

"That . . . that can't . . . That cannot be."

"It is."

"You are mistaken."

I picked up my phone and found the text Elaine had sent me. I enlarged the download and handed her the phone. "See? That's his mug shot. See the date?"

She stared at the picture. Her hands trembled. A tear spilled down her cheek and hit the screen.

"Alena," I said. "Are you all right?"

A car horn blared behind me. The light had changed to green, and I pressed the accelerator, following the GPS's directions to Bethany's house.

"I need to tell her," Alena kept saying. "I need to tell her."

When we got to Bethany's house, she opened the door and hurled herself out of it before I was even able to turn off the car.

As I grabbed my bag and chased her across the lawn and

up the walkway to the front door, I noticed the garbage can at the end of the driveway, the car parked farther up. But it was Spike's car, not Bethany's, and when Alena started pounding on the door, it was Spike who opened it.

I wasn't surprised that Spike had arrived here before me—not with the way he drove. I might have remarked on it, just to lighten things up a little, had I not seen the look on Spike's face.

"Where's Bethany?" Alena said.

"She's not here," he said. He was holding her cat, Mr. Francis.

Alena tried to push past him. But even with a freaked-out cat in his arms, Spike held his ground.

"Are you sure?" I asked.

Spike nodded. "I searched the house," he said. "But somebody *was* in here. That's for fucking sure."

THIRTY-FIVE

O h my God," Alena whispered.

We were standing in Bethany's once-tidy living room. It had been completely ripped apart, destroyed, the cushions on the beige couch slashed open, along with all the corduroy pillows, down feathers leaking out of them and settling on the floor in drifts. The ceramic vase was smashed to bits, the dried flowers crushed into the carpet. Someone had even disassembled that cheesy Eiffel Tower wall hanging, dropped the frame on the floor, and left the paper poster curling miserably beside it.

Alena picked up the poster and gently placed it on the coffee table. "What happened?" she said. Mr. Francis rubbed against her leg. She picked him up, holding him much the same way as she'd held that purple stuffed bunny—too tightly.

Mr. Francis stuck all four paws straight out, his eyes huge and unblinking.

"Someone was either angry," Spike said, "or they were looking for something."

"Seems kind of like both," I said.

He nodded. "What's interesting," he said, "is what isn't here."

"What do you mean?" Alena said.

"No car in the garage," he said. "No gun in the kitchen. Her bedroom's like this—ransacked. But far as I could see, the only thing missing was the phone."

"So maybe she came back," I said, "tried to find something, took what was important, and left again."

"If that's the case, though, why do you suppose she murdered the couch and all the pillows?" Spike said. "I mean, I'd understand if her decorator did it, but—"

"Money," Alena said.

I looked at her.

She plucked at her lip. "Bethany hides money in all sorts of strange places," she said. "Sometimes she cannot remember where."

Spike and I looked at each other.

"She told me this once," Alena said. "She does not trust banks."

"Well," Spike said. "I hope she found it."

Alena said nothing. She looked at Spike, then at me. Her eyes glistened with tears. She let out a long, anguished sigh.

Mr. Francis pushed his way out of her grip, scurried across the room, and hid beneath the coffee table.

I moved to comfort Alena. She turned away. "No," she said. "No. He can't be alive."

Spike's eyebrows shot up. He mouthed words at me: *What is she talking about?*

I shook my head and mouthed, *Later.* "You know what? I think we should all go next door and talk to Glenda," I said. "She did say she saw Bethany last night. Maybe she came in contact with her before she left today."

"That's a good idea," Spike said.

Alena followed us wordlessly.

It was almost as though Glenda had heard my thoughts, because when Spike, Alena, and I got outside, I saw her standing on her front porch, holding Happy in her arms.

Glenda waved at me. Then she raised Happy's little paw and made him wave, too. I waved back. Happy struggled against her. He didn't look very comfortable.

As we jogged down the walk and up to Glenda's front door, it occurred to me that I had spoken more to Bethany's neighbor in the past two days than she had in the past two years. As extroverted as she may have seemed to her clients, Bethany was clearly an entirely different personality type when she was off the clock.

"You just missed her," Glenda said. "That woman is always on the go."

"Yeah. Well, I wish we could catch up to her, because we're

having a problem reaching her on the phone," I said. "I think she's got it turned off but doesn't realize."

"That happens to me all the time," Glenda said. "Of course, she seems like someone who would value their phone more than I do."

"Right? She values her phone more than anybody," I said.

Happy started to whine. Glenda shushed him.

"Glenda," I said, "did Bethany say anything to you before she left?"

"No, nothing. I just saw her pull out of the driveway."

"How did she look?" Spike said.

"Pardon?"

"Did she seem relaxed? Agitated?"

"Her top was up again. I didn't see her." Glenda peered at Spike. Happy squirmed in her arms.

"So, to be clear, it was just her car that you saw," Spike said.

Happy yelped.

"What is wrong with you, sweetie?" Glenda set Happy down. He started dancing around in circles. "He's never this antsy."

"Glenda," I said, "Have you seen Bethany at all today? Like . . . has she been in her yard? Did you see her getting the mail? I know her garbage pail is out front, and you saw her wheeling it down the driveway. But that was last night, right?"

"Yes. It was very late."

"You're sure of that?" Spike said.

"Sure of what?"

"That it was Bethany in her driveway."

"Well, it was dark out, and my night vision is not good. But I did see a woman wheeling Bethany's trash can down Bethany's driveway, so . . ."

"You're sure it was a woman?"

Glenda gave Spike flat eyes. "Well, I didn't run up and give her a squeeze-check, if that's what you're asking."

"You literally saw her."

I could tell she was getting annoyed. "I heard her, okay? I can't see at night. I heard the wheels of the trash can on her driveway. What's with the third degree?"

"He's just worried about Bethany," I said. "They're very close friends."

"Is that so?"

Spike squinted at me, then looked at Glenda. "Okay, well, I heard her taking her garbage out last night," she said. "And I'm ninety-nine percent sure it was her, because I've heard her taking her garbage out probably a hundred times and my ears are quite good and it sounded the same."

Spike exhaled. He turned to look at me. "So she ripped apart her own house, disposed of something last night for the sanitation department to take away, and left again this morning."

"Assuming it was really her," I said.

"Yes. Assuming."

I peered up and down the street, at all the driveways, including Glenda's. "Bethany's the only one who took her garbage out," I said.

"Pickup isn't till Monday, actually," Glenda said.

Spike and I looked at each other.

"Are you all right, young lady?" At first, I thought Glenda was talking to me. But she was watching Alena, who stood apart from us on the grass, her back hunched, her hair curtaining her face. It looked as though she was crying.

"Young lady?" Glenda said again.

Alena lifted her head and turned to us. She wasn't crying. She had been texting. Her phone was cradled in her hands and her eyes were unexpectedly bright. "Blake is texting me," she said.

"What does he want?"

"He said he has huge news, and he wants to know where I am."

"Don't tell him yet," I said. "Ask him what the news is."

"I will say that I am still at the gym."

"Good."

Alena thumbed her phone.

Happy yelped again. Glenda shushed him. He sprung from the porch and took off down to the edge of her property, barking furiously. "What is wrong with you, Happy?" Glenda said.

He was on the driveway now. I hurried after him.

"Don't let him go into the road," Glenda called out.

I shouted Happy's name.

He didn't stop. Not until he was at the base of Bethany's driveway. Then he got quieter.

Happy growled, his back stiff, his little body an arrow

pointed at the lone garbage can. He made a snarling sound, then barked once and growled again. My stomach dropped. I knew why dogs made noises like that. It was never for pretty reasons.

I made my way toward Happy. The air around me was warm and thick, and it felt as though I was moving through it in slow motion.

As I got closer to the dog, I caught a scent. Sickening and familiar. Out of the corner of my eye, I saw Alena hunched over in front of the porch, tapping at her phone.

"Guess who Blake has been texting with?" Alena's voice was bright, cheerful. "Guess who?"

I reached the garbage can. The smell was unmistakable, even with the lid closed. My eyes started to water.

Happy was barking now.

"Guess who?"

"Alena, please—"

"Bethany!" Alena shouted. "Blake has been talking to Bethany since yesterday! That's why he's been so sneaky. It is a surprise! It's why she was gone! Meetings! She's found a new sponsor for us both, and—"

"Alena, wait," I said. "Just please—"

"I cannot wait, though! He says he is going to meet her at her office and they will come and get me at the gym! What should I say, Sunny? Should I tell him—"

"Tell him not to meet anyone!"

"What the hell is happening down there?" Glenda said.

I threw the lid open, that putrid, dirt-sweet smell barreling out. The smell of death, stronger than I'd ever known it to be, due to the heat. My stomach heaved. I grabbed the hem of my T-shirt, put it over my nose and mouth, and breathed in to keep from retching. But I made myself look inside, my eyes finding the Prada dress. The black hair. The delicate rose tattoo. Those few parts of Bethany that I could still recognize and identify.

"It wasn't her," I said. I swayed on my feet, my head light. My pulse pounded up into my ears. "It wasn't Bethany taking out the trash, because she's . . . she's . . ."

"What is wrong?" Alena said. "Oh my God, what is that smell?"

Happy kept barking.

I spun around. Dug my fingernails into my palms to keep from passing out. "Listen to me, Alena. Call Blake. Now. Tell him to stay where he is. Tell him do not open the door for anyone."

"You're scaring me!"

"That isn't Bethany he's texting with."

"What is in there?"

"Call Blake NOW!"

My voice echoed. I was dimly aware of draperies shifting in neighboring houses, of Glenda shouting for help and grabbing Happy and running back to her house. Of Spike calling 911, telling them about a dead body.

And then Alena was right beside me, falling to her knees. Screaming.

THIRTY-SIX

After she stopped screaming, Alena couldn't speak. Couldn't move. She couldn't even make it up to standing.

I grabbed my phone out of my bag and called Blake. He answered fast. "Hi, Sunny! Did Alena tell you—"

"Blake, I need you to lock the door and stay where you are until I get there. Do not let anyone in. I have the key, so if someone rings the buzzer, it's not me. You got that? Anybody tries to get in, you call the police."

"Wait, what? I'm supposed to meet—"

"No one. You're not meeting anyone. *Under no circumstances are you to leave my apartment. Do you understand?*"

"Okay." He said it in a small, frightened voice. I could hear Rosie barking in the background.

"Have you told Bethany where you are?"

"No . . ."

"Good. Don't."

He didn't respond. For a few seconds, I heard nothing but the sound of Rosie barking and Blake's breathing.

I tried to make my voice as calm as possible. "I'll be there in about half an hour," I said. "Just do everything I said and you'll be fine."

More breathing, quick and shallow. I was afraid he might hyperventilate.

"You okay, buddy?"

"Yeah . . ."

"Seven Seas, Blake," I said. "Your feet in the water."

"S-Seven Seas."

"I'll be there before you know it. Everything will be fine."

I heard sirens. I said goodbye quickly, and hung up before Blake heard them, too.

I turned to Spike. "I've got to go."

"I'll talk to the cops," he said.

Glenda was holding Happy in her arms. "She's in shock," Glenda said. "What should I do?" She was talking about Alena, who was sitting on the grass, her head pressed against her knees. I knelt down beside her.

"Alena?" I said. "Listen to me. It's going to be all right. I'm going to go get Blake. I'll bring him back here, and we'll figure everything out."

Alena said nothing. She didn't even look up.

"Go on," Spike said. "Get out of here before the squad cars get here. I'll make sure Alena sees the paramedics."

I dug into my gym bag, searching for my keys, but felt only my clothes, my toiletry bag, my wallet, my gun.

Why could I never find things when I needed them?

After what must have been a full minute of this frustration, I realized that, in all the excitement of arriving at Bethany's house, I'd left the keys in my car.

The sirens were growing closer.

I hurled myself at my car and jumped behind the wheel. The key wasn't in the ignition. "Shit," I whispered.

I searched the front seats, the floor of the car.

When I finally gave up and opened the door again, I spotted a glint of metal beyond my right front tire, my key chain with Rosie's picture on it.

I dove for the keys, grabbed them off the pavement, got back behind the wheel.

I shoved the key into the ignition, my hand shaking, the wheel locking momentarily until I put my foot on the brake and yanked at it. At long last, the key turned easily, the engine roaring to life. "Okay," I whispered. "That's more like it."

As I shifted the car into reverse, someone started pounding on the passenger-side window. "What the fuck?" I shouted, expecting some annoying teenage cop, a nosy neighbor, anybody but the desperate-looking person I saw.

It was Alena—hyper-alert and animated, her eyes blazing. "Let me in! Unlock the goddamn door! I'm going with you!"

She said it loudly. Forcefully. And without a trace of a Bosnian accent.

THIRTY-SEVEN

I drove. Alena talked. And talked.

She told me in her flat Southern California drawl that it was just like Blake to get catfished by someone pretending to be Bethany, that he was the most gullible person she knew and that to love him was exhausting, debilitating even.

She talked about how much of a relief it was, speaking without having to worry about how to pronounce words and how when she was staying at my place, she'd been afraid of talking in her sleep because she did that sometimes, and it was never with an accent. "I mean, of course it wasn't, right?" she said. "You can't make your subconscious, like, put on a performance."

Then she told me she'd probably be having nightmares for the rest of her life after what she saw in the garbage can, and how Bethany didn't deserve that. No one deserved that, especially Bethany, who had given up so much for Blake and herself. "Her whole, entire life," Alena said. But she veered away from that topic before I could respond.

Clearly, Alena was still in shock, and speaking incessantly was a form of self-protection. So while I obviously had a lot of questions for her, I decided I was better off focusing on getting home to Blake as fast as I could, rather than trying in vain to get a word in edgewise.

"You know I've never been to Bosnia," Alena was saying now. "I haven't even been out of the United States. I learned how to speak Bosnian from Duolingo. I figured out my life story by reading about European models on Wikipedia. Ever listen to any interviews with Paulina Porizkova? You really should. She's super-interesting." I hit a patch of traffic and I abruptly switched lanes.

Alena gasped, which meant she'd finally took a breath. I seized the opportunity.

"Why did you lie about where you're from?"

"A lot of reasons," she said.

"Such as . . ."

"Well, they all had to do with Bethany."

I glanced at Alena. "She gave you and Blake fake personas and narratives," I said. "Because she thought they'd get you more followers?"

She looked at me. "That's part of it," she said. "But there were other reasons why we needed to change our identities."

"Were you guys in trouble?" I said.

"Yeah."

"Did you really meet Blake at the gym?"

She picked at a nail. "Maybe I need to stop talking for a while," she said.

I didn't want her to stop talking. Not now. But I didn't want to push her, either. "You know, Alena," I said, "we all do what we have to do, in order to survive."

We rode in silence for several minutes. I pushed the speed limit, swerving around slow drivers, trying my best to channel Spike on the road without getting pulled over.

Traffic was interesting for a Saturday—smooth sailing for about a mile, then a sudden slowdown. An accident. It had to be. Or roadwork maybe. I jammed my foot on the brake and slowed to a crawl. For quite a while, I rode it out, listening to horns blaring, wondering who exactly was sitting in my passenger seat and how I could get her to reveal herself.

As it turned out, she didn't need my help. "You studied art," Alena said, after what had felt like an endless stretch of quiet. "Why did you become a cop after that?"

"Because I'm curious about people," I said. "I like trying to figure them out." I gave her a quick smile. "In some ways, I think I paint for the same reason."

She nodded. "That makes sense, I guess."

"It's not the only reason."

"Yeah?"

"I mean, my dad's a cop," I said. "Well, he's retired now, but he always loved it. He lived for it, and in a lot of ways, he still does. I think the main reason I became a cop was because, you know . . . I love my dad."

Alena turned. I could feel her watching me. "What's it like?" she asked.

"Being a cop?"

"Loving your dad."

I took a breath. "It's kind of a pain in the ass, actually," I said. "He gets himself into trouble a lot."

"Like Blake."

"Different trouble," I said. "But yeah."

More silence. I kept my eyes on the congested road and let her watch me.

"You're interested in my tattoo," Alena said.

I glanced at her. She tapped the cross on her cheek.

"Oh."

"I've seen you staring at it."

"Yeah," I said. "You're right. I am interested. Who gave it to you and why?"

She closed her eyes and took a deep breath, exhaling in a huff. "I gave it to myself," she said.

"Really?"

"I did that prison-tattoo thing where you get a needle really hot and . . . shit, you know, it still feels weird talking in my real voice."

"Didn't it hurt?" I said. "The tattoo, I mean."

"Oh, yeah. But it was worth it."

"How come? Are you very religious?"

Alena snorted. "Hardly," she said. "I did it to protect myself."

"From what?"

"The fucker I used to live with," she said. "He used to beat the hell out of me every chance he got. Closed fists. I was even unconscious once. I thought, if he sees the sign of Jesus, maybe he'll stop." She let out a long, trembling breath. "It actually worked, kind of. But now he's gone and I'm stuck with this ugly thing. I have to wear foundation every time I go to the gym, or even when I go down to the lobby to get my mail."

I ventured a glance at her just as traffic started to speed up again. "Who is *he*, Alena?"

"Come on, Sunny. You know."

My eyes went big. "The Preacher?"

"Yep."

"How did you know him?" I said. "Were you involved with him a long time? Did you meet him through Bethany?"

She shook her head and let out a mirthless laugh that lasted long enough to be uncomfortable. "I gave myself this tattoo when I was nine years old," she said finally. "My real name is Alicia Walls. That crazy asshole is my father."

THIRTY-EIGHT

It was the well-placed ace that toppled the house of cards. The lone bullet hole that drained the massive tank of water. The perfectly placed explosion that launched the avalanche. Whichever metaphor you chose to describe it, revealing her birth name to me opened up something within Alena—perhaps because it drove home the fact that Bethany was dead, and that at last, she was truly her own boss, capable of revealing any secret she chose to.

And she started with a doozy. "Bethany killed my father," she said.

My jaw dropped. *"What?"*

"I mean, I thought she did. And she thought she did, too. For fifteen years."

"Bethany was the one who shot him?"

She nodded. "How the hell does somebody survive a bullet in the brain?"

I didn't know what to say. I could barely speak. Alena described her childhood, which was rife with physical and emotional abuse, warped Bible study (in Gideon Walls's version of the Old Testament story, Abraham happily sacrificed his son), and, when he deemed her old enough to work, hours of slave labor cleaning his house and delivering illegal drugs for him. As young Alicia got bigger and more cognizant of her grim surroundings, she said, she tried in vain to protect her mother from the Preacher's violent outbursts, his sadistic attacks. But she was just a little girl and only wound up getting hurt herself.

"When I was about eight or nine, I heard them fighting one night," Alena said. "It was bad. Really awful. Even for him. I slept with my head under the pillow. And the next morning she was gone. He said God took her away from me as a punishment. I knew he killed her. As young as I was, I knew it. I hated him so, so much."

"Of course you did," I said.

"I was terrified the same thing would happen to my baby brother and me." She turned and faced me. "I used to carry him everywhere with me, just to make sure he wasn't alone with Gideon long enough to piss him off."

"You have a brother," I said.

"Yeah," she said. "Billy," she said. "My mom used to call him Bubba, and he was so little when she died. Just three years old. He barely remembers her. When we're alone, when no one is listening, I tell him stories about her. To keep her in his thoughts."

I looked at Alena, everything starting to make sense. The lack of chemistry between them, the protective way she treated him, the fact that, after two years of dating, this inseparable, exclusive, loving couple still lived in separate apartments. "Your baby brother is Blake," I said.

She nodded. "I'm sorry we lied to you, Sunny."

"Don't apologize," I said. "Just help me understand."

She cleared her throat. "All these years, we thought Bethany had killed Gideon," she said. "We were scared she'd be wanted for murder. We lived off the grid for a while, then we started moving all over the country, from town to town. We never made close friends at school because we were too scared to tell them who we really were. And anyway, just when we would start feeling settled in, Bethany would tell us it was time to move. Pick up. She'd have new birth certificates for us. She said we had to be 'vigilant.' She used that word. First big word I ever learned."

I nodded.

"And then one day, she saw my Instagram. She read up on influencers, how much money and free swag they got. She told us, 'Here's a way we can support ourselves. Get rich, even.' We all got excited. But it was a big risk. We all knew that. Bethany was still scared she'd get caught. And being successful in this business means being visible twenty-four/seven."

"So you invented other personas."

"Yes."

"You obtained new birth certificates, driver's licenses. You had plastic surgery . . ."

"A little. Bethany went for the works. But I just colored my hair and got a boob job that she paid for." She smiled. "Bubba didn't need to do anything. He just grew up."

We were back in town now, a few blocks away from my loft. I turned and looked at her. Her blue eyes were bright with tears. She yanked her gym bag out of the backseat, pulled out a package of Kleenex, and blew her nose. "All these years. He was alive. He was in jail. We didn't have to hide like that."

I looked at her. "He's out of jail now, though."

"I know. That terrifies me."

She chewed on a nail. I thought of the shoebox underneath Bethany's bed. The driver's license. The child's drawing. The lock of fine brown baby hair, tied up in a pink ribbon. "Your mom," I said to Alena. "She was Betsy Rosanski."

She nodded. More tears spilled down her cheeks.

"Then can I ask you . . . who was Bethany?"

"My aunt Linda," she said quietly.

"Oh." I remembered Betsy's rap sheet, the arrests for pickpocketing with her sister, years before she married Walls. "I . . . I heard about her."

"I never knew her before she shot my father. And I know Gideon had no idea who she was when he brought her home that night. He shut us in our room like he always did when he took women home. Bubba and I fell asleep. The gunshot woke me up."

"She went home with him and tried to kill him."

"Yes."

"Why?"

"She'd been in touch with my mom. They wrote letters and told each other everything," she said. "When Bethany stopped hearing from her, she must have known he finally made good on the threats. She tracked him down. It took more than a year. She found out what bar he liked to go to. What type of woman he was into. She got all dressed up. Went to that bar so many nights until finally he showed up. She acted like she was into him. He took her home. She drugged his drink . . . And when it was over, she took us with her."

We were nearing my loft. I found the first space I could and parallel-parked. "She saved you," I said.

"Yes."

"She planned it all." I took the key out of the ignition and looked at Alena. "She planned it perfectly."

"You know Bethany," she said, tears still trickling down her cheeks. "She can make anything happen."

We both got out of the car. I grabbed my gym bag, and the two of us ran to my loft.

As we reached the door, I heard someone shouting my name, and when I turned, I saw my fourteen-year-old neighbor, Cara. She had Rosie on a leash.

I checked my watch. It was noon. On a weekend. She normally walked my dog at three on weekdays, if I wasn't around. "What's going on?" I asked.

"Rosie was barking like crazy for a really long time," Cara said. "I knocked on the door and no one answered, so I opened it and she was all alone, so . . . you know. I figured she had to go out?"

"Rosie was alone?"

"Yeah, I'm sorry I used my key, Sunny, but it seemed like she really had to go."

"No, no. That's okay."

Alena and I stared at each other. I asked Cara if she could take Rosie to her place after the walk, and at the same time I called Blake. He picked up fast. "Sunny? Are you with Alena?"

"Yes."

"Okay. Okay."

"Where are you?"

"I'm in the guest room."

I exhaled. I looked at Alena and mouthed, *He's there.* "That was just my neighbor Cara, Blake," I said. "Good for you for not answering, but—"

"Come up now. Please."

"I am. We are. We're on our way."

I put my key in the front door. Rather than wait for the elevator, Alena and I ran upstairs. As we reached my floor, I plunged my hand into my gym bag and pulled out my gun. I decided to keep it out for the drive back to Sudbury, just in case anybody was following us. I couldn't risk rummaging around in my bag for it, the way I had with Dylan Welch. After I unlocked the door, Alena slipped around me and hurried into the apartment, shouting her brother's name, the door slamming shut behind her, locking automatically. *Great.* I unlocked the door again.

"Blake!" I called out, once I got in.

"Drop it," said a man's voice. It wasn't Blake.

"Drop the gun," the voice said. And then I saw them in front of the open guest room door. An enormous bald man—his ropey arm around Alena's neck. A knife in his hand, the tip of the blade at her chin. He glared straight at me, and the first thing I noticed was the thick purple scar on his forehead, like a mountain range on a relief map. The teardrop tattoos were subtle by comparison, and I found myself thinking about the way Eddie had described him, never mentioning the scar, just the tattoos and the shaved head. And his suit, of all things. *What a shit eyewitness Eddie Voltaire was,* I thought. Because you couldn't control where the mind went at times like this, and in my case, it usually fled to ridiculous places.

Alena whimpered. Blood trickled down her chin.

I dropped the gun. There was nothing else I could do.

"Preacher," I said.

He smiled—if you could call it that. It looked more like a baring of teeth. "I am not the Preacher today," he said, as Alena started to cry. "Today, I am the Reaper."

THIRTY-NINE

Walls kicked my gun across my living room floor and gestured with his bald, scarred head at the guest room door. "Get in front," he said to me. "Unless you want me to slit her throat."

"She's your daughter," I said.

He stared at me, his eyes the same shade of blue as Alena's, but with a deadness to them. A dry, cold calm. It was unnerving, his gaze. I wondered if it was the result of the gunshot wound, or if he'd always been like this. Cold and inhuman, the only tears he was capable of tattooed on his cheek. "My daughter is a sinner," he said. "She will pay for her sins."

Alena began to shake. Tears streamed down her cheeks. "Please." She said it to me. "Please."

He told Alena to shut up. She bit her lip. Caught her breath.

I got in front of Gideon Walls. He yanked the gym bag from my arm and dropped it, then told me to hand him my phone. I did. He shoved it into his back pocket.

He kicked open my guest room door. "Go in," he said.

The room reeked of sweat, of fear. The blackout curtains were drawn. The desk lamp was turned on, but it didn't give off much light, and it took my eyes a few moments to adjust.

I heard someone crying softly in the corner, and I knew it was Blake. "Don't hurt her," he said. "Don't hurt her, please."

My eyes got acclimated to the darkness and I took in the sight of Blake. He was tied to my hard-backed wooden desk chair. His arms bound behind him, his feet splayed and duct-taped to the chair's legs. Duct tape dangled from his cheek—removed, no doubt, so he could answer his phone. (Where was his phone? My eyes darted around the room, from the two unmade beds, to Blake and Alena's overnight bags, to the throw rug, to the desks, to the bookshelves, that big purple bunny rabbit in the corner, which no longer gave me the creeps. Everything was relative, I supposed . . .) Walls moved toward Blake, his grip still tight around Alena's neck. He slapped the tape back over his mouth.

As he did, Blake's head moved into the light. I noticed a deep gash on his forehead. Another on his cheek. "It's going to be okay, Blake," I said.

"Don't lie," Walls said. He was wearing a black T-shirt. Black jeans. A gold cross around his neck. He was a few inches taller than Blake, with a big chest. His arms bulged. *Prison muscles,* I thought.

"The Lord detests lying lips," Walls said. He socked me in the stomach. I fell to the floor, the wind knocked out of me, bright specks dancing in front of my eyes. I gasped for air and he hit me again.

I tried to stand, but fell back. Walls had a roll of duct tape now. He'd forced Alena to her knees and he was binding her hands together behind her back as she struggled against him. He did her ankles next—all very quickly. He didn't have the time for the harsh precision with which he'd bound and gagged his son. I hoped that would work in Alena's favor.

"Stop!" Alena yelled. He slapped a length of tape over her mouth.

Blake let out a groan and pulled at his restraints. The legs of the chair squeaked.

How were we ever going to make it out of here?

Walls strode to the corner of the room. He switched on the light, and I got a better look at the knife. An extra-long push dagger with a drop-point blade. Sharp and deadly. He returned to Alena's side and put the blade to her throat. "It's judgment day," he said. "At long last, you will both reap what you have sown. The same as your treacherous aunt, who paid for her sins with the blood of thirteen stab wounds. One for each of the apostles."

Alena screamed, but it was stifled by the tape. I wanted to tell her to save her breath, to save her strength. *Use your energy to escape!* I wished I could will the thought into her head.

I heard myself say, "How can you call yourself a servant of God?"

Walls turned around.

"How can you call yourself a servant of God," I said, "and do this to your own children?"

He glowered at me, those hollow shark's eyes trained on my face. "If they were truly good children," he said, "they would have called the cops on their aunt. They would have gotten help. They wouldn't have left their own father for dead and run off with his murderer." He stared at Alena. "She introduced herself before she shot me," he said. "She said, 'This is for Betsy.' You heard her from your room. Don't tell me you didn't."

I stared at him. "They were little kids," I said. "They were frightened. They didn't know or hear anything."

Blake moaned beneath the duct tape. Walls moved toward him, the dagger gripped in his hand. "You're a weakling," he said. "A sheep. Following your heathen sister around. The Lord would be ashamed of the likes of you."

My mind raced, grappling for Sunday school phrases. *Something, anything.* "Jesus said, let the little children come to me," I tried. "The kingdom of heaven belongs to them."

Walls slashed Blake's arm. He cried out.

"The eye that mocks the father," Walls said. "The ravens of the valley will pick it out. And young eagles will eat it." He held the blade to Blake's eye.

Alena sobbed.

My gaze shot from him, to Alena, to the floor next to me. I scanned it, looking for anything that could be a weapon. I landed on Alena's red stiletto heel, which was behind me, under the nearest bed.

"He was making pornography," Walls said. He slapped Blake across the face. "This . . . sick pervert."

"How did you know that?" I slipped my hand under the bed, grabbed the shoe. "I don't believe you."

"A man I used to be in prison with, a member of my congregation. A holy man. He saw this . . . this filthy bastard. He paid for a video just so I could see it. 'He looks like you,' he said. 'Could he be the son you've been searching for?' I watched as much as I could stomach. And I recognized you in an instant. I found your Instagram. I found all of you. Your sister. Your aunt hiding in the background of one of Alicia's shameless pictures. Her hand in front of her face. Hiding. With Betsy's ring on her finger. The Lord works in mysterious ways."

Tears streamed out of Blake's eyes. He murmured something behind the tape.

"What?" Walls said. "Are you going to tell me now? Have I finally gotten you to see that I'm serious?"

Blake said it again, louder.

Alena made a grunting noise. I looked at her, and she locked eyes with mine. My gaze traveled down the length of her arms, the tightness of the muscles. She'd managed to loosen the duct tape. She was nearly free. I showed her the shoe, and she nodded. Kept working.

Slowly, I edged closer to Walls, then closer still. I gazed up at him, the shoe tight in my hand. The floorboards creaked. I held my breath, waiting for him to turn and see me. But he didn't. He was that focused on his son, that intent on frightening him.

Walls crouched down, put his face next to Blake's. "Are you going to tell me where the money is?" he said. "Or shall I send you to hell with your mother and aunt?"

Blake tried to speak again. I moved closer.

"Betsy might still be alive, had she told me where it was," Walls said softly. Sweetly. "Stealing is a sin. Stealing from a man of God, a mortal sin. She was a bad, bad wife."

Blake groaned.

"If you are prepared to tell me what she did with my hard-earned savings, Billy," Walls said, "I may rethink your punishment."

Blake nodded.

"You will tell me?"

Blake nodded again. I moved closer, until I was less than a foot behind them.

Walls ripped off the duct tape.

Blake said, "Your holy man friend likes to look at dudes on OnlyFans." Then he bit Walls's hand.

Walls shrieked. Blake clamped down harder. Walls hand was bleeding. He reared back and raised the knife and at the same time, I lunged forward, slamming the stiletto into his face with all my strength.

I felt a sickening give—the heel connecting with his eye.

He howled, blood streaming down his face, the shoe clattering to the floor. He lunged at me with the knife, this figure from a nightmare, this bleeding cyclops. He slashed blindly at my arms, my chest, my cheek.

I pushed open the guest room door and he followed me out. My T-shirt stuck to me. Blood bloomed from my cuts. I put a hand to my face. It came back bright red. *At least it's me he's after,* I thought. *At least it's not them.* I could see my gun across the room; I ran for it. He slashed at my back. My skin stung, and then there was pressure, as though someone had kicked me in the spine. I turned around in time to see Alena bursting out of the room. "Get out!" I shouted at her. "Get help!"

Shouting took more out of me than it should have. I felt woozy. Light-headed. I saw a thick smear of bright red on my polished wood floor. It looked like paint. But it was blood. My blood. "Get help." I said it again. At least I thought I did.

But Alena didn't leave my apartment. She rushed straight for Walls. Butted her head into his stomach and knocked him off-balance, his feet sliding out from under him. He landed on his back, *Just like Dylan Welch,* I thought.

Alena landed splayed beside him. But she got up on her knees fast. She punched him in the stomach, pounded her fist into his face, his bloody eye. He groaned.

"I hate you," she said again and again. "You killed my mother because of some money! Some stupid fucking money! You killed my aunt. I fucking hate you!"

I stumbled toward the gun. I was aware of Walls pushing Alena off of him and rising to his feet, the two of them grappling with the knife.

My .38 was on the floor right in front of me. I saw the blood on my shirt, my arms, as I collected it into my hands. It was hard to balance. I turned toward Walls, the gun slippery in my hands.

Walls won, I thought. *He won.* Because, injured as he was, bloody as he was, he still had the knife. He grabbed Alena by the wrist and raised the blade over his head, an awful guttural noise escaping from him, filling the room.

Alena screamed. The blade came down.

I shot Walls. The bullet connected with his neck and he grabbed at the wound, he clawed at it, the knife falling from his hand. Alena pushed him onto his side. She took my phone from his back pocket. I recited my passkey, and I heard her calling 911, letting them know what happened.

I felt faint. I lay down on the floor near Gideon. He moaned softly. His eyelids fluttered.

After she was done with the call, Alena moved closer to him. She knelt beside him. Whispered something in his ear just as his body went still.

I heard what she said. No one else ever would. Blake was still in the guest room, way out of earshot, and the paramedics and police had yet to arrive.

I closed my eyes, replaying that moment in my mind as I began to lose consciousness. Alena Jade crouching next to her dying monster of a father, and whispering those words to him—the last words he would ever hear on this earth. "The money's in the purple stuffed bunny," she had told him. "Mom gave it to me. It's mine."

I heard sirens outside my building, Alena telling me not to worry. And then everything went black.

FORTY

Four days later

"If you wanted me to stay that badly," Richie said, "why didn't you just tell me?"

He was in my hospital room—my last visitor of the day. I'd already spent time with my parents and Elizabeth, Spike and Flynn Tipton (who had clearly made it past the one-night-stand phase), and Lee Farrell (who'd come both as a friend and in an official capacity as he wrapped up the Rose and Voltaire murder cases). Alena and Blake had visited me as well, and stayed for well over an hour, during which I marveled at their resilience—both physical and emotional. Blake's injuries had already faded and, despite their obvious and understandable grief over their aunt, he and his sister both seemed so hopeful, with Blake gearing up to shoot the *Shred*

Shed pilot and Alena making definite plans to apply to college. Before saying goodbye, they'd left me with a gift: a framed photo of the two of them, plus Mr. Francis, whom Blake had adopted—and Rosie and me. They'd Photoshopped us in; a picture Alena had covertly snapped when they were staying at my place. I'd found it so funny—the idea of my dog and me plugged into their happy family—that I hadn't even noticed the sizable check taped to the back of the frame. Not until Blake and Alena were long gone.

"You could have even written me a letter," Richie said.

"I dunno," I said. "I thought nearly getting stabbed to death would make more of a statement."

Richie touched my cheek, very gently, as though he was afraid I might break. The surgeon, Dr. Ortega, had assured me I'd be "right as rain" after a couple months of rehab, and if I kept healing as well as I was, I could go home as soon as tomorrow. But it had been really touch and go there. I'd suffered major blood loss, and had been unconscious for nearly three days—during which, according to my dad, Richie had hardly ever left my bedside. "Please don't make that statement again," he said.

"As long as I feel heard, I have no reason to."

Richie sighed. He pushed a lock of hair out of my eyes and gazed at my face. The stitches. "Seriously, Sunny. Please be careful."

I wanted to kiss him, but I couldn't sit up. "I'm always careful," I said. "It just doesn't always work out for me."

Richie said nothing. He didn't realize that I knew he'd been at my side when I was unconscious. I figured he'd tell me himself if he wanted me to know, and so far he hadn't.

"I'm sorry I screwed up your Jersey plans," I said.

"Don't be," he said.

I knew Richie was still moving. He had a job in New Jersey now. A home he'd started paying rent on. A life. It was where his kid would be starting school in the fall. But the fact that he'd postponed that move meant so much to me—and his choosing not to set a date for now meant even more. "Can I get you anything?" Richie said. "Water?"

I shook my head, which kind of hurt. As impressed as I was with Mass General as a whole, it seemed to me that the staff was a bit stingy with the pain meds. "Just stay here with me," I said. "Okay?"

He nodded, and took my hand in his, and I felt the way I always did when the two of us were together, but most of the time chose to ignore.

During my visit with Blake and Alena, we'd talked about Blake's "happy place," the Seven Seas, which, as it turned out, was not some storybook locale but a motel on the outskirts of Las Vegas, where Blake, Alena, and Bethany had stayed for several weeks following their escape from Reseda and Gideon Walls. The Seven Seas had a small swimming pool—the first one Blake had ever seen. It had made such an impression on him that he'd drawn a picture of the pool two years later—a bright blob, surrounded by stick figures—and given it to his aunt. Soaking his feet in the water with Aunt Linda while watching Alicia do flips off the diving board, Blake recalled, *I felt safe for the first time in my whole life.* To this day, he'd go there in his mind whenever he felt stressed, just as Bethany used to take out her shoebox full of family keepsakes and gaze at her sister's driver's license.

She used to call it "taking a trip home," Alena had said. And though that may have sounded a little strange, it made sense to me. Home didn't have to be an actual place. It could be a memory or a photograph or a pet, or a big, stuffed bunny full of cash from your mother—anything that made you feel loved and happy and safe.

Home could be a person.

I watched Richie's face. I felt the warmth of his hand in mine. He smiled at me, and I wished I could flick a switch and freeze this moment, just before I felt my heart starting to break.

"Penny for your thoughts," he said.

"Six and a half hours," I said. "It's not that long a drive. Is it?"

"I bet you dinner and drinks I can do it in six," Richie said. "Five and a half, once I get a little practice."

I smiled back at him, and held his hand a little tighter. "You're on," I said.